Where to Find Me

Alba Arikha

ALMA BOOKS

ALMA BOOKS LTD
3 Castle Yard
Richmond
Surrey TW10 6TF
United Kingdom
www.almabooks.com

First published by Alma Books Limited in 2018
© Alba Arikha, 2018

The W.G. Sebald quote is from *The Emigrants* by W.G. Sebald, published
by Harvill Press. Reproduced by permission of The Random House
Group Ltd © 1996

Alba Arikha asserts her moral right to be identified as the author of this
work in accordance with the Copyright, Designs and Patents Act 1988

Printed in Great Britain by CPI Group (UK) Ltd, Croydon CR0 4YY

ISBN: 978-1-84688-448-1

FOR TOM

And so they are ever returning to us, the dead.

W.G. Sebald

*Si c'était à recommencer, je te rencontrerais
sans te chercher.*

Paul Éluard

Where to Find Me

Part I

1

Jean is my first boyfriend. We are nineteen years old, students at the Sorbonne. In our spare time, we ride bicycles along the Seine and discuss literature. We both want to be writers and change the world. "I could become the next Proust," he tells me.

It is the summer of 1939, two months before Britain and France declare war on Germany. Jean writes poetry for me on the backs of bus tickets. He kisses me on street corners and tells me I'm the one. We linger in Montparnasse cafés, hoping to catch a glimpse of Jean-Paul Sartre. We see him once, sitting alone. He seems to have a cold and wipes his nose several times with a handkerchief. We don't dare approach him.

At night, we drink cheap rosé from a bottle and smoke Gauloises. We go dancing. I wear red lipstick and a black turban hat. I lose my virginity to Jean in the backroom of a jazz club. A saxophone soars as he removes my stockings. Jean's arms are soft and warm and I think I love him, although I'm not sure. Perhaps it is the thrill of knowing that our meetings are illicit which contributes to the rise in my feelings: Jean has been given strict instructions to stay away from me. I am a Jew, the daughter of a shopkeeper. Jean is from a rich bourgeois family. His father is the CEO of a major car factory that supplies trucks to the Germans. He is a close friend of Pierre Laval, the former Prime Minister. The relationship is too dangerous, and we separate. Jean writes me a farewell poem on the back of a last bus ticket. I never hear from him again. But I still have the ticket.

On a rainy dawn, 14th June 1940, German tanks stream into Paris. A man's accented voice comes on the loudspeaker and announces that the capital is now an open city. A curfew is being imposed from 8.00 p.m. that evening. A large swastika flag is raised over the Eiffel Tower, and the Hôtel de Ville is draped, like a fallen woman, in another. Thousands flee that same day. The traffic signs and street names are now in German. Paris time becomes Berlin time. I pass the Arc de Triomphe and see German soldiers goose-stepping at a ceremonial changing of the guard.

A week later, Hitler comes for a visit and poses for a picture in front of the Eiffel Tower. "He's only visiting," my father declares. "He'll be gone soon. Hitler will fall."

But he won't. I can feel it. Our town is unrecognizable. Something awful is about to happen to us.

"We should leave," I tell my father. "We shouldn't stay here." But he disagrees and accuses me of being weak. "Courage is facing the enemy, not fleeing from it," he says. "And in any case, no one has the right to tell you how to live. No one human being can decide the fate of another."

He is wrong, but he is my father and I must listen to him.

The drip-drip of elimination. This is how it begins. Small drops at first, propaganda material disguised as anodyne images meant to reassure an uncertain public: happy schoolchildren with a skipping rope, fashionable young women posing for the camera and flirting with German officers, churchgoing families dressed in their Sunday best. We need to believe these are realistic snapshots of life. We need to pretend that nothing has changed and that life goes on as normal, even though giant swastikas line the quiet streets. No traffic, no construction work, no pedlars selling their wares. Instead, police sirens rend the air and foreign soldiers patrol the pavements. Nevertheless, I continue to attend my classes at the Sorbonne. I'm studying English literature. I love the teacher, André Stein, who speaks about Victorian authors, especially George Eliot, as if they were personal friends. I lose myself in his words and the books he recommends. I read them at night, in my small room, and I dream of a better world.

The drip quickly turns into a steady flow. The curfew is imposed every night. The streets are dark. I stay home. We listen to Radio Londres, transmitted by the Free France resistance movement. My father strongly disapproves of it. "Troublemakers," he scoffs. "Sowing discord." Yet he listens. A man, a professor, explains that the word "occupation" has taken on a new meaning. It now means vandalized, taken, closed down: bookshops, parks, apartments, bakeries and brothels. What next?

"Not toyshops," my father declares. "They would never dare. Anyway, this man doesn't know what he's talking about."

During the day, my mother sets off for work, wearing vermilion lipstick and tailored dresses. She has recently been promoted to manager of stockings and tights at the Galeries Lafayette, a job she loves. One morning she returns home, her lips pale, her eyes red. "I've been fired," she says, holding back her tears. "I'm no longer allowed to work."

"But why?" my father asks, startled.

"Because I'm a Jew, Maurice."

My father looks at her and says nothing.

*

My father's toyshop, Maurice Baum: Jouets, stands on the Rue des Rosiers, right next to our apartment. It is a well-known and much loved institution, nestled on the ground floor of an eighteenth-century building. Toys of all shapes and colours line the shelves, and its pervading smell is akin to a musty book. When I was a child, that shop, that smell, was my haven. Now it feels unsafe. What if the Germans close it down? What will happen to us then?

My father's brother and his children live above the shop. My cousin Pierre, who's outspokenly political, attends the Sorbonne with me, and studies physics. He's arrested on a Sunday morning, and we are all shocked. "He should have shut up instead of spouting his views on street corners," my father says. "No wonder they arrested him."

Pierre is eventually released, but I feel more nervous than ever. There have been further arrests of people we know. The fact that my mother has lost her job and that my father's Gentile clientele has dwindled only makes matters worse. Yet, it seems to leave my father undeterred. He attributes the situation to general panic, to overreaction, not to the anti-Semitic propaganda which is spreading insidiously, like the plague.

I begin to wonder: is my father losing his sanity? Everyone else I know is concerned, but not him. I share my thoughts with my mother, who immediately puts me in my place. "Don't you dare question your father. He knows what he's doing. If he says we're safe, you must trust him."

I visit my friend Françoise, who would like to become a concert pianist. She lives with her parents in a large apartment near the Panthéon. We listen to music together, Mozart and Schubert mostly. We talk about my wanting to leave France and what's happening at home. "I don't understand my father," I tell her. "It's as if he doesn't want to believe that we're at war. He keeps saying that everything is all right. But it's not, and I'm scared."

"Maybe he knows, but doesn't want to admit it to you," she ventures. "I'm sure he's as scared as you are. But no matter your differences, Flore, you still can't leave," she adds. "You can't do that to your parents."

Françoise has nothing to fear. She's a Catholic girl, the daughter of a prominent historian. "No one will touch my father," she tells me. "He knows important people."

Afterwards she plays me a Chopin Prelude. I look at her and realize that I know no important people. Would it be different if I did? Yes, it would. But Jews no longer have the option of being important.

I close my eyes for a short while and listen to Françoise play. I forget where I am. Who I am. Not a Jewish girl. Not the daughter of a man who cannot see what is happening outside his toyshop. Because my father's reality has become warped. The Germans are like toys inside his imaginary playground. Like the marching-soldier collection displayed in the front window of his shop.

Soon, the springs will unwind and no one will be able to fix them.

2

My father comes home one day with two puppets from his shop. The paint on their faces is chipped. I still remember what they look like. One of them is a harlequin with a tricorne hat and a diamond-patterned costume. The other is a witch. She wears a pointy black hat and a polka-dot robe, and she carries a broom. I find them slightly sinister, but my father seems utterly enchanted by them, like a small child. I can see him, sitting at the kitchen table, carefully painting over those faces with a small brush. His dexterity and concentration are fascinating to watch. But there is something else. Something teetering. Foreboding. As if he may be losing control. And yet his discourse is strangely coherent. "Don't you understand that this is just a temporary state of affairs? You must be patient! You must believe me! Why don't you believe me?"

"Because you're wrong, that's why!" I shout. "Look at what's happening around us!"

"Don't you dare contradict me!" he shouts back. "I know exactly what's happening!"

My mother intervenes. "Please," she says. "Let's not argue about this." She gently grabs my father's hand. "There is no man more patriotic than your father," she tells me, with a note of pride in her voice. "He would fight for this country, if he could."

"But the Vichy government doesn't care if Maurice Baum the shopkeeper wants to fight for his country, don't you understand?" I exclaim. "They will do nothing to save us! Nothing!"

"Stop talking nonsense," my father snaps. "And don't you forget that Charles de Gaulle's niece is one of my biggest customers. She always comes into my shop to buy toys for her children. She will have a word. She told me she would. And I believe her."

"A word with whom, Papa? With Charles de Gaulle?"

He hesitates. "With who matters is with who," he finally answers. He stands up and suddenly appears small to me. Diminished. His black shoes need a polish; his blue suit has little specks of dandruff on the collar. His usually gentle face is taut and serious: perhaps he is worried after all. Perhaps Françoise is right. Perhaps nothing is wrong with him and he just doesn't want to admit the truth: that we're in danger. All Jews are in danger. Yet, here we are, sitting in our living room, passing time.

I look around us. A sliver of light falls in the centre of the room, revealing imperfections. The particles of dust. The cracks in some of the chairs. The hole in the colourful rug. The cobweb on the window sill. We have fallen from grace.

I can only watch as strands of darkness slowly coil themselves around us.

3

Every morning, after she has ensured her yellow-star badge is pinned to her chest, my mother leaves the house in search of food. We can no longer buy meat, eggs or milk from the usual shops, so we have to search elsewhere.

She finds us bread on the black market. The only vegetables available are yellow turnips and Jerusalem artichokes. I hate them, but I eat them anyway. We have no choice. We have become pariahs in our own land. I am no longer allowed to attend the Sorbonne. My beloved teacher, André Stein, has been arrested and taken away; we're still waiting to hear news of him. Jewish children are banned from all playgrounds. We say nothing. When we're made to sit in the last car of the Métro, we still say nothing.

At home, meals have become oppressive. My mother and I sit in silence while my father does all the talking. About his toyshop, his loyal customers and how the nation is being fooled into believing that the Germans will actually manage to keep their promises – and that includes deporting Jews, or whatever it is people are saying. "Never believe what you hear," my father repeats, like a mantra.

After dinner, he puts a record on, usually Maurice Chevalier. He particularly likes the song 'Pour toi Paris', which he knows by heart. Once, he grabs those puppets with their newly painted faces. He stands in the middle of the room and starts to make them dance to the music, as he sings along with them. "*Pour toi, Paris. Pour la route qu'avec toi on a suivie, pour toi, Paris.*"

It is an indelible image. My father holding up those stringed puppets as they pivot from one leg to the other and he sings along to Maurice Chevalier's voice in the dim light of our sitting room. Outside, German boots crunch past our front windows, heavy footsteps like a drum.

*

The French police come to arrest Jewish families who live on our street. My father insists we will be spared. He knows best. "Those Jews they're arresting are foreigners. Immigrants. We're not. We're French citizens through and through."

Then he is ordered to close his toyshop. But he still doesn't want to hear of it. "It's my life," he keeps saying. "My shop. I'm not closing anything."

My mother begins to cry. "Please Maurice, they'll arrest you if you don't, please."

But my father doesn't budge.

I will never forget this day. Monday 12th July 1943. My mother is wearing a blue polka-dot dress cinched at the waist. Her hair is curled. On her feet, wooden platform shoes. They clunk like hooves. I can smell her perfume. Shalimar, by Guerlain. My cousin Sarah is holding her hand. Sarah and her mother were taken away in the middle of the night to Drancy. The child was released after a few days. She is seven years old and she is sick. My mother is taking her to the doctor. She knows it is risky to walk the streets, but she must. Her niece is very sick. "It will be all right, Maurice," she repeats, several times, as if to convince herself. At first my father says nothing. But he knows. By now he knows how dangerous it has become for Jews. We're being singled out and taken away, like sheep to slaughter. That is what my uncle has told my father, who said nothing. This is his tactic. To say nothing, as if admitting the truth were a form of defeat. It makes me so angry I no longer talk to him. When my father speaks to me, or asks me a question, I answer curtly. But that day, something is different. I'm not sure whether he has heard a piece of news he hasn't shared with us, but he looks tense rather than defiant. Angry too, when Sarah starts to cry. "Stop crying!" he shouts at her. She stops, surprised, and looks at my father. We all do. There are lines on his face. His lips are pursed. The sun is shining outside. The weather is beautiful. All the horrible things in my life happened when the weather was beautiful. "I'm going to the doctor," my mother declares. "It's no good you just standing there."

"Be careful," says my father. Then this: "You shouldn't go."

"But Sarah's ill…"

"Don't go, Clara."

"It'll be fine. We'll take the back streets."

She kisses us goodbye and leaves with Sarah. I am twenty years old. The French police stop her on the Boulevard de Beaumarchais. My mother is wearing her yellow star, but my cousin is not. Any child over six years old has to wear the star, and Sarah isn't. My mother was distracted. I know this because our neighbour saw it all. The soldiers stopped my mother and took her and Sarah away.

I never saw either of them again.

My father knows they will come for us next. But he does nothing. I tell him that we have to leave our apartment. There is a look on his face which I've never seen before, as if blood had momentarily stopped flowing through his veins. As if he had already given up on life. A man he knows offers to hide us in his basement.

M. Bonnet and his wife Jacqueline. They own a restaurant and live on the Rue des Francs-Bourgeois, near the toyshop. Their daughter always stops by the shop after school. She especially loves the porcelain dolls. She also loves my parents. My father tells me to go there, says he will meet me the next day. Why? Why the next day? Why not now? Maybe he wants to take a last look at his beloved shop. Maurice Baum: Jouets. "Go, go," he says.

So I walk to the Rue des Francs-Bourgeois alone. I've removed my star. I am terrified I will get caught. I cannot get caught. I want to live in London one day. I cannot get caught. I want to become something. Someone.

I cannot get caught.

They come for my father that night. They cannot find him at home. So they go to his shop and there he is, sleeping among the toys, clasping those puppets against his chest. The police smash them up, together with everything else. Then they take my father away.

M. Bonnet inspects the shop the next day. Amongst the wreckage he finds five precious dolls inside a trunk the police hadn't bothered to open.

*

My father is released after six months. M. Bonnet knows someone important at the Commissariat de Police. My father looks the same physically, but something has changed inside him. Whatever it is I had suspected about his state of mind has now been confirmed. "I've lost my balance," he tells me, sounding like a child.

He returns home. He doesn't want to stay at the Bonnets'. He wants to play with his toys, he says. His eyes are darting around, like those of a madman. I leave him alone; it frightens me to see him this way.

The police show up at the Bonnet home. They look around, but don't find me. "You have to leave, Flore," they tell me.

I can no longer stay in the basement room. I leave that evening. I do not dare say goodbye to my father. I fear getting caught. I cry for him. For what has become of him. For my mother. I say goodbye to the Bonnets. A friend of mine has found me a new place to stay. An older couple, communist farmers in the Vaucluse. It takes me a month to get there. A fixer leads me, and a Jewish family travelling with us, through fields and woods under the cover of darkness. We sleep in barns and abandoned houses along the way. Whenever we hear someone approach, we fear for our lives. It is hard to distinguish between the Nazi patrols and the villagers. When I finally arrive in Vaison-la-Romaine, Marie and Antoine Thibault greet me warmly. They are very poor, but they are kind. I'm not sure I'd still be alive if it weren't for them. I stay with the Thibaults until the war is over. When I return to Paris, I am told that my father was arrested again, not long after I fled. No one is sure of his whereabouts.

4

It is 1945. The temperature has dropped to -14 Celsius. There is snow everywhere, no heat, no food. Electricity is only on for an hour at noon. Families have placed advertisements in *Le Monde* looking for their loved ones. I do the same.

Someone comes forward. An old friend of my parents, Roger. He tells me that my mother, father and Sarah died in a concentration camp. Bergen-Belsen. Roger knows, because a friend of his, who has survived, was there with them. He said that my father had stopped speaking. That he didn't care whether he lived or died. That he had gone mad.

That night I dream of the toyshop. Its musty smell. The way my father greets the children. Stooped, twinkle-eyed. The way he displays the marbles: mica, devil's eye, opaque, cat's eye. *Can we play? M. Baum, can we play?* The miniature circus where the clown turns round on a wheel. The wind-up soldiers. The rosewood music box with the dancing ballerina. *Oh, comme c'est beau!* The porcelain dolls. *Les Parisiennes*, they are called. Valuable, nineteenth-century dolls clothed in silk, velvet, cashmere, patent-leather shoes. Some like Marie wear jewellery. Rose has a wig made of human hair. M. Bonnet tells me he'll give me the dolls when I'm ready to have them. When will that be?

My mother can hear me. Feel me. So can my father. I speak to them at nightfall. Their breath has vanished into a place with no name. But I can feel particles of their spirit float around me.

We are about to enter France's Fourth Republic. I am twenty-five years old and a painter's model at the École des Beaux-Arts. I like sitting in the nude. I make money that way, but not enough to sate my hunger. So I take on another job as well, translating poetry from English to French. One night I go to the Comédie-Française to see Jean-Louis Barrault perform in a play. On the way to my seat I bump into Jean. He looks different. Richer. He introduces me to his wife, who is pregnant. Her eyelashes are pale. A small diamond sparkles around her neck. Jean tells me that he is working for his father now. "So you never wrote your novel?" I ask him. "No," he answers, looking as ill at ease as does his wife. Does she know about us or has she spotted the Jew in me?

We say goodbye quickly. The meeting leaves me feeling unsettled. I wonder what I ever saw in Jean. Then I think of that evening in the jazz club, of the way we used to ride our bicycles along the Seine, of Paris before the war.

But I must not think about those days.

The theatre is very crowded: we're all squeezed next to each other, and there is an unpleasant smell of unwashed bodies. But the play is so gripping, albeit tragic, that I eventually forget about the smells, although my empty stomach grumbles. Theatres and music halls may be full in Paris, but grocery shops are bare, and we're going hungry. Thank goodness for Charles-Henri, my lover. His parents have a house in the country, and he goes hunting for food there, and when he's lucky he returns to Paris with large sacks of meat and potatoes. I'm never sure what the meat is, but I eat it anyway. We've long given up being fussy. People eat their own guinea pigs and pigeons from public parks. The government has had to warn the public that cats are unsafe in stews. Charles-Henri assures me that his meat is perfectly edible, and I believe him. He cooks dinners in his apartment and invites his friends over. Not mine, because I don't have many friends. His are raucous and pretentious, and I don't like them much, but I don't want to be picky, because at least I have a lover. Charles-Henri is very good-looking and writes bad poetry. He's also jealous, especially of the painters I meet at the Beaux-Arts school or in Montparnasse cafés. Picasso tries to seduce me. But I don't find him attractive. He says he will draw me, but it never happens. He has a thick Spanish accent. He buys me a drink one day at the Café de la Rotonde. His new lover, Françoise Gilot, is with him. It doesn't stop him from flirting with me.

I live on the Rue Saint-Jacques. I am trying to rebuild my life.

When I am alone, away from the Beaux-Arts or Charles-Henri, I am overcome by grief and despair. The familiar space I once inhabited has lost its meaning. Everything has lost its meaning. Sometimes, at night, my breathing feels constricted, as if I were choking on splinters. I wake in a sweat and sit upright. It takes a while for my breathing to slow down. I close my eyes and I can hear the first sounds of morning. The cry of a child. The distant roar of a car. Someone walking quickly down the street. A bird chirping on my balcony. Isolated sounds which will only later gather into the tumult of an ordinary day.

When I open my window and look outside, the sky is a smoke-less blue, the air is thin, like glass. I lean forward, and the breeze blows smoothly against my skin, still pale, not freckled, like my mother once was.

My mother. Now dust, now gone. And my father? I can under-stand him now. He lost himself in an imaginary world because the reality was too painful to accept. When he finally did accept it, after my mother was arrested, it was too late: madness had taken over. Did he feel responsible for her arrest? Would she have been spared had we stayed at home and not left the house?

I will never know the answers. Every day I ask myself, but I will never know.

There are many who say it wouldn't have made a difference. Nothing would have, except for luck. It stood by my side, not theirs. I loved them and lost them. Why? Because of a religion I barely believe in. Judaism is the bane of my existence. Yet it is an indelible stamp on my skin. I cannot make it disappear. No matter how hard I rub it off, it will always remain.

There are good men and women in my life. The Bonnets and the Thibaults. "Never forget the good people," I can hear my mother say. Never forget them, even though they will never replace the dead.

My English is nearly fluent now. I could leave France and my memories behind. Throw them into the Seine and watch them drown. But memories never drown. They always rise again to the surface.

5

In the fall of 1945, my father's shop is sold to someone else. A man who paints it white and changes its name. I split the money from the sale between the Bonnets and the Thibaults. Both these families saved my life. I keep only a small amount for myself. With this money, I will buy myself a ticket for Palestine. Not London as I had dreamt of. London is too close. I need to go farther, away from my memories, away from the ghosts of my parents. Not for ever, just for a while. Roger and Catherine, his wife, inform me they are looking for French teachers in Palestine. Catherine's brother Samuel settled there a few years back. He's become an architect and is happy. I could be too. I could change my life and reinvent myself in the land of milk and honey. Catherine knows a man who could help me get on a ship. "But it's not necessarily going to be the most comfortable of voyages," she adds. "They're not taking in refugees any more."

"What do you mean by that? Who aren't taking in refugees? The Jews?"

She shakes her head. "No. The British. They have quotas. It's outrageous, really, given what's happened," she mutters, under her breath.

"So immigration to Palestine is illegal?"

She hesitated. "We call it clandestine rather than illegal. You might be stopped by a British patrol, or you might not. But it's worth it. It's worth the risk." She pauses and looks at me. "The boat leaves from Italy on 17th September . If I were you, I would go. There's nothing left for you here. And you're young. You have your whole life in front of you."

Yes, but would I be willing to risk it once again? I hadn't given Palestine much thought before, because I wasn't a Zionist. I loved my country and had never seen a reason to leave it. If any movement tempted me, it had to do with literature, not the Promised Land: Dada and Surrealism, Symbolism and Existentialism. That's what I was interested in, and I didn't want to give it up. "Why should you?" Catherine says. "Take what you know with you! Write the novel you always wanted to write!"

"I don't know if I can," I tell her. "And I don't know if I still want to."

"You might change your mind when you get there," she says. "And at least you'll be far from those degenerate art schools."

Catherine strongly disapproves of my being an artist's model. Doesn't understand how I can strip naked for strangers. Doesn't understand art in general. I don't mind what she thinks, because I know what I like. Although, in truth, I don't see myself being a model in Palestine: I'll be exposing myself enough by going to a foreign country; I do not wish to expose myself further.

What awaits me there? I know hardly anything about Palestine, aside from the fact that the Mediterranean divides us. And I know no one who can enlighten me about the country's mores. What do people read there? Can one buy foreign books? What food do they eat? Do they have good coffee? How many languages do they speak? Will I be understood?

Too many questions, yet I know that I must go. I must sail as far away from Paris as possible. There is nothing left for me here, whereas in Palestine I will have a purpose. And I am bound to find others who have shared my plight. In Paris there is no one. I no longer see my old friends from the Sorbonne. I had close friends there. But many have moved away, or seem awkward in my presence, as if I had been the perpetrator of this war, rather than its victim. Or perhaps I'm over-interpreting. Perhaps their awkwardness stems from an unease, a difficulty in commiserating with me, because what I have lived through is bigger than anything they can grapple with. None of my friends have lost their parents. All they seem to have lost is their ability to speak with me. The war is a taboo subject, like a curse. So we avoid each other, like cats in the night.

*

Catherine is cooking me dinner, my last one before my departure tomorrow. We eat potato-and-carrot soup. Bread has been rationed again, as there is a wheat shortage, but she has managed to find us a small loaf on the black market. "I also saw a grapefruit in the shop today," she announces, excitedly. "The first grapefruit I've seen since '39."

There is a pitcher of watered white wine. It tastes like medicine, but we drink it anyway. Roger arrives late. He has had a meeting with someone from a publishing company who might have a new job for him. Roger used to be an editor before the war. He spent some time in the Resistance and managed to escape before the Germans uncovered his cell. But he became ill with tuberculosis while in hiding and hasn't been well since. He coughs a lot and looks pale. They have no money for a doctor, although Roger doesn't like doctors anyway, so it wouldn't make a difference. He coughs throughout dinner and he wheezes when he laughs. For dessert, we all smoke Gauloises. "You're doing the right thing by leaving this damn country," Roger declares, before heading off to bed. "And you should change your name to Flora. It's more international."

6

My first impression of Palestine is one I will never forget. The blinding white light. The dusty heat. The resinous scent of pine. The cyan blue of the sea. I haven't seen anything like it before. Paris is thin and hungry, but at least I know her. Here I know nothing and no one. There are nurses and soldiers on standby when we disembark from the ship. They take our temperature and whisk away the frailer ones. The streets of Haifa echo with the cries of vendors and the laughing of Arab children running around barefoot. A chicken squawks desperately before it is slaughtered in broad daylight by a man wearing a keffiyeh. There are Jewish women dressed in sandals and shorts, soldiers in khaki uniform with Mauser pistols hanging from their holsters, carts being pulled by tired donkeys. The air is filled with salt and the sound of foreign languages. Everything is loud and carefree. A seventeen-year-old girl who has sailed with me asks if we can stick together. She's French and quiet. She's been to Buchenwald and seen horrible things. This is what she tells me, without elaborating. We share a room in a hostel our first night in Haifa. It is dirty, and the bed has a few springs missing, so we decide to head for Jerusalem. It's where I want to be anyway. We take a bus there and find another hostel near Damascus Gate. It's much nicer, and we stay there for a while. The French girl cries a lot. I've tried to remember her name several times, but cannot. All I know is that she cries a great deal and reveals very little. Then a teacher at the Hebrew school I enrol in tells me about a Polish family. They're looking for someone to teach their son English. In exchange, they will give me a room with a small basin. I would rather it had been French lessons, but I say yes anyway. I have to do something, and it seems too good an opportunity to pass up. So I move in. The French girl announces that she is going to a kibbutz in the north, and I never see her again.

*

I find it difficult to learn Hebrew, and I am not the only one. There are many people like me in the classroom who struggle: orphans and refugees, but also Zionists and activists who claim that they want to change the world. I am not in Palestine to change the world, just my life. I want to leave my past behind and forget the traumas of the war. I am a twenty-five-year-old woman who has never been outside France. But Paris without my parents has been stripped of its meaning. Everything has been stripped of its meaning.

In the evenings, I usually have dinner with the Polish family. The mother is called Sonia. She has two boys: David, my seven-year-old pupil, and a small baby who hardly sleeps. I can hear him wailing every night in the room above me. He often keeps me awake, but I don't complain. I feel sorry for Sonia, because she looks so tired and fraught. She speaks no English, so it is difficult to communicate with her. Her husband is called Mordechai. He wears short-sleeved shirts and smokes a lot, and his skin is always sunburnt. He used to be a mathematician in Warsaw, before he was deported. Now he's making up for lost time. "I have many things to do aside from mathematics," he once tells me. "I want to live everything again."

"I do too," I say; there is no need to ask him what he means by that. Mordechai and I understand each other. To a large extent, we all understand each other in this strange land. There is an urgency here, as hard and hot as the stones that dominate the landscape. Many of us have suffered, but it is time to heal. "We have to reduce the six war years into six minutes," says Mordechai, puffing on his cigarette. "In mathematics it is called the beta reduction: you substitute one function for the other. I am doing it in my every day. Substituting life for loss. It doesn't mean you suppress, but compress. That is the way forward."

I listen to Mordechai. His words resonate more than any words of wisdom I have ever heard.

And it is in that small room, below the wailing infant, that I begin to write. At first it is a diary – a garbled one at that. Later, long after the events depicted had unfolded, I rewrote it in the form of this fragmented memoir. While many events have been indelibly imprinted on my mind, I find that others have dimmed, like a fading fresco. Yet, through the process of rewriting and remembering, some details have reappeared, hints of hues rising, opening that small door into the repository of my memory.

*

I go to restaurants alone in the Jerusalem evenings. I don't want to have dinner with Mordechai and Sonia every night. Besides, she isn't a very good cook. So I find a lively restaurant on Jaffa Street, in the centre of Jerusalem. I bring a book with me and pretend to read. I don't mind. I'm used to being on my own. I enjoy watching people, listening to all the languages spoken around me. Sometimes young men come to the table and strike up a conversation with me. I suppose I must not be very forthcoming, because they always end up walking away.

I start to make friends at the Hebrew school. One of them is a Hungarian woman my age, Ada. We make it a habit to meet at Café Atara, where many writers congregate. One evening, after we have just sat down for dinner, a man called Ezra Radok comes to our table and asks if he can join us. Ada has met him before and is secretly in love with him. His looks are striking, with searing blue eyes and dark hair. He is a poet from Prague. She doesn't know much about him aside from the fact that many women are in love with him and that he is said to be related to Kafka.

It will be a few months before I dare tell Ada the truth. That I too have fallen in love with Ezra Radok. That he isn't related to Kafka, although his parents had known him. That, although he has written a book of poetry, he has decided to give it up in favour of prose, and that he has become a significant part of my life. Just how significant, I don't know. How can I presage the future? I can barely understand the present. I don't watch out for its crevasses. I don't even know they're there. Why would I? I want to live again. Love again.

Hope again.

*

I returned to Israel thirty-eight years later, when my husband Henry gave a concert with the Israel Philarmonic Orchestra. He had played with them once before, under the baton of Zubin Mehta. It had been an important event, and I had missed it. I couldn't bring myself to return, because of my memories of Ezra. He had blood on his hands, and I had been an unwitting accomplice to his crime. Not because I had been involved in any way, but because I had never thought the man I loved would be capable of murder.

But this time Henry convinced me to go, and I finally relented. "You can't let the past take over your present," he said. "You were innocent then and you're innocent now."

"I know, but I can't forget," I said.

"I understand," he answered. "But it was a long time ago. And Ezra is dead. It would mean the world to me if you came."

The blinding white of the Jerusalem light was the same. So were the stones and the smell of pine. The streets were as I had remembered them, as was the Old City. The Arab man with the blue eyes was still selling fruit by Damascus Gate. I greeted him like an old friend, but he didn't remember me.

The small house with the peeling paint I had lived in with Mordechai and Sonia had been replaced by an ugly office building. The house Ezra had lived in was still there, even more beautiful than I remembered. It belonged to a family now. A German shepherd ran towards the gate and began to bark furiously. A woman appeared at his side – slim, stylish. "*Sheket*," she admonished him. "Be quiet."

Did she know who had once lived under her roof?

On the way back to the hotel, I passed Café Atara, then Fink's restaurant, where Ezra and I had spent many an evening. Years later, I found out that the barman who served drinks to the British officers plotting against the Irgun was one of its members. I remember the waiter. He had light hair and a dimpled smile. He was a friend of Ezra's.

"In this country, everyone is plotting against each other," Mordechai had once told me. "You cannot trust anyone."

I should have listened to Mordechai only.

No one else.

Henry and I stayed at the King David hotel. It seemed taller and more majestic than I remembered. Its pink sandstone gleamed in the sunlight. A man was playing the piano in the near-empty restaurant, which overlooked the Old City walls. The atmosphere was staid and quiet. Everything shone. The leather chairs, the marble floor, the turquoise and gold-corniced ceiling.

But I knew what had happened beneath the shine. What lay beyond the rebuilt rubble of war and memory. I wondered, as I walked past the numerous bellboys and hotel staff, whether they knew it too. How many of them had witnessed what I had? Were they able to live with it, or had they chosen to forget?

Until now, I have kept the truth to myself, entrusting it only to this blue spiral notebook. An amalgamation of history and memory – not suppressed, but compressed, just as Mordechai saw it.

For twenty years it has crepitated, like embers, in the third drawer of my old walnut desk. I've occasionally taken it out to look at its cover, but never dared reread its contents – nor shall I do so now. I would like my past to be revisited, but not by me. I do not need to be reminded of what happened. I know what I wrote. I know what happened. And I am ill now. Trouble with the heart, the bones, the spirit. I am eighty-two years old and tired. Sometimes so tired that I can barely make it out of bed. My doctor says it's the heart pills. But he also thinks that I am depressed. Has thought so for years. He has suggested I seek help, or take medication. "I know a good psychotherapist," he told me, more than once.

But the notion of seeking psychological help is an ungraspable one. I have never been an admirer of Mr Freud or Mr Jung. I have done what I needed to do, and I did it on my own. I have delved deep inside my psyche and reignited those dormant embers.

Those fragmented memories. I have given words to the images and images to the words. I do not need my Pandora's box to be opened. On the contrary, I need it to be firmly closed. And only my son can do that. The hole of Maurice's absence has never been filled. I have waited every day for him to reappear in my life, but it hasn't happened. Perhaps he never wanted us to meet. Or perhaps he didn't know how or where to find me. I will never know, and I have given up trying. It is now up to someone else to do the work for me. For someone else to inform my son that for him I have recorded history as I experienced it. For him, I have attempted to retrace my steps, follow the arc of my destiny from that summer morning in Paris, right before everything I had taken for granted vanished before my eyes – a door slamming into darkness.

7

Ezra and I are eating schnitzel at Fink's restaurant. It is 12th April 1946 and I am in love. My first true love. There he is, sitting in front of me, eating, dipping a piece of pitta bread in some olive oil. He hasn't eaten since that morning, he tells me, and he is ravenous.

Although he holds a part-time job in a British government office, where he processes the applications of Jews seeking asylum in Palestine, Ezra is always broke, because the pay is very low – "as low as the number of Jews they let in," he tells me. The food is good here in Palestine, and there's much more of it than in France. We eat hummus and fresh courgettes, bread and eggs, spicy cracked olives and Hungarian pastries. I make a habit of paying for the two of us when we go out, because I'm happy I can look after him that way. I've saved money from my year modelling, although Ezra doesn't like to hear about it, because it makes him jealous to know that men other than him saw me naked. I laugh, and he laughs back. He moves his hands animatedly when he does so, and barely breathes between bites. "I'm hungry all the time," he says.

We meet up in cafés or restaurant after work. I no longer teach David English, but French four times a week now, in a school near the King David Hotel. I enjoy it. The headteacher has asked me to commit to another year, and I have agreed.

Ezra doesn't really enjoy his job. He complains that he has no time to write his novel, and when I mention that I would love to read it he becomes agitated. "Stop asking me." The book in question is a love story set in 1920s Prague, and everyone seems to know about it. I have a feeling he hasn't written much of it yet, but doesn't want to admit it, although one drunken night he does reveal that the whole story has been written in his mind – that's why people know it, because he's given it away before writing it. It is just a matter of giving life to the characters. "It shouldn't be too difficult, " he says, although I wonder. I should know. I have tried to write my novel, but have given up on the idea. I don't think I have it in me. And there is only room for one writer in this relationship.

Ezra's first collection of poems was very well received, and he was fêted as a wunderkind, a Rilke in the making – and suddenly "the whole town wanted a piece of Ezra" is what I've been told. This was before we met. Now things are different, because we're always together, at least in the evening, so if they still want a piece of him they keep it to themselves. But that doesn't detract from the fact that there is something magnetic about Ezra, and the result is that we are seldom alone, except in restaurants.

We have been to Fink's several times before. It is, I am told, an institution. A place for intellectuals, artists and politicians. There are also plenty of British soldiers who flirt with the Jewish girls. The barman, Yuri, is a friend of Ezra's. He's Russian and is very good-looking. There are pictures of famous painters on its walls, and in the evening the bar is so full it is intimidating. Hoards of people shout and drink too much. Parisians may indulge in the same activities, but they do it with more reserve. Here, in Palestine, everyone is loud, and reserve is a byword for complacency. No one ever seems to sleep, and Ezra is no exception. He drags me everywhere and introduces me as his girlfriend. My relationship with him is unlike anything I've ever experienced with Jean or Charles-Henri – and I like it. I feel proud being Ezra's girlfriend. A few times he takes me to have drinks at the King David Hotel, said to be the best in the Middle East, and even though Ezra and I cannot afford to become regulars, I realize exactly why people love it, because when I'm there I never want to leave. The waiters are all Sudanese, and so many languages are spoken that it's easy to forget which country one is actually in. Men are dressed in suits, and women smell like flowers and wear high-heeled shoes and summer dresses and flirt with men who might or might not be strangers. Ezra tells me that the southern wing of the hotel is rented by the British to accommodate the Chief Secretariat of the Mandate Administration, and it is where they conduct their business, entertain and take their tea. The notion of "taking tea" is not as foreign to me as it is to Ezra. He hasn't read the English classics I pored over at the Sorbonne. England is not, admittedly, a country he wishes to know more about, because he doesn't have much sympathy for the British, whose presence he resents – although he doesn't discuss it in public, because he doesn't want to lose his job. But aside from the British, Ezra seems to know everyone else, from writers to politicians to Bedouins and the Arab fruit sellers in the Old City, like the blue-eyed man by the Damascus Gate, who gives him oranges and dates for free because Ezra once saved his small boy from getting run over by a passing donkey cart. It happened quickly. Everything here happens quickly. Jerusalem is beyond anything I could have ever imagined. The energy is kinetic. I often wonder if it might spontaneously combust one day. Or perhaps it irradiates from its ancient soil. I am swept up by it all, and for the first time since 1943 I am happy. I can feel it swell inside me like a torrent of water rising through cracked, sore earth.

*

There is a friend of Ezra's called Lotta, a musicologist from Berlin. The front door of her house is always open, and every Friday night people pour in and out like a swarm of hungry bees. Lotta is in her early thirties – a sophisticated, attractive woman with long black hair and dark skin. Her husband, a clarinettist, has recently left her for another woman, who is now pregnant with his child. For a while Lotta's house was closed to family and friends, but now she's reopened it. "I don't have a baby, but at least I got a house out of the bastard," she declared.

One can just walk into Lotta's living room and someone will be playing the piano or reciting poetry. There are conversations in German, Hebrew and English – sometimes Russian or French. People often sleep over at Lotta's, because there are no cheap hotels in Jerusalem, and there is no way of contacting her in advance because very few people have telephones. "Her house is like a literary salon," someone once says about Lotta. "But not everyone can be a member."

I often wonder whether I would be a member if it weren't for Ezra. I'd like to be friends with Lotta. I find her impressive. She writes, she sings, she speaks several languages, she is everything I am not. But there is something aloof about her, or perhaps it has to do with me. I try to speak to her several times, but she seems distracted, as if she'd rather be talking to someone else. Ezra once mentioned that she was "sort of in love" with him, and I wonder what he means by "sort of". But I know better than to ask. I also know that, if I could, I would make Lotta like me more. Show her my steelier side.

But something about her defeats me.

*

Ezra is fluent in French, so this is the language we speak together. He has a faint accent, which he calls "the lost Empire accent". "Where I come from no longer exists," he says. "Unlike your Paris."

"Paris may still exist, but it's no longer mine, and it's been bruised."

"It will recover," Ezra says. "France always recovers."

"Yes, it does," I concede. "Its vanity is too deeply anchored in the national psyche."

"Were your parents vain?" he asks me, a question which takes me by surprise. If anything, my parents were the opposite of vain. They were modest, hard-working, humble. "They didn't know what vanity was. Although my mother was coquettish," I tell him.

"Was she pretty like you?" Ezra continues. "She must have been."

"I think she was beautiful," I answer. I describe my mother and her elegance, how she loved clothes and how loud her laugh was for such a delicate woman. Then I find that remembering her laugh makes me want to cry, so I tell Ezra that I'd rather hear about him now, his childhood in Prague, his mother and father. His face tenses up a bit when I mention him. "I never really felt I knew my father," he says.

Ezra was brought up in an affluent family in Prague, in an apartment housed in a former palace overlooking Wenceslas Square. There were so many rooms in that apartment that he could ride on a bicycle through them. There were two servants and a French nanny, Simone, whom he adored. He spoke German to his parents and French to Simone, who had sole charge of little Ezra, because his mother, a famous beauty and socialite, was too busy to take care of him. He never resented her absence – so he says – because he loved his mother and she loved him back, and when she was there for him she was "entirely there". She was very bright; "a well-read woman with a voracious appetite for life" is how Ezra describes her, as if he were talking about a female version of himself. "Our house was always filled with people, especially in the spring and summer. My parents had many parties. There was a playwright, Jaroslav Hapvil, I think she had an affair with him. I'm sure my father thought so too, though I wouldn't know, because he was a difficult man to talk to – very reserved, a rich textile manufacturer, a cold man, just like the rooms in our apartment in the winter. When guests would come to visit, the stove had to be lit two days beforehand to ensure they would be comfortable. That's why most of our parties took place in the warmer seasons. I met Kafka's parents because they came to a few or our parties, and they knew my mother – everyone did. They all loved her – even Kafka's father loved her, although he was not a nice man. Like us, they spoke German at home, and Franz wrote in German and the Czechs didn't like that: they wanted him to write in Czech. But then that didn't matter, because he died in 1924, and we all thought that grief would make Franz's father softer – but it never did. He was also a manufacturer, a clothing retailer, like my father, but he wasn't elegant like him. He was overbearing and loud. My mother used to say that it was because he had grown up the son of a ritual slaughterer from Southern Bohemia. A religious Jew. "He's got the sensitivity of a slaughterer," she would say about Hermann Kafka. She never really had much patience for Hermann or religion. Although we were Jewish, it was seldom discussed. Until 1938, when there was a big Wehrmacht parade on Wenceslas Square and our lives changed overnight."

I never hear the rest of the story, because Ezra stops it right before the gates open into Auschwitz, where he was deported. "I don't want to open those gates again," he says. All he does tell me is that he contracted typhus, then tuberculosis, and the fact that he survived made him stronger.

He doesn't hear the rest of my story either, as mine stops after my mother has walked away in her blue polka-dot dress, the smell of perfume trailing behind her. I do not describe the heaving hole of her absence, how I circumvent it every day. In general, Ezra and I do not feel the need to put our pain into words. We continue eating our schnitzel and potatoes, followed by strudel with a hint of cinnamon, and leave our pain wordless.

Ezra is thin, painfully so, and appears younger than his twenty-three years. When he speaks and laughs, there is something iridescent about him. Being with him jolts me out of my sadness. If he can live again, so I must. "The inferno swallowed up my parents, but not me. I am lucky. There is no guilt to be had in luck, only gratitude," says Ezra.

I learn from him. I grow with him. Ezra has had many girlfriends before me, and his physical prowess take me by surprise.

He is man, he is mine, he is desire. He is poetry, passion and fire. He is cigarettes, carnal words and moist fingers. He is pale skin, like a high moon.

At night we speak loss, that silent language the departed have left behind. The vortex of war has spared us, and we lie entwined, our bodies glistening with drops of pleasure as we defy the spectre of our common history.

In the morning, when Ezra lights his cigarette, I see his shadow on the wall, the movement of his hand towards his mouth, the way the smoke blends with the first rays of the hot, burning sun.

8

Ezra and I have been together for a few months. His landlord, an unpleasant Romanian shop owner, has found us in bed and has kicked him out. He cannot stay with me, because my room at Mordechai and Sonia's, a single bed with a small desk, is too small for the two of us. And also they probably wouldn't approve. So he is temporarily living with Lotta. I should be jealous – Lotta is pretty, albeit much older than us – but I am not. I trust Ezra with all my heart. If he were to ask me to marry him, I would say yes.

Unequivocally yes.

And then perhaps that would solve the accommodation problem.

*

Something has happened and I am nervous, although Ezra tells me not to be. "Don't worry: we're safe," he says, running a finger along my bare skin.

We are sitting on my sofa on a Saturday afternoon. Outside we can hear voices, the occasional sound of gunfire – a reminder of war, of Paris, which until now had seemed so far away. But then everything here is done differently, including this curfew, which has been imposed throughout the country. In France, the concept of safety was reserved for all non-Jews. Here it is the opposite: we are being told to stay in for our safety. The Mandate government has dispatched seventeen thousand troops and arrested members of a paramilitary Zionist organization, in retaliation for attacks on government buildings, railways and British troops. They have called the operation "Black Sabbath". Documents have been seized and taken to the King David headquarters for safekeeping. The government has promised to eradicate terror and violence, a promise which has been met with a tepid response. Why is that?

When I raise the topic with Ezra, he appears bored; I am surprised. "The government will never be able to tame the people. There is too much anger. And anyway, politics doesn't interest me," he mumbles.

"But how could it not? These Irgun people are savages! Look at what they've been doing to the country! They're destroying everything!"

I think I catch something in his eyes, a blink of unease.

"I suppose they are," he finally answers.

*

I stop by Lotta's a few days later, as I occasionally do after work. In general, I prefer meeting Ezra elsewhere; Lotta's presence still makes me nervous. This time, I'm relieved to see she isn't there, and the house appears empty. Ezra isn't in the kitchen or his bedroom. I'm about to leave when I hear voices. I follow their trail and I find Ezra in a room at the back of the house, speaking to a man I've never seen before. He is short and pudgy, with an unpleasant face. I cannot hear what he and Ezra are saying, but it looks important, because they are standing close to each other and seem to be very concerned about something. I stand by the door briefly, then walk away. That is when Ezra calls out my name. "Flora, come here! Come and meet my friend!" he says, as if there is nothing untoward about what I have just witnessed.

So I go back in and am introduced to Shlomo. He has small eyes, and his face is bruised, with patches of dried blood near his nose. He looks unlike Ezra's regular circle of friends. He says something in Hebrew and smiles wanly. "Shlomo has just had an accident," Ezra translates. "Which is why he looks a bit red in the face."

"What happened?" I ask.

"He got beaten up by an Arab," Ezra answers. "Wrong place at the wrong time."

"What do you mean? What happened?"

"Stupid, really. All about a pack of cigarettes."

I've heard of several incidents between the Jews and the Arabs, but not among my friends and acquaintances. They, as well as I, respect the Arabs. No one wants trouble. Those who do are part of those radical groups the British Mandate is trying to eradicate. I look at Shlomo and wonder whether he might actually be part of such a group. He is speaking quickly in Hebrew, and I cannot understand what he is saying. He is sweating now and looks distraught. He glances at his watch and mumbles, in broken English, that it was nice to meet me. He bids me goodbye and Ezra walks him to the door. When Ezra returns, I badger him with questions. "How come I've never met him before? How do you know him? What happened with the Arab?"

Ezra explains slowly. "The Arab got upset over money Shlomo owed him. Nothing to do with cigarettes. He just didn't want to get into it in front of me. And I know Shlomo because we work together," Ezra adds. "We're not really friends, just colleagues at the British government office. We process naturalization papers together." I look at Ezra as he speaks, and I can tell that there is more to the story.

"What else do you do there? I'm sure you do something else."

"That's all," he says firmly.

"You don't lie well," I remark. "It shows on your face."

Ezra raises his head and looks at me quizzically. "Does it?" He smiles. "Yes, it's true. There is something else. But I'm not sure you're going to like it."

"Try me."

He hesitates. "Are you sure?"

I nod. "Yes."

"All right then," he says slowly. "As you know, we handle the applications of Palestinian Jews. All above board. Except that we also happen to have the files of those who have disappeared during the war. So we help smuggle Holocaust survivors into Palestine."

"How?"

He speaks cautiously. "I know a forger. He's been able to copy government stamps."

"Really?"

I'm not sure whether to condemn him or say nothing. After all, we were both smuggled into Palestine. I can hardly hold it against him.

"So who's the forger?"

"An Arab, in Jaffa. And you are not to tell a soul, do you hear?"

"Of course." I pause. "So you smuggle Jews into the country?"

He raises his voice. "Is that a problem for you? Are you going to tell anyone? You know I could go to jail for that, right? Do you know that? The British have a quota they have to respect. I disrespect it. Do you understand? I was in the camps and I thoroughly disrespect their quota."

"Yes, of course. But they're not the ones who put it in place, are they? That would be the League of Nations, not them. They're just following orders—"

"They follow orders like dogs. Do you hear? Rabid fucking dogs!" His voice has risen, and his eyes are shining in a way I've never seen them shine before.

"Ezra—"

"No, now you listen! Do you know how many refugee-filled ships are sent back by the British?"

"No. Please don't shout. I understand this is important, but calm down. Don't shout."

"I'm not shouting. The French, the Italians and the Americans are prepared to take the Jews in. But the British? Nah... Not even when it's a matter of urgency. Like the *Struma*, in 1942. Do you know about that? You must – it was a big scandal."

"I'm not sure."

The truth is that until I arrived here I knew little about the British Mandate or Palestine. But I don't feel comfortable admitting it.

Ezra looks at me intently. "The *Struma* was a ship – actually, not a ship, but a lousy wreck of a boat – which had 769 refugees on board, many of them rich Romanians who had paid a fortune to escape the Nazis. It left from Romania bound for Palestine in 1942. There was a short stop in Istanbul, because the engine failed. But the Turkish government wouldn't let the passengers off the boat, so they ended up spending weeks awaiting a decision about their fate. The Jewish Agency pleaded with Palestine to take the refugees in, but the answer was a resounding 'no'. The British ambassador in Ankara said that he didn't want these people – *these people* – in Palestine. And so what happened?"

"I don't know."

"I'll tell you what happened: the boat was torpedoed by the Soviets, and they all died, except for one survivor. They all fucking died." He pauses and breathes deeply. "Another time, a submarine – a Soviet one again – machine-gunned four hundred Holocaust survivors in the water."

"That's awful," I whisper. "But why?"

"They thought they were Germans." He pauses. "So say the Soviets. That they thought they were Germans."

Ezra lights a cigarette and blows the smoke towards his open window. I can hear children singing in the street.

"There're many more stories like this one," he says. "So yes, I think that every Jew should be let into this country. I think that we have suffered enough. Those quotas should not be in place."

I nod. I cannot speak. The image of the *Struma* ship and the machine-gunned survivors is haunting me. But there is something else. Ezra has revealed an anger – more than anger, a rage – which takes me by surprise. How come I didn't detect it before? Why did he lie and claim that he wasn't interested in politics? He is more than interested. He is committed. But to what? To peace? Or something murkier?

"Are you involved in anything I should know about?" I ask him straight out.

"No," he answers firmly. "I knew you would ask that, but no. All I am is a holocaust survivor. The British have to stop intercepting our boats and putting our refugees in concentration camps. They must stop behaving like Nazis. The Jewish people will never again capitulate. We have suffered enough."

I reach my hand out towards his. "It's true, Ezra. We have all suffered enough, especially you. But I don't think the British are behaving like Nazis. They're just doing their job. I'm sure many of them feel bad about it. They're human after all."

Ezra continues to smoke and says nothing. I look into his eyes and see flecks of black, like tiny bullets, against the blue of his irises.

Ezra has found a new place to live. It is in the German quarter, on Emek Refaim Street, an old stone house with purple bougainvillea dripping down its whitewashed walls. It has a room with a large bed, a bathroom and a kitchen. The furniture is elegant, and from his window one can see the Scottish Church of St Andrew. It is a beautiful, peaceful place, and for the first time I am jealous. I wish I lived in an apartment like his. To make matters worse, the rent is low, because it belongs to a friend of Lotta's, who has spread the word that everything must be done to help Ezra the "wunderkind". So the words come out before I can stop them. "Lotta always wants to help, doesn't she? I mean, does she ever NOT do anything for you?"

Ezra's face darkens. "I'm not having an affair with her, if that's what you're thinking."

"No, no of course not."

But there is something about the way he says it which makes me think otherwise. Why would he jump to such a conclusion so soon?

I tell him I need to get back to work, I have papers to grade. It's getting late. My voice is wobbly – soon I will cry, and I'd like to leave before that happens, because I don't like anyone to see me cry. But Ezra doesn't give me that option. He comes towards me and takes me in his arms. "What's the matter? Don't be upset. There is absolutely nothing for you to worry about, do you understand? I love you, don't you know that? I love you, Flora Baum."

He has uttered those words before, but this time, more than any other, there is an urgency, a despair nearly in the way he holds me against him. "I need to go," I say, pushing him away. "I have a lot of work to do."

He grabs my shoulders. "Nothing happened between us," he says sternly. "Nothing at all. Lotta may want something to happen, but I'm not attracted to her. I never will be. Do you believe me?"

"Yes," I answer softly. "I believe you."

"I don't want to lose you," he whispers, his eyes resting on mine. "We cannot lose each other."

"No," I whisper back. "We cannot."

"I'll see you tonight. I love you," he says again.

It is 21st July 1946. Ezra has to spend the evening in Haifa. His superior wants him there for an early meeting the next morning. It will be easier for him to spend the night. "I'll be taking a train straight after work," he says.

Because he is employed by the British, Ezra has a special pass that enables him to travel wherever he wants. But I worry about him travelling, because there have been many incidents lately: bombings, kidnappings, people being shot in broad daylight. Last month, five British officers and one RAF serviceman were kidnapped. For all I know, Ezra could be next. "Be careful," I tell him.

"Of course," he reassures me. But he seems nervous. He holds me tightly against him and begins to kiss me and fumbles with my bra and tells me that he wants me, even though he should really be going back to his flat. "But it's 'that time of the month'," I tell him shyly. I also have stomach cramps – although I have kept those to myself; I find it embarrassing to discuss such matters, and so clearly does he. "OK," he mumbles, as I button up my blouse. I grab a hairbrush and brush my curly black hair more vigorously than I should. Ezra lights a cigarette and paces around the room. "What are your plans tomorrow?" he asks, tapping his ash into a cracked coffee cup. "Will you be home in the morning?"

Because he has never asked me anything of the sort before, I become suspicious: "Why are you asking?" I say, holding the hairbrush in mid-air.

"I'm just wondering, that's all. Is that bad?" he asks, sounding defensive.

"No, no of course not," I retract. "I don't know what I'll be doing. I may go for a walk with Ada. I don't teach tomorrow."

"OK."

I wonder, not for the first time, whether he's cheating on me. If so, is it Lotta? Is he really going to Haifa? Or am I being paranoid?

"I'll see you tomorrow," Ezra says.

We kiss at the door. He smells of soap and summer sun.

*

Yael, the headteacher at the school, has asked to see me. She wants to discuss the curriculum for next year, and is also interested in my teaching English. She suggests we meet at 12.00, in a café near the school. It's a hot and muggy day, and my stomach cramps have been replaced by a bad headache. But I don't dare cancel the appointment, because I need to display enthusiasm and I need this job. I'm starting to run out of money.

Yael is in her late thirties. Her hair is prematurely grey, which makes her look much older. She has two children, one of whom is at the school, an intelligent girl who has learnt to speak French very quickly. Yael seems to think it's thanks to my teaching, whereas I'm inclined to believe that her daughter just learns fast. Whatever the reason, Yael is happy and I'd like to keep it that way.

She's a bit late for our meeting, so I order coffee and a pastry while I wait for her. I'm hoping the food will make my headache go away. But if anything, it makes it worse.

By the time she arrives, my head is pounding. "Are you OK? You look pale," Yael remarks.

I explain and apologize profusely. "I'm so sorry, but I think I need to go home."

"Of course." She looks at me. "Have a lemon juice before you leave and don't drink any more coffee."

I do as she says. I drink the lemon juice slowly and it does alleviate the pain, but not enough. I apologize again, and Yael walks me to the door. She stands close to me and I can smell her armpits. "Take care of yourself; we'll speak tomorrow, it's fine," she says gently.

I walk back slowly. My head is throbbing. I cross the street and increase my pace. I look at my watch. It is 12.30. I wonder whether Ezra is back from Haifa, and if I should go and visit him. I miss him suddenly. I shouldn't have overreacted the way I did. I shouldn't get so jealous. He doesn't have another woman. He only has me. Then again, he gets jealous too, even more than I do. I realize that we've seen each other practically every evening since we first met. Last night was the first time that we didn't. And we left on a sour note, all because of me.

I cross the lights at King George Street. The King David Hotel stands in front of me, like a fortress. I think of the evening Ezra and I spent there only a week ago. There was an Egyptian man who spoke perfect French. He was very elegant and courteous. We talked about André Gide and Paul Éluard, and drank champagne. The Egyptian said he was a foreign correspondent from Cairo, and the King David was his pied-à-terre. "Nowhere else in the world will you find private detectives, socialites, Zionist agents, journalists and Arab sheikhs all in one place," he said, laughing. I asked Ezra to join in the conversation, because the man was so interesting. But he didn't, because he was jealous. He said that he wanted to leave early, so we did, even though I would rather have stayed. As we walked back, I realized that the man hadn't even told me his name. For all I knew he could have been a spy. Jerusalem is filled with spies, and I suppose that's what makes it exciting.

My headache is starting to lift. I walk by Steimatzky, the book-shop. Perhaps I should go inside and get a book or two. I wonder if Ezra has read *The Great Gatsby*. He must have. Ezra has read everything. But something is happening. A thunderous, deafening eruption. What is it? The ground beneath my feet is shaking. Is it a bomb? I look up, and then I see it and gasp: the south-west wing of the King David Hotel has just collapsed into a mass of stone, cement and twisted iron. There is a billow-ing of black smoke and charred debris everywhere. There are screams, and people running and cars overturning on the street, and broken trees and shards of glass everywhere, and men and women covered in blood and white dust, then sirens blasting from fire trucks, ambulances and police cars – and I fall to the ground. A man helps me up. He is covered in white dust, as I am. He says something to me in Hebrew. I don't answer. Time passes. Or does it? Palestinians and British soldiers are digging in the rubble for survivors. Dead bodies are strewn around me. I gasp. I see my mother, my father, and I begin to wail, because the void of grief Ezra and I had kept so tightly sealed has burst open, like an abscess. Then I see a man lying near me on the ground: he is wearing his British soldier's uniform; his black boots are covered in debris, and a woman rushes towards him. "James!" she is screaming. "James!" She is young and pretty, probably my age, and her pale-green dress is smeared in filth and blood – and James, her husband, is dead. He has managed to open his eyes and see her one last time before dying, and she is holding him against her and swaying back and forth and touching his boots and speaking to him as his head now tilts backwards. I rush towards her and say a few words of comfort – I don't remember exactly what – but I do remember that she listens and I get her to release her husband's corpse and gently close his eyes – and she kisses his eyelids, then kisses his still, white face, covers him with kisses while the sun burns hot above us, and she leans him gently back on the ground and then turns towards me and whispers that he was the love of her life, no other man like him, that she's expecting their first child, that nothing will be the same without him ever again, that he was her life, her love.

"What's your name?" I ask her.

"Claire Betts," she answers, in a faint voice. "We were supposed to go to Aden in a week. Start a new life. Not finish one."

She falls on her knees and covers her face with her hands, and I hold her against me and she begins to howl and cannot stop; she has a dainty pearl necklace around her neck, and she howls on her knees and now so do I – for her, for James, for my mother and father, for the black of death and for the pale green of Claire's dress which James saw one last time before dying.

Now there are paramedics and policemen everywhere. They lift Claire up. Someone places a blanket over James's face. Claire turns around as she walks away, and she looks at me, almost as if she wanted to tell me something. Then she disappears into the cloud of black smoke, the smell of burning, and into the dust.

*

The sun is impossibly hot, impossibly heavy. I don't remember getting home. Perhaps someone walked me there. The same man who had picked me up? My head is throbbing so violently I cannot see straight. I'm in bed. Mordechai and Sonia have come to see me. They feed me and take care of me. But the light hurts my eyes. The heat is unbearable. I vomit a few times. Then I fall asleep. I wake up at dawn to the sound of the muezzin's call for prayers behind the Old City walls.

The next day, Mordechai sits me down in his kitchen. "Ezra won't be coming back," he says. He explains why. He heard about Ezra and Shlomo. His brother told him. He knows about most of the Irgun members, because his brother has been working for the British intelligence for the past four years, helping them track down the radical elements within the community. Ezra, who was the second in command of the organization, is the mastermind.

"What?" I gasp. "The mastermind?"

"Yes," says Mordechai. "My brother was about to close in on Ezra and his friends before this happened. A serious slip-up. I'm told they managed to arrest a few hundred of them. They're all at the Rafiah detention camp. But they want Ezra. They got Shlomo, but they want Ezra. And Shlomo won't give him up."

I cannot speak for a long while. Mordechai's words have clogged my throat. I can hear myself breathing quickly.

"I'm sorry to have to tell you," Mordechai says, squeezing my hand gently, "but I thought that you should know."

"He never went to Haifa," I finally murmur. "He was here the whole time… He lied to me over and over again. He wasn't working for the British but against them…"

Mordechai nods slowly. "He wasn't the only one. Right now, in this country, everyone is plotting against each other. You cannot trust anyone."

"Including you?"

He smiles. "I suppose so, yes. Including me. But I'm one of the good ones," he hastens to add.

I fall silent.

"Why did he do it, do you think?" I finally ask.

Mordechai removes a pack of cigarettes from his shirt pocket and lights one. "In retaliation for the Black Sabbath raids," he says, blowing the smoke away. "He and his friends wanted to strike where it would hurt most. And they didn't go at it gingerly. They used TNT which was hidden inside seven milk churns, 50 kg of explosives per churn. Ezra is the one who drove the van dressed as a Sudanese waiter, and who placed the churns inside the basement kitchen of the restaurant before leaving the premises. The bomb went off at 12.37 p.m. Three separate phone calls were made, warning the hotel that the explosives were about to go off. The one thing my brother and his men don't understand is why the hotel dismissed the calls. But they'll focus on that later. The important thing now is to catch Ezra and his fanatical comrades."

Mordechai finishes his cigarette and crushes it forcefully with the tip of his nicotine-stained finger. "The death toll is approaching ninety people." He lifts his head and looks at me. "We are now witnessing the last days of the British Mandate, mark my words. The Irgun has won its battle. Palestine will from now on be left to its own devices."

Everything he says shocks me to the core. How could I not have known? How could I have been so naive? Because I loved Ezra. I was blinded by my love for him. I curse him. I loathe him now. I'm ashamed of him. Ashamed of myself. The image of James Betts floats through my mind. His body lying on the ground. His wife kissing his closed eyelids. I would like to find her and tell her what I know. I would like to find her and say how sorry I am.

"There was a woman," I say to Mordechai. "Her name was Claire Betts, and I saw her in the rubble next to her husband, kissing him a last goodbye. It was devastating."

Mordechai nods. "It's terrible. I'm sorry. For her, for us, for England."

Then a thought occurs to me. "Does your brother know that you're telling me all of this? And how did he find out about Ezra?"

"He had an informer – and yes, he knows."

"Who was it?"

He lights another cigarette. "I have no idea."

"I bet you it was Lotta," I mutter. "I'm sure it was her..."

"I don't know," he says, smoking. "I think that Ezra tried to recruit her, but it didn't work."

I freeze. "Did he try to recruit me, do you think?"

Mordechai looks at me and smiles. "I wouldn't be able to tell you. Only you know, Flora. No one else. So let me ask you this question: did he try to recruit you?"

I shake my head. "No. He never said a thing. I suppose I'm not committed enough to this country."

He takes another puff of his cigarette. "But you were committed to him. Do you have any idea where he might be?"

I shake my head again. "No idea. Whatever he did tell me was clearly a lie. You should try speaking to Lotta. He didn't lie to her. They were very close."

"Yes, I know. She's being interrogated as we speak."

I turn abruptly towards him. "What do you mean by 'I know'? Did they have an affair?"

He looks at me. "Do you still care?"

"No," I retort. "I don't."

"Good. He was a traitor and she was in love with him. That's why we think she might have information. That's why they're holding her. Because she was angry with him for loving you, not her."

The following day a party of British officers shows up at Mordechai's. My room is searched, my identity card checked. I am driven to a police station for questioning. A tall English officer with an alert face and a cut-glass accent sits behind a wooden desk. The room is stiflingly hot, and there is a smell of stale tobacco in the air. I tremble, despite the heat. The officer asks me questions about Ezra: how we met, what I knew about his job, his friends. I mention Shlomo and Lotta, and the Arab passport forger from Jaffa. The officer presses me for details about the forger, but there isn't much I can tell him other than what Ezra shared with me.

"I never suspected anything," I say. "I had no idea that Ezra led a double life – no idea at all." It is the truth, and I can tell that the officer believes me.

"If I had known," I add, "I would have left him."

"Yes, but would you have reported him?" he asks, his eyes settling on mine.

"Of course I would have," I answer firmly. "I would have had no problem with that."

But I wonder. And I can tell, by the way he looks at me, that the officer does too.

"We are looking for Ezra Radok," he states firmly, "and we will find him. He has killed ninety people." He pauses. "No one can be allowed to get away with killing that number of people. No one."

There is another interrogation: another officer, a new set of questions. About my last evening with Ezra, then Lotta, then Ezra again. I answer as well as I can and must sound convincing, because they let me go. "We'll be in touch if we need to talk to you again," I am told.

I wait a few days. I hear about more arrests, Ada being one of them, though I'm not sure why. All I know is that I must leave. My time has come. The land of milk and honey has turned charcoal-black. Ezra is still on the run. If they catch him, he will probably be hanged. I cannot stand the thought. That the man I loved and touched and kissed and trusted might be hanged. Because I do believe that although he lied about his covert activities, he did truly love me. I could feel it. One cannot pretend to love. Nor can one pretend to hate. And now I hate him. He cannot get away with what he's done. Still, I must leave before they find him, if they do. They might never. Knowing him, they might never.

He is a murderer, yet I loved him. He is a murderer who betrayed me. He is a murderer whom I trusted with all my heart.

If there is a lesson to be learnt, it is that I must not love again.

Not for many years to come.

Later, I found out that Mordechai lied to me as well.

There was no brother. The brother was him. Mordechai. He was the agent working for the British. He was looking out for me, Yael told me. And he knew I was innocent. He knew many things. What those things were, she didn't elaborate and I didn't ask.

The image I carry as I sail away is not of Ezra, but of Claire Betts clasping her dead husband, and the way she turned round and looked at me, standing in her blood-stained pale-green dress, under the heat of that impossible midday sun.

HANNAH

1

We were friendly with all of our neighbours on Oxford Gardens, except for Mrs Dobbs, who lived across the way. She was a grey-haired, rather elegant lady of indeterminate age who, despite her slow gait and lined face, had a certain aloof self-sufficiency about her, which hinted at an interesting history.

For four years we tried to befriend her. My father, based on the fact that she had once complimented him on one of his plays, was convinced that she had been someone or done something important. "There's a secret there, waiting to be deciphered. Or plucked, like ripe fruit."

"Good luck and good plucking," said my mother.

My father had an infectious ebullience about him, which touched most of those who crossed his path. But not Mrs Dobbs.

She remained immune to our niceties, our invitations to tea, the fact that my father was renowned in his field. She was always polite – how do you do, yes what a lovely day – but no more than the minimum required.

From what we gathered, she lived alone and had no children, no relations. The neighbours told us that her husband had died in 1981. He had been a famous concert pianist, Henry Dobbs, and a gentle man. They could often hear him play, and he was very good indeed. I know this because as soon as my father found out who her husband was he bought two of his records and played them at full volume, hoping the familiar sound of her husband's Schubert interpretation might entice Mrs Dobbs into our house.

I still remember what that Schubert record looked like. On the front was a photograph of Henry Dobbs, a man with a large mane of white hair sitting at a piano. Underneath it was a quote which my father liked to read out loud: "Dobbs's superb virtuosity never supplants his heart-rending musicality. If Glenn Gould were to have an heir, Henry Dobbs would be him."

"Imagine that!" my father would exclaim. "Imagine that such an impressive man was married to that very warm and delightful woman."

But if anything, hearing Gould's heir apparent blasting from our sitting-room window defeated my father's purpose, because now, whenever she saw him, Mrs Dobbs barely said hello, as if he had offended her in some way. So my father stopped playing his records and declared that it was a relief, because Henry Dobbs really wasn't such a great pianist after all, so why bother.

Occasionally Mrs Dobbs had visitors. Once I saw an elegant man with a cane standing by her front door. He wiped his feet on her doormat before entering. There was also an older woman, and a young man carrying a violin, who rang our doorbell by mistake.

"Is this the house of Flora Dobbs?" he asked with a strong accent.

I pointed him in the right direction. "That was a German accent," my mother declared, as soon as he had gone. "There must be some German connection there."

We told my father when he came home. "Her name is Flora," I said to him. "And Mum thinks Flora has a German connection."

"German?"

His face sank. "She's a Kraut. Of course she's a Kraut. That would explain everything."

"What would it explain?" I asked.

"Never mind," my father sighed.

"I don't think she's a Kraut," my mother ventured. "I've heard her speak, and she doesn't sound German."

My father turned towards her. "You say you heard her speak? As in more than three words?"

My mother gave it some thought. "I can't really remember how many words it was," she finally said.

I couldn't understand what all the fuss was about. I didn't really care whether or not Mrs Dobbs had a connection to anything German or otherwise. As far as I was concerned, she was a lady my brother Ben and I often passed on our way to school, who wore flowing skirts and lived in a slightly grubby street in Notting Hill, like us. When it rained, she carried an umbrella that was too large for her small frame. She used public transport. We knew this because we often saw her struggling to get aboard the 31 bus. But we didn't find her particularly interesting. She was old, at least to our eyes, and she was curt and unfriendly.

"I wonder where she's off to," my mother said, when Ben mentioned seeing her get on the bus.

I shrugged my shoulders. "I don't know. And anyway, who cares?"

"There's something mysterious about her, that's all," my mother said.

Eventually, my parents gave up conjecturing. And as the years went by and Ben and I grew older, leaner and pimplier, Flora Dobbs seemed to remain just as she had always been, stuck in time, a mysterious lady of indeterminate age who wanted nothing more than to be left alone.

*

In 1986, I received a letter of acceptance to the sixth form at St Paul's School. I was sixteen years old and thrilled. When I got home, my father opened a bottle of champagne and my mother had to remind him that Ben and I were too young to drink. So my parents drank the champagne instead, and we got into the car and drove to a nearby French bistro to celebrate, even though Ben had to get up early to go on a school trip to France.

He was surly, as he often was, and nearly destroyed the evening, not by being boisterous or rude, but through the harshness of his silence.

What Ben had witnessed as a young child had settled inside him like a chemical. His stability had been challenged. And as he turned into a young man, that instability became part of his DNA.

I watched my brother grow like a sick plant. I saw how his roots became tangled and contorted, how the blossoming of his youth was stunted, contaminated by a rampant intruder. He was still beautiful. He would always be. But his beauty was tainted by guilt. Deep, solidified guilt, like mortar. He seldom communicated. He kept his head lowered when he walked, when he talked, when he ate. There were moments of respite, but few of them. When they happened, we latched on to them, trying to keep Ben going for as long as we could, attempting to draw him in, to make him laugh, to ask him questions, to hold what we loved of him until the tentacles of his mind drew him back into their Stygian, muted fold.

It was painful to watch. I could see lines on my mother's face that hadn't been there before. My father, vivacious outside the house, was tense around his own son. I assured my parents that Ben would climb out of the hole of his own accord. "Most teens do," I added, though I wondered how true that was. I was after all still a teen myself.

"Of course he'll grow out of it," said my mother, trying to sound reassuring.

"Is that right?" my father mumbled.

After nearly five years, Ben's behaviour had sapped the energy from my tired parents. Although I shared their concerns, I blamed them for allowing my brother to drag them into his vortex of negativity. The atmosphere at home had become stifling and heavy. Silence-heavy. Tiptoe-heavy. Ben-heavy.

*

The temperature was below freezing the following day, but when we kissed, my boyfriend Arun's lips felt warm. "I'll see you tomorrow," he said. "We could do something after school. Like a film maybe. Or you could come to my house," he added, sounding nervous. "My parents will be out."

I had met Arun at an afternoon party. He was rumoured to be some sort of maths genius who went to the nearby Latymer School. He was of medium height and very thin. He had deep brown eyes and wore his jet-black hair parted to the side. He had been educated in an Anglo-Indian school in Calcutta. He found it hard to make friends and concentrated on his work instead. Until he met me.

I was his first girlfriend; he was my second kiss. When we held each other I could faintly smell the brilliantine in his hair. He had a way of telling stories that entranced me, not only because of their exoticism, but because of the rich imagery he used. He described a "moon like ice" above the mountain ridge of the Sikkim Himalayas. He told me about the "shimmering rainbow of saris" hanging from the Calcutta clotheslines, and the way they twirled in the wind. He described his house and how its walls were streaked with rain from the monsoon.

"One day, if you like, I'll take you to Calcutta," he once told me.

No boy had offered to take me anywhere before, and I could feel my cheeks burn.

And now, hearing him invite me to his house, I felt them burn again. "Yes, I'd like to do that. You know, see a film or come to your house or something," I answered.

The thought of what might happen between us made me feel queasy and elated at the same time.

"See you," he said.

We kissed one last time and parted ways. I walked towards the Tube, my gloved hand clutching the acceptance letter, feeling a heady whirl of giddiness and love.

By the time the train pulled into Ladbroke Grove Tube station, I realized I had lost a glove and my fingers had become painfully cold. I walked hurriedly home. It was five o'clock, and Oxford Gardens was deep in winter darkness. A prostitute Ben and I called Hairy Mary, because of her unruly mane of thick dreadlocks, was smoking a cigarette on the corner of Ladbroke Grove, wearing a short dress and high heels. I remember thinking how cold she must have been, and wanting to say something empathetic, but was suddenly unsure of the etiquette required when speaking to prostitutes.

I just lifted my one gloved hand and waved at her quickly, and she waved back. Then she walked away, teetering tentatively towards St Mark's Road. I could hear the click of her heels in the cold of the night, and I decided that there probably wasn't such a thing as etiquette with prostitutes, that we were all human after all and therefore next time I would say something to Hairy Mary no matter what.

By the time I got to our house, a freezing rain was coming down.

I rang the doorbell, but no one answered. The house was empty. I remembered that Ben was away in France and my parents were out. I fumbled for the keys in my bag, but they weren't there. I emptied the bag by the front door and searched frantically, my fingers now wet and painfully numb: still nothing. I was drenched. I had no money on me, no way of getting in touch with my parents. We knew other neighbours, pensioners and professionals, who would have been more than happy to let me in. They, unlike Mrs Dobbs, whom they treated with contempt – "She gives herself airs," they said – had no trouble in accepting and returning our niceties.

But perhaps because I was in such a good mood, knowing that my future was going to change radically and that a whole new world awaited me, or perhaps because I thought this would make my nosy parents happy, I decided to knock on Flora Dobbs's door instead.

I ran across the street, covering my head with my schoolbag.

I waited, raindrops dripping down my face, my frozen hand more painful than before.

Then I heard a key turning in the lock: "Yes?" she said in a harsh voice, her eyes peering at me from behind the door, which was held open by a latch chain.

"I'm so sorry, Mrs Dobbs," I said quickly, "I'm your neighbour and my name is Hannah. I got locked out of my house – well, not really locked out, but I can't find my keys and my fingers are frozen, and I have no way of getting in touch with my parents. Would you mind if I came in and used your phone and waited till they get home?"

Her face registered an expression of discontent. I had been too blunt. Yes, she clearly minded. This had been a bad idea. Anything that had to do with this woman was a bad idea. The neighbours were right: she put on airs, and she was also rude.

But then her face softened. "All right then," she said. "Come on in."

I was so astonished I remained on her doorstep. "Are you sure?" I asked, the rain pouring down my face.

"Yes, I'm sure," she answered, undoing the latch and letting me in. "But you're very wet. Please remove your shoes, leave your coat by the door, and I'll get you a towel. I'll be back in a moment."

I closed the door behind me and did as I was told. Her hallway smelled damp. I removed my coat and my shoes. My feet were wet, but I didn't dare remove my socks.

She came back with a towel and I roughly dried my hair, my hands, my face.

"Thank you," I said, handing her back the towel. I was already starting to feel better.

She opened a door at the end of the hallway. "Follow me," she said.

I imagined a room with flowered wallpaper, vases resting on doilies and tired sofas upholstered in canary-yellow fabric. But what I saw caught me so unawares that I gasped.

There were rows and rows of books, from floor to ceiling. Plush velvet armchairs and a coffee table with intricate carvings. Gilded chandeliers and a life-size African sculpture of a man leaning against a door. Oriental rugs of all shape and sizes covered the floor. On the spare bits of wall were abstract paintings and framed photographs of people and places.

This house belonged to a woman with expensive, refined taste. My father's assumption had been correct: her life must have been special. And then there was the piano. A shiny baby grand with the words Bösendorfer inscribed on its ebony lacquer. I knew about Bösendorfers. A friend of my parents had one in his sitting room.

He was a famous pianist and was paid large amounts of money to perform to packed audiences. I also knew how expensive they were. This had to be the piano Henry Dobbs had played on. I wondered if she knew our famous friend, but didn't dare ask her.

"Do you play?" I asked her instead.

She looked at me and shook her head sadly. "My husband did. But he died a few years ago. I used to a bit, but I no longer do."

I wondered what her husband had looked like. Had they had children?

"It's so beautiful," I couldn't help but murmur, running my fingers on the cool surface of its black veneer; I wondered why she still kept it if she didn't play.

"Is your hand all right? Would you like to rest it on the radiator?"

I looked at it. My skin seemed to have turned a pale white. The pain was still there, though it had slightly abated. "That's very kind, thank you," I said.

I placed both my hands on the radiator, but felt self-conscious. What an awkward thing to be doing in a stranger's home, I thought. But then again, I could feel the heat restore movement in my frozen fingers, so I kept it there a while longer.

"My husband suffered terrible frostbite in Sweden once," Mrs Dobbs volunteered. "We had to go to the hospital. We thought he might actually lose his hand."

"Oh, that's horrible!" I exclaimed.

"Yes," she answered calmly, "it was. But in the end he was all right. Now, would you like a cup of tea?"

"Yes, that would be lovely," I answered, taken aback by the friendliness of her tone.

In truth, I was taken aback by almost everything in the room, including Flora Dobbs herself.

I had been mistaken about her. We had all been mistaken. She wasn't rude at all, just guarded. But about what? Underneath her perfect English, I had detected the faintest of accents. Where was she from? Would it be rude of me to ask? And she was elegant too. I could see it clearly now. She wore a ruffled blouse with a dangly necklace and a paisley skirt. She had high cheekbones and wore the faintest of make-up. She must have been pretty once, not so long ago.

I asked to use the bathroom. Mrs Dobbs pointed upstairs. "One flight up, first door to the left," she said.

The door was a faded green, and its knob had fallen off. There was a poster, *Hommage à Claude Monet, Grand-Palais, 1980*, on its frame. It pictured a sailing boat, with trees in the background. There were ripples of light on the waves. I wondered if she had seen the exhibition and brought the poster back with her to London. I walked into the bathroom, turned the light on and closed the door.

The wallpaper was a faded *toile de Jouy*, featuring a pastoral scene. There was a large, rusty bathtub with black cast-iron legs and a cracked ceramic basin, its surface decorated with printed flower tiles. I used her loo and went to wash my hands. I sighed with relief as the hot water restored my hand to its previous colour. Her soap, old and hardened, had lost its lather. There was no hand towel to dry my hands, so I had to use a bath towel – hers presumably – which felt improper. A set of slippers – small, pale blue – stood in the corner of the room, yet another unsettling glimpse into the more intimate side of Mrs Dobbs.

I quickly turned away and looked out of the window. I could see our street and the front of our house. Someone had forgotten to turn the light off in the attic bedroom. Or perhaps my father had left it on for a reason: there had been a spate of burglaries in the area. "We need to be aware," he had said. Was Mrs Dobbs aware? I wondered.

A strong wind was cutting through the air, making the windows rattle. The branches of the trees were swaying. A car drove by, then disappeared. I could hear the distant sound of music, but I wasn't sure where it was coming from. As I was about to leave the bathroom, something made me look up: there, right above my head, was a collection of seated, antique porcelain dolls. I gazed, wide-eyed. There were five of them, looking at each other as if they were friends deep in conversation. I had seen dolls like this before. On Portobello Road and in French flea markets my parents used to drag us to when we were younger. But never had I seen a row of them in such good condition. They were beautiful, with combs and jewels in their locks, miniature flowers and feathers on their clothes: petticoats and silken dresses, varnished shoes and lace cuffs, and I gazed at them in wonder.

Why had she chosen to put them in such an unlikely room? Had it been me, I would have displayed them proudly. Perhaps she was embarrassed, I reasoned. After all, there was something incongruous about collecting dolls, wasn't there? Or perhaps not? Perhaps they weren't even hers?

I returned to the sitting room, my head filled with those dolls and how beautiful and strange they were. I found Flora seated, pouring some tea from a flowered teapot. I was about to ask about her collection, but something held me back. She looked at me and smiled. "How do you like your house?" she asked, sipping her tea. "The man who used to live there before you was a friend," she added. "He lived there for nearly fifty years."

"Oh really? Wow... What was his name?"

"Bert Moser. He was a painter. A good one. He and his wife had four children. They're all big now."

"Wow," I repeated. "Well, I like the house very much. We all do."

"Where did you live before?"

"In Hammersmith. We sold our flat because there was an accident."

"I see," she answered slowly. "What accident?"

I backtracked, my heart beating quickly, as it always did when the recollection slipped into my thoughts, like a contaminated letter.

"Oh, nothing serious. My father wasn't feeling well, but now he's fine. He's a theatre director," I added proudly, trying to conceal the tremor in my voice.

I couldn't tell her the truth: that my father was only a small part of it. None of us had felt well for a while; some of us still didn't.

"Yes, I know about your father," she declared, slightly cryptically. "You wanted to ring your parents, didn't you?" she added, smoothing her skirt around her knees.

I jumped up. In all the excitement, I had forgotten. "Yes, please."

She pointed to a small table, behind the piano. I rang my mother, hoping she wouldn't be with a patient. Ever since becoming a therapist, a few years back, she seldom got home before dinner time.

But she did answer, and I explained about the keys. "Where are you now?" she asked. "I have a patient coming in five minutes, I can't really talk."

I told her where I was. There was a silence on the line. "You're where?" she repeated. Then she cleared her throat. "All right, we'll discuss it later. Your father should be home in about forty minutes. I'll find a way of letting him know."

She hung up immediately.

"Everything all right?" Flora enquired.

"My father will be home in forty minutes," I replied. "I hope that's not too long," I added, suddenly worried.

"Not at all," Flora reassured me.

I picked up the teacup and took a few sips. "Your tea tastes good," I said.

"It's Darjeeling. I like it too." She looked at me inquisitively. "Tell me, how old are you, Hannah?"

I told her that I was sixteen, and had just been accepted at St Paul's.

I described my current school and my parents, my brother and my friends. I'm not sure why I did, nor what prompted me to tell her my life story. One explanation is that I tended to speak too much when I was nervous. And she made me nervous.

The other explanation is that I wanted to impress her and, in doing so, hoped this would result in her inviting my parents over for tea.

Whatever the reason, I spoke freely. I told her that I loved books and wanted to become a writer. That one day I hoped to go and read English at Oxford. I nearly told her about Arun, and how he wanted to go to Cambridge and study astrophysics, but then I decided against it; if I hadn't told my parents about my boyfriend, I certainly could not tell her. Or could I?

I found it difficult not to think about Arun all the time. It was as if he had lodged in my mind, like a secret guest. Sometimes I felt I had to shoo his image away, because it was blurring my vision. And now, just thinking about him was blurring my vision again, especially because I was going to be alone with him tomorrow. So under those circumstances it was definitely not a good idea to discuss him with Mrs Dobbs, who thankfully didn't seem to notice anything was amiss. She looked at me and smiled. "I hope your wish will come true," she said, and for a brief moment I had to gather my thoughts. "My wish?"

"Yes, Oxford. It's a very good place to study."

"Oh, I know. I can't wait."

I looked at her. Something in her tone made me wonder whether she'd been there herself. But again, I didn't dare ask. I would do so at the next visit, I reasoned. Somehow, it seemed obvious to me that there would be a next visit.

"I see that you have many books," I ventured instead, pointing at her collection. "Do you write as well?"

This time, the words slipped out of my mouth before I could control them. She had a way of making me feel comfortable and intimidated at the same time.

Mrs Dobbs stirred her tea with a silver spoon. "I suppose I do," she said quietly. "I'm working on a book now."

"Really? What's it about?

"It's about the composer Robert Schumann. Do you know his work?"

I thought quickly. Did I? No, I didn't. Or perhaps yes, I did.

"I think I do," I answered firmly. "He's very good."

She nodded. "He is indeed."

"Is it being published?"

"I hope it will be," she answered, after the briefest of pauses.

"That would be so nice," I said. "I mean to be published."

"It would be," she smiled.

I cast a glance at her bookshelves again. "Have you read all of these?"

I didn't want to spend too much time talking about her book and Robert Schumann, because I wasn't sure what questions to ask about him.

"Not all, no, but many." She dabbed the corner of her mouth with a napkin. "Are there any particular authors you like?" she asked me.

I mentioned a few books, and the conversation started to flow. She told me that she was particularly fond of French literature, and that she too had wanted to become a novelist when she was younger. Then the war had broken out, and life as she knew it had changed.

"How did it change? Your life I mean?" I was hoping she would answer.

"Well," she said slowly, "I left France and came to settle in England. That was many years ago."

I tried to contain my excitement. "So you're French?"

"Yes, I am."

"From where? From Paris?"

"Yes. From Paris."

"That's really nice." The news made me happy. I couldn't explain why, but it did. Sitting there talking to her also made me happy.

"Do you know Paris?" she asked me.

"Not really, no. I mean I've been there, like twice, but I don't really know it. My parents do, though. My mother used to live there. She speaks a bit of French. She went to a cooking school there. She's a really good cook."

"I see." She didn't appear particularly interested.

I took a sip of my tea, then placed the cup on its saucer. Pale violets dotted its surface. "I like French literature too," I ventured. "We read Victor Hugo at school. And I love Marguerite Duras. I thought *The Lover* was really good."

Mrs Dobbs seemed surprised. "Really? I haven't read it, so I couldn't say." She poured herself another cup of tea. There was a large ring on her finger. Its stone sparkled. I wondered if her husband had given it to her. I also wondered whether she deemed me too young to read *The Lover*. If she did, she was wrong. There was a lot about me she didn't know. Like the fact that I had a boyfriend, for example.

"It's really good," I repeated. "I like François Mauriac too. *Thérèse Desqueyroux*. Is that how you pronounce it?"

"Indeed it is," she replied. "You have a good accent."

Did she mean it? It was hard to tell. But it didn't matter, because I was very much enjoying my time in her company. We went on talking about books: she was clearly well read. "What about English literature?" she asked me.

"I love the Victorians. Especially George Eliot," I said. "I think I know her better than she knows herself," I added forcefully.

Flora Dobbs looked at me again, and this time her whole face lit up.

"That's very interesting," she said. "Very interesting indeed. Would you care to tell me what makes you say that?"

But I didn't have time to answer, because then there was a knock on the door and she stood up. "Follow me," she said. "That will be your father."

She closed the small door between the room and the hallway and we walked towards the door. I gathered my coat, my bag, my shoes, and put them back on; they were still damp.

She lifted that same latch and opened the door. There was my bearded father, wearing his beige raincoat. He looked even taller than usual, standing in the rain, holding an umbrella.

"I'm here to fetch my daughter," he said to Flora Dobbs. "And I must thank you for looking after her." he said. I could see that he was trying to crane his neck and catch a glimpse of her sitting room.

But there was nothing for him to see.

"It was a pleasure," Flora answered, shaking my hand and ignoring my father.

Then she closed the door firmly behind her. The freezing rain had turned to snow.

*

I never got to tell Flora Dobbs why it was I felt such a kinship with George Eliot, or many other writers we hadn't yet discussed.

I tried to, but she never seemed to be home. Two weeks later, I knocked on her door again. I was carrying a lemon cake my mother had baked that morning. This time I knew she was there, because I had seen her enter her house a few minutes before.

I waited a long time before she came to answer her door. And when she did, she seemed odd, almost as if she didn't remember who I was. "Yes, hello," she said, her face upturned towards me. "What can I do for you?"

I was so surprised I fumbled for words and nearly dropped the cake. "I... I just wanted to thank you for the other day. I really enjoyed talking to you. My parents wanted to thank you too, and my mum made this lemon cake."

I handed it to her with shaky hands, and she hesitated before accepting it. "That's very kind, thank you," she said.

Her voice sounded darker than the other day. Sterner. What had happened?

"Is everything OK?" I asked. I couldn't keep it back. I had to know. Had I done something wrong?

Flora Dobbs rested her eyes briefly on mine. "I'm sorry. Something has happened, I'm afraid. We will not be able to see each other for a little while. Perhaps in the future, but not for the moment."

"But why?" I exclaimed. "Have I done something?" Strangely, I felt my throat constrict, as if I were about to cry.

"It's nothing to do with you at all," she reassured me quickly, her gaze much softer. "It's all to do with me. I'm sorry. I wish you much luck with all your studies. Goodbye."

Then she closed the door gently behind her.

What had happened? It was incomprehensible. Nothing to do with me, all to do with her, she had said.

But what could that be? Was she ill? Had she received some bad news?

I was upset. Hurt. We had established a connection that day, in her sitting room. There was something special about Flora Dobbs, and I could tell that she felt the same about me. So why stop it there?

It had to be something serious. No one behaves like that without a good reason. Unless this was a French way of doing things? No, it wasn't. Of course not. It was a Flora Dobbs way of doing things. I had to accept that I would never see her again. She had mentioned "perhaps in the future", but I could tell that she didn't mean it. She was only saying it to be polite, to make it seem less incomprehensible than it was. And after all, I barely knew her. I had a whole lifetime to meet other men and women with whom I could discuss George Eliot and other matters.

She was hardly the only one.

But no matter how much I tried, every time I passed by her house I felt a strange flutter in my stomach, like a longing, or a yearning to see her again. There was something about her that had resonated with me. But I couldn't put it into words.

For a while after my visit to Flora Dobbs, I got into the habit of standing at my bedroom window, searching for hers. I had located her bathroom, to the left of the building opposite. I could see lights going on and off, shadows moving behind a curtain.

And then, one morning, I saw a figure standing there.

It was Flora Dobbs. She was looking in my direction – a short figure wearing a dark blouse. I thought I could even see her eyes flashing at me. I looked back at her, transfixed. I even waved, a short friendly wave.

She didn't wave back, but drew the curtain abruptly, as if she were frightened.

Not long after I had begun at St Paul's, she moved out of her house.

It happened on a weekend, when we were in the country.

No one saw her leave, and no one said goodbye. No one knew where she moved to or what happened to her. Her timing was impeccable.

My father took to scanning the obituary pages, in case she had died. "Where the hell has she gone? What made her leave now? It's such a strange thing to do," he kept repeating.

After I left Flora's house that evening, my father and godfather Walter, buoyed by a steady stream of single-malt whisky, had besieged me with questions. "What does her house look like? What did you talk about? What does she do all day? Was she a nice person? Do you think she's a spy? I think she works for MI5." (That was Walter.)

But in the end, the conjectures we came up with were insubstantial. She was gone, and we would never find out the truth about her.

The house remained empty for a while, until a bearded television producer and his Spanish wife showed up on our street one day.

I was on my way back from school when I saw them. The woman had short dark hair and was very tanned. The man was dressed expensively and looked serious.

Soon after their visit, there was a "SOLD" sign outside Flora Dobbs's house.

The couple dug a basement and added a loft. They renovated the kitchen and knocked down walls. The building works lasted a year, and the noise became unbearable. We decided to go on holiday earlier than usual. My parents had rented a house in the foothills of the Pyrenees. At the last minute Ben had declined to join us, choosing to stay with his friend James instead.

My parents, to their credit, didn't challenge his decision, and the holiday was all the more peaceful for it.

When we returned to London, trucks were still parked outside our house, and Polish builders smoked and spoke loudly as they hammered and drilled.

By the time the producer and his wife moved in, the whole street was cursing them.

And slowly, Flora Dobbs's name sank into oblivion.

2

Walter was a tall man with an angular face, bushy eyebrows and hair the colour of straw. His eyes had a continuously mischievous sparkle, as if he were about to do something naughty. As far as Ben and I were concerned, Walter was like family. A dapper dresser with a preference for red corduroy trousers and pink shirts, he smoked a pipe that smelled of dead leaves. I can still see the small red tin of tobacco – Dunhill London Mixture written on its top in yellow letters – and the way his long and feminine fingers removed the tobacco and placed it in the pipe bowl.

He spoke a cut-glass English and liked to recite dead poets only. "Not interested in the living ones," he would say. He would declaim Keats and Shelley in slightly bombastic fashion, a habit which seemed to have been put on hold now that he had met Lucie, whose interest in poetry was minimal, as he politely described it.

Since he was an inveterate bachelor, the notion that Walter would ever settle down with anyone seemed unfathomable. But then Lucie Canton appeared, an average French actress from an insignificant French town, as my father remarked – then later tried to retract. Walter declared himself smitten, and the next thing we knew she was wearing a large diamond on her nail-bitten finger.

The wedding was held in our house on the Dorset coast in April 1982, the day after my twelfth birthday. I was the bridesmaid.

Lucie wore a pale-yellow dress with matching flowers in her braided hair. She seemed elated and drifted through the room on tiptoe, like a ballet dancer. Her extended French family all came, and a man with an accordion crooned French tunes they all knew by heart and sang heartily, including the bride.

I had never seen Lucie so visibly moved, singing the songs and raising her fist in the air with patriotic ardour.

Ben and I played with some of her French nephews. None of us spoke the other's language, but we managed to communicate nevertheless. One of them, fifteen-year-old Julien, asked me to dance with him "*le rock and roll*". He had a handsome face, though there were red acne spots on his forehead. He wore pointed boots and had very large feet. It was the first time I had danced with a boy, or at least attempted to dance with one. I could smell aftershave on him as he twirled me around and tried to teach me a sequence of steps, which I struggled to follow. In the end he left me to my own devices, and I felt humiliated.

Later on, as I was eating a slice of cake, I caught him staring and he blew me a kiss, and my cheeks burned red-hot.

After the wedding, Walter whisked Lucie off to Italy for their honeymoon. Not long after they got back, we began to see her behind the till at Pebbles, Walter's antique shop on Bridport's South Street. "Lucie, my beautiful wife, is now my new manager!" Walter announced enthusiastically to a luke-warm audience.

He had opened his shop in the early Seventies, and it was admired by locals and Londoners alike – not to mention my mother, his biggest fan. She had furnished our house mainly thanks to Walter's keen eye, and she wasn't the only one. People came to Pebbles for Walter's finds, but also for his charm, his humour and his knowledge.

Lucie's arrival changed the dynamic. It was going to take some getting used to: she was shy, and she struggled with the language. She seemed ill at ease in England, and complained about the weather and the food. She often prefaced her sentences with "in my country", which irritated my father no end. But she knew about furniture, especially nineteenth-century French, and more than once my mother declared herself surprised by the extent of Lucie's knowledge.

She and my father stressed how important it was to make Lucie feel welcome, though Ben found it difficult. I tried to be sympathetic, and made a point of asking Lucie questions when I saw her. She would answer in a thin voice, stumbling on her words. I felt sorry for her, though Ben didn't. "She hates us," he said. "And I hate her back."

My mother admonished Ben sternly: "Stop saying such silly things. What's to hate? She's lovely. Nobody hates anyone here, and she finds you and Hannah very sweet."

"Does she?" I asked, surprised.

"Yes, she does," my mother answered, not entirely convincingly. "Lucy's main problem is that her English isn't very good. It's difficult to move to a new country, and she's struggling. I would like you to promise me to be nice to her. She makes Walter happy, and that's the most important thing."

Ben shrugged his shoulders. "I liked Walter better before her," he said. "He used to play with us."

"Walter is the same as he always was," said my mother. "And he loves you and your sister – that will never change. Just promise to do as I say."

"I promise," Ben said, sounding serious.

"Good."

Lucie had olive skin and brown hair cut in a bob, and though her face was pretty, there was something sad about her which I overheard my mother attribute to the fact that she wasn't able to have children. When I pressed my mother for further details ("How does one know if someone can't have children?"), she feigned ignorance, and I understood that the comment was not destined for younger ears. We didn't know much about Lucie's film career, though my mother said she had been "on the road to stardom" when she met Walter. There was a large poster of her hanging at Pebbles. *L'Arrivée du mendiant*, the film was called – *The Vagrant's Arrival*. It was a swashbuckler set during the French Revolution. Lucie, dressed in a close-bodied purple gown, her hair piled high in enormous curls, was gazing lovingly into her co-star's eyes, a handsome French actor – who, I was told, "made women swoon". From the way he was dressed, in a dark coat and matching waistcoat and breeches, I deduced that the waistcoat-wearer wasn't the vagrant.

Soon after the film was released, Lucie met Walter, and now that she lived in England she wasn't working as much. "It will do her good to swap the *boudin noir* for a proper G&T," my father quipped.

"That's not funny," my mother had said. "No one wants to give up a career."

"What's noir whatever?" Ben asked.

"Something disgusting the French find delicious," my father answered. "It's a blood sausage."

"Yuck," I said.

"Barf me out!" Ben shouted.

"No need to shout, and no one's asking Lucy to give her career up," my father continued.

"Walter should give her up," said Ben. "He was more fun before. Now he's become boring, like all married people."

"That's enough, Ben," my mother said sternly.

Of all the adults we knew, Lucie was the only one Ben taunted. Perhaps he felt her vulnerability. Or perhaps it was his own way of venting his anger towards Walter. Whatever it was, there was something deliberately cruel about the way he shunned her, or left the room when she attempted to speak to him, staring at her with mocking eyes. When my parents were around, he was on his guard. When they weren't, he took full advantage. A few times, I was able to nip it in the bud, and apologized to Lucie for my brother's behaviour, but she seemed to take it in her stride. "It is not important," she'd say, smiling wanly. "*C'est pas grave.*"

I couldn't understand why she didn't retaliate or put him in his place. After all, Ben was only eight years old. Instead, she said nothing, though I could imagine that, had he been French, she would have reprimanded him.

I was never sure whether Lucie told Walter about my brother. Perhaps she had, but Walter didn't believe her. Or he might have told her that it would sort itself out. And sometimes, despite it all, it was funny. Ben imitated the way Lucie spoke and wiggled his body like she did, smoking an invisible cigarette and pouting his lips – Ben was very good at imitating people, and was often asked to perform in front of my parents' friends.

Once he went behind Lucie's back and made horrible faces while she was drinking tea. "Stop it!" I mouthed, as he stuck his fingers up his nostrils.

But it was too late.

Lucie turned around quickly and spilled her tea, burning her leg in the process. She got up quickly and screamed, "*Petit con!*" as Ben fled to his room, followed by my irate father.

Another time, Ben found a spider in the garden and stuck it in Lucie's handbag when she wasn't looking. He had heard her mention that she was arachnophobic. When she opened her bag, a large black spider crawled out and she screamed again.

Ben feigned utter surprise, and even offered to fetch her a glass of water.

"Did you do this?" she asked him for the first time, her green eyes burning bright.

They could have been welling with tears, though I wasn't sure.

"No, of course not!" he cried vehemently.

"Ben would never do such a thing," said Walter, grabbing Lucie's hand.

"Yes, he would," said my father.

He dragged Ben away, and we all heard him shout at him.

Ben cried, but didn't confess. Only I knew the truth. And when Ben came out of his room a few hours later, his eyes red from crying, I made him promise that he would never do anything of the sort again. "You're being cruel to her. Imagine if anyone did the same thing to you. How would you feel?"

Ben shrugged his shoulders. "I wouldn't care," he said.

"That's a lie, and you know it."

"It's just for fun," he mumbled.

"Ben," I said firmly. "It's not fun. And Walter will never leave Lucie, because Mum says that he loves her lots. When you're older, you'll understand."

"Love is boring, and I understand everything."

My brother had blue eyes, blond hair and an angelic face. I instead had inherited my father's Mediterranean looks: black curly hair, dark eyes, pale skin. I looked nothing like my brother, and I envied him. A beautiful boy, people often commented.

But to me, he was a monster. A miniature, albeit irresistible monster.

"Be careful," I warned him. "You're going to get into trouble. And then you'll be grounded, and you'll cry and I won't care."

Ben shrugged his shoulders. "I won't care either," he said.

*

My parents liked to tell the story of how they met, in 1968. My father had contacted my mother, Anita, because she had translated a Norwegian playwright, little-known outside her country, whose play he wanted to direct.

Anita had arrived for their first meeting, at the Chelsea Arts Club in London, wearing black bell-bottom trousers and an orange blouse. "Your mother dazzled me instantly," my father said. "There was another man who was dazzled too, and I had to get rid of him quickly," he added, in a conspiratorial tone.

"How? Who was he?" we asked him.

He never said, and over the years I wonder whether there even was another man. But even if there wasn't, it didn't matter, because my mother had chosen him instead. They had discussed theatre and life until the bar had closed. By the time they parted, "filled with vodka and Norwegian secrets", my father knew that he would marry her.

"All my male friends were very jealous," he told us. "Your mother took our breath away."

I looked at my mother, remembering his words. She still took his breath away, I was sure of it. Once, not long before, I had found them dancing in the kitchen. The radio was on, Ray Charles was singing and at one point my father held my mother's waist, and she threw her head back laughing, her long mane of hair nearly touching the floor.

Their love was pure, unimprovable. I clapped loudly. "Again!" I cried out. "Dance again!"

I cannot remember if they did. All I know is that after that summer of 1982, when the shadow of loss altered our lives, their happiness faded into something more muted. And as it faded, so did their fascination with one another. They seemed to have found a more discreet way of communicating their love. Or was it something other than discretion? I worried. Our parents were together, but on either side of the family there was a history of betrayal and tragedy. My paternal grandmother, Anna, had died young. Her husband had remarried another woman he did not love and, by all accounts, had treated badly. After a few years, she left him. My grandfather realized the error of his ways, but it was too late. She never returned, and he became an alcoholic. As for my maternal grandfather, Fredrik had fathered a child with another woman. My mother had never forgiven him. She was still very upset with him. Whenever his name was mentioned, her face turned red.

Was history contagious? Something told me that it was. A hereditary pattern which spread its germs and spawned other variants of the same condition. I needed to ensure I would be immune to those symptoms. I wanted to create my own permutations, my own history, untainted by its predecessors. Because although my parents had been spared, there was no telling what might happen to them tomorrow.

*

"Dip-dip all blue!" my father cried out, throwing me high into the air before I landed in the water, shouting and laughing at the same time, my feet kicking against the waves, small peaks of foam which gathered me in their wake.

It was a very hot day. Lucie was in the sea with us. She was wearing a yellow bathing suit, and her face was sunburnt. She laughed when I landed next to her. Walter was ill that day, she said – he had some sort of stomach bug. "Actually, I don't think Walter really likes the sea," she confessed. "But I do!"

She rode a wave and looked, for a brief moment, like a young girl cavorting in the water, like us. It made me like her much more.

"I want to play 'dip-dip all blue' too!" cried Ben.

"All right then," my father said. "Here we go!"

"Dip… dip" – he lifted Ben – "all blue!" he said in his booming voice, as he threw Ben upwards and watched him drop into the water just as he had done with me.

The hoarse cries of seagulls pierced the sky. They flew in a circle above us, flapping their grey wings. A trail of clouds scudded across the blue horizon. Was the heat finally breaking?

I was about to point it out to my father when an unexpected wave surged upwards and broke over my head, churning me around as I gasped for air. For a few long seconds, everything went cold and dark, and I tried desperately to fight my way back to the surface.

I succeeded, just in time to see Ben's body being crushed by the same wave, and we lost sight of his small head.

I screamed, my mouth full of salt water. The wave wasn't even that big, and yet its pull was unlike anything I had ever experienced, as if a hand were grabbing me from below. Everyone began to shout and scramble away.

"Riptide!" someone cried. "Get out of the water!"

"Go back to shore!" my father shouted.

"I've got him!" Lucie shouted back.

I saw her dive under, then re-emerge holding Ben, her eyes looking startled and wide.

My father grabbed Ben's limp body and struggled with him to the shore, to my mother who began to scream, "Ben! Ben!" Two lifeguards rushed over and laid him on the sand. His eyes were closed, his face was green and it made me want to vomit.

A crowd gathered round him, their bodies glistening wet from the water.

One of the lifeguards turned Ben's head to one side and began to administer mouth-to-mouth resuscitation.

Nothing happened.

I dug my toes into the sand, feeling my heart pounding against my bathing suit. I even held my breath, just to feel what my little brother was going through.

The thought that he might die was inconceivable.

My father was standing by my side; he was dripping wet, and I could hear him breathing heavily. I closed my eyes. It was too awful to bear.

But then there was a sound, and I opened my eyes and saw that Ben was throwing up half the sea, and the lifeguard was now holding him upright. Everyone clapped, and my mother, who wanted to hug him, had to be restrained.

"He's going to be fine," the lifeguard declared. "But we still need to take him to hospital."

"Leon!" my mother cried out. "He's alive!"

We all hugged each other, and my mother began to cry.

"Where's Lucie?" I suddenly asked. "She saved him!"

My mother stopped crying immediately and clasped her hand to her mouth. We called out her name. "Lucie! Where are you?"

But only the sound of the waves gave any clue to her whereabouts.

Lucie had dived in to save Ben, and all that time we had assumed that she was standing with us.

My mother went pale. "Lucie," she said hoarsely, grabbing the lifeguard's arm. "Our friend Lucie was in the sea with my son – she saved him. She went to get him and she's still there, in the sea."

She began to tremble from head to toe. My father told us to stay there while he drove to the hospital with Ben. He looked utterly distraught. "I'll be back as quickly as I can," he said.

I ran towards my mother, and we held each other tightly as the two lifeguards walked quickly towards the sea, now ominously calm. The sky was cloudless. The sun was shining. The seagulls were gone. The ambulance drove away with Ben, its siren wailing in the distance. Another one arrived, and more lifeguards. My mother and I stood on the beach, on the pebbles that hurt my feet; I had lost my shoes in the commotion. A few people remained, out of concern and sympathy. Or was it? I wondered. They said a few words to us, but I can't remember what or whether I answered. The only thing I do recall is that the girl who had drowned two summers back was mentioned. "Do you remember that poor lass? This is a dangerous beach," a man said. "I'm not coming here any more."

My mother and I said nothing. We didn't want to think of the other girl, only of Lucie. We just stared at the wide, glittery expanse and held hands tightly, quietly. "Someone needs to tell Walter," she said finally.

The lifeguards were gone a long time. When they came back, looking exhausted, they shook their heads, looked at my mother and said that they had done all they could, but hadn't been able to find Lucie. "But that doesn't mean anything yet," said the lifeguard. "And a helicopter's on its way."

Soon enough, it arrived and began to circle the beach, its engine roaring above the sands.

I looked at my mother. Her face seemed to have shut down, her emotions sealed away somewhere distant and unreachable.

It frightened me. Everything frightened me.

My world was crumbling, piercing my heart like the rocks had pierced my skin. How would Walter react?

They had to find Lucie.

They had to.

She had saved my brother and had drowned instead of him. Instead of Ben.

I clutched my mother's hand. Her fingers felt brittle, as if they might break. I'm not sure how long we stayed on that beach. I watched as the sun became paler, colder. "Find her, find her, find her," I repeated to myself.

Ben was being kept in hospital overnight – just to be safe, the doctor said.

My mother had gone to stay with him.

Walter was in our kitchen, smoking his pipe. My father was sitting opposite him, drinking.

Neither of them spoke. There was nothing to say.

We all knew what had happened. None of us said it, but we knew. The helicopters wouldn't find her. No one would find her.

Only the sea knew where she was.

*

The weather changed the day after Lucie disappeared.

The clouds turned black. Sunday black. The heat dropped and the rain came down. The possibility of finding her became increasingly unlikely as the rain continued and a gale-force wind of 70 mph whipped up the foam-crested waves. In the middle of the night there was an explosive noise followed by a flash of lightning. I ran to the window: shapes were illuminating the sky, like neon branches. I rushed back to my bed. I was frightened. Ben woke up shouting. I heard my mother comforting him. "It's only the thunder, my angel, it's only the thunder."

It was calmer by morning. I went into the garden and looked around me. The landscape I had loved had been altered, stripped of its beauty. The sea and its briny smell, once the panacea for all my childhood ills, had turned dark and foreboding. Now, even the air reeked with the tang of disappearance. I could envision Lucy's body being tossed by the waves, crashing against rocks – her skin scorched, blistered, ripped apart.

How long had it taken her to die? Had her body started to decompose under the water? Would they ever find her?

It was a terrifying thought. Only a few days back, this shy and innocent woman had been sitting with us at our kitchen table. Now she was no more.

Our house felt different too, like a station does after the last train has departed: empty, forlorn. And the press had found out: Lucie's face stared at us from the front page of the local paper. "After Little Wilma Fathers, Lucie Canton: Are Our Beaches Safe?" was one of the headlines written in large, bold letters.

A television crew showed up at our house unannounced, as did a few journalists. The phone rang off the hook. Articles were printed, mentioning my father and Lucie, "the theatre director and the famous French actress".

All of us longed to flee and return to London. But we couldn't. We were stuck. My father tried to calm us. "She might still be all right. One never knows," he said.

Did he really believe it?

By the next morning Lucie was still alone at sea. I read up on riptides and rip currents and sneaker waves. Lucie was sand. A grain of sand: pale, soft, warm, insoluble.

Maybe my father was right. Maybe she was still alive. Maybe she had managed to clamber over the rocks and swim ashore. Maybe she had found shelter somewhere.

"Let's call Cristina and Peter," I overheard my mother tell my father. "They should come over. They're good with this sort of thing."

"They're Trotskyites," said my father. "Radical Labour Trotskyites. How does that make them good at anything? And what 'thing' are we talking about here, and why do we need to see anyone at all?"

"Come on, Leon, you know what I mean," my mother answered wearily. "Peter's been grieving all his life."

"It was a bit different, wasn't it? He didn't even know his father…"

"It's for the children," my mother insisted. "This is a very, very difficult time for them, and Ben loves your sister. I think it will be a good idea. And Salisbury's not far. They could get here quickly."

"And their children? What if they show up with those insufferable twins of theirs?"

"They won't. Not under these circumstances. And they're not insufferable. They're just boys."

"Fine. Give them a ring, then."

I didn't know much about my Hellenic past, except that my great-grandfather had been born in an Epirus mountain village, somewhere near the Albanian border, and had emigrated to the UK in the 1880s. My paternal grandmother had died young when my father and his sister Cristina were children. His father had raised them alone. The Greek connection, tenuous at best during their lifetime, now disappeared altogether. My father, despite his Mediterranean features and Greek surname, knew very little about his ancestors. Nor did he seem to care, and neither did Cristina, who, with her husband Peter, was a politically committed, prominent Labour activist, deeply involved with various causes, including the Palestinian one and its promotion as a democratic, secular state. They were both members of the Palestinian Solidarity Campaign and believed the state of Israel should be eradicated from the map, a viewpoint my father didn't share, although my mother was dabbling with the thought of joining the campaign as well, not because she necessarily believed in the cause, but because she found her life too cushy and wanted to give more to the oppressed around the world. "So give your clothes away and join the Anti-Apartheid Movement or the United Democratic Front, a much better cause," my father had retorted. "South Africa needs us more than the Palestinians. Solidarity is not only about shouting radical slogans like Peter and my sister do. It's about doing something about it. Apartheid in South Africa can and should be eradicated, but not Israel."

Peter's father James had been killed at the age of twenty in the 1946 bombing of the King David Hotel in Jerusalem. His mother, Claire, had been pregnant with Peter at the time and returned to England a broken woman. The repercussions of this attack, both in the world at large and within his own family had a strong impact on Peter. Spurred on by his mother, who had laid the blame firmly at Israel's door and had struggled thereafter to make ends meet in her native Kent, Peter came to view Israel as the prime reason for all their ills.

When he turned twelve – at which point Claire had found a good job as a librarian – she took her son to visit his father's grave at the Ramleh War Cemetery, in the Judaean Hills. "We need to find Plot 7 Row G," she told him.

Peter was the one who found it, and he felt deeply moved to see his father's name inscribed on the headstone: "James Francis Betts, Private Rifleman, Royal Artillery 1926–1946". He claimed it instilled in him a desire to become a voice for the oppressed around the world, although my father argued there was more to it: "At first he believed in it for the right reasons. Then, when he became older, it turned into the wrong reasons, like a vendetta."

In the early '60s, Peter left for South America, where he spent two years with Voluntary Service Overseas, an experience he described as "seminal". In 1968, as a King's College student, he wrote his first pamphlet entitled, *The New Apartheid: Plot 7*, calling for a national boycott of Israel. The pamphlet gathered numerous signatures, including Cristina's, which is how he met her, and Peter contemplated interrupting his studies in order to devote more time to Plot 7. But his mother thoroughly dissuaded him, explaining that James would never have wanted his son to abandon his university studies in favour of political activism.

By then Claire had long since remarried a notary from Kent, with whom she had two more children, and politics were relegated to a distant past for the now plumper though still attractive Mrs Plendon from Tunbridge Wells. But for Peter the seeds of dissent had been sown: his half-siblings had a loving father, and he didn't. His mother, whose grief had defined his younger years, who had cuddled him at night so tenderly, was now happy and seemed to have forgotten the battle for James's memory, which she and Peter had forged together.

In truth, the ghost of his past never left him. As I grew older, I wondered whether his ongoing battle for justice wasn't a way of regaining his mother's love rather than honouring his father's memory. To this day, I don't know. What is clear is that the story of James Betts, murdered by Zionist radicals on a hot day in July, was a tragedy which left a mark on our family. Despite Peter's "terribly tiresome activism", as my father called it, I don't believe any of us was able to view the politics of the Middle East with an impartial eye. If my uncle didn't entirely persuade us of the unmitigated evil of the Israeli regime, he certainly came close to it, and made sure we, just like him, would never forget: Peter kept a meticulous record of what had happened on that fateful day of 22nd July 1946, in a large folder which contained several articles and photographs of the hotel before and after the event. There was a picture of his parents on their wedding day: his mother, wide-eyed and demure; his father, young and boyish-looking, smiling at the camera, his arm round his bride's waist. There were clippings about the 6th Airborne Division, which James had belonged to, and a letter from his mother Winifred to the *Nottingham Evening Post*, written shortly after her son's death. Entitled "Goodbye My Golden Son", I found it more heartbreaking than any of the other paraphernalia Peter regularly brandished when we went to visit.

In 1977, Cristina gave birth to twin boys. Night feeds and nappy-changing curtailed their various activities, and the folder was momentarily shelved, especially because baby James was unwell for a while. They weren't sure why, but then he recovered quickly – "a strong boy, just like his grandfather once was".

Once the twins had started nursery school, Peter, who was by now teaching English at the local university, picked up where he had left off, although by now "Plot 7" had assumed a more generic name, which also involved South Africa and any cause he thought was worth fighting for – of which there were many.

I liked having someone like Peter in the family, because he made us question everything we took for granted. Thanks to Peter and Cristina, I was afforded a glimpse into what it meant to be a victim of war. To be oppressed, or unfairly judged. To fight for freedom and civil rights. I was proud of my aunt and uncle. There was something authentic in their desire to make a difference. They meant it. They lived it. And even as a child I could see that made it laudable. If my father disagreed with some of their views, that was his loss. This was about justice. The Jewish extremists had killed Peter's father for no reason other than the fact that he happened to be a British soldier. They had deprived a child of his father, a heinous crime in itself. I felt for Peter, even though 1946 seemed a world away from mine.

Except that when they came to see us that day in Dorset, after Lucie disappeared at sea, Peter, especially, seemed strangely subdued. "We're with you with all our hearts," was all he said, while outside the rain continued to fall relentlessly.

Peter's voice, usually so loud and clear on public platforms, was remarkably quiet in our private surroundings, almost as if he wasn't sure of what to say. Was it because my parents weren't fighting for a cause? Or was it because he found it difficult to relate to the death of a stranger? He barely knew Lucie, although he and Cristina had been at the wedding. I remembered him there, fiddling with his tie, standing by the buffet on his own while everyone was dancing. He seemed shorter and pudgier, and his hair was parted on the side. His large eyes looked worried – not the committed, passionate eyes I was used to, filled with the verve of his regular railing. There was no outcry that day, just a feeling of deep unease on his part, although not on

Cristina's. She was drinking copious amount of champagne and dancing; she was wearing a low-cut red dress and high-heeled sandals. I could hear her laughing on the dance floor: she was very loud, perhaps even drunk. Cristina taught art in a grammar school, but she also showed her paintings in local galleries, and someone in London had expressed interest in her work, is what my mother told me, which had made Cristina happy, so she was especially ebullient that day.

Cristina was different from Peter. They shared the same political and moral values, but there was a certain grace and ease about her which her husband lacked. I could see it now in the way Cristina took Ben aside to talk to him. She did so spontaneously, with great confidence. For all his talk of international boycotts and social justice, Peter did not match her confidence. Cristina had a special way with people, especially children. I enjoyed her company, and so did Ben. I couldn't hear what she told my brother, but I could see his small face momentarily light up as she spoke, stroking his hair as she did so.

Then his face fell again, and Cristina went to find my mother in the kitchen. They began cooking together, and I could see them from outside peeling vegetables, their heads bent as they spoke, their faces looking grave. I was in the garden, so I watched them through the kitchen window during that small pause in the rain, before it lashed down again and their faces became as fuzzy as an old photograph.

But rather than go inside, I chose to stay where I was, in the wet garden. It was an impulsive reaction, as if I needed to commune with the elements, so I lifted my face and arms, and let the blustery rain soak me – my hair, my cheeks, my clothes, my sandalled feet. My mother came outside and grabbed my arm. "Hannah, what are you doing – are you mad? You're going to catch pneumonia! Don't you think we have enough worries as it is?" she shouted. "Go and dry yourself. And I mean now!"

Her tone was sharp and angry, and I cursed her under my breath as I ran upstairs to change. How could she not understand? Nothing was the same, and nothing could be explained – that's why I had done it.

But now was not the time to argue with her, as she had pointed out.

I threw my wet clothes on the floor. I dried my hair and grabbed a dress from my wardrobe and went back downstairs. My parents had lit candles and set the table beautifully. Ben was sulking. We all sat down to dinner, and just as we did so, the rain turned to hail. It smashed against the window pane before it turned to rain again. My mother had made mashed potatoes with chicken breasts and carrots, but none of us was really hungry.

Ben kept his head lowered and didn't speak, even when Cristina tried to communicate with him. So we ignored him and tried to pretend that everything was all right, and Peter began to talk about his children and their school, then about the war in Lebanon, but was quickly interrupted by my father, who diverted the conversation to Margaret Thatcher instead ("No wars today Peter – no wars"), except that Thatcher was intrinsically linked to the Falklands War, so my mother deftly launched into a lengthy reminiscence about Argentina and how she had once been as a young girl, and how we should all go there some day – South America is where it's at.

But none of us really cared. About South America or the children's school, or the Falklands War. All I could think about was Lucie, alone at sea.

I'm sure that Ben was thinking the same thing.

Then my father mentioned the Beatles, and we began to talk about John Lennon. Ben lifted his head briefly: he was a Beatles fan. I said that I wanted to go to New York and see Strawberry Fields in Central Park. Ben said he didn't want to, then fell silent again. My mother looked worried. "Ben, darling, please don't be upset. Tell us what you'd like to talk about! Anything you'd like."

Ben fiddled with his food and said nothing. My mother then declared that it didn't matter, he didn't have to eat if he didn't want to – she was happy to just talk about the Beatles and Strawberry Fields and anything he wanted to. "But I don't want to talk!" Ben cried out. "Don't you understand? I don't want to talk about anything at all! Don't you see? Don't you see?"

He began to squash the mash harder and harder with his fork, and bits of potatoes started to fly everywhere. My mother shouted something, but it was too late. Ben grabbed the plate with two hands and smashed it on the table, breaking it into several pieces as the food spilled everywhere. We looked at him, bemused. My mother turned white. "Ben," she whispered. "Ben please—"

Ben threw his chair back and ran to his bedroom, leaving the floor covered in bits of mash and porcelain. Peter and Cristina were stunned into silence. For a long while, none of us said anything.

Eventually, my mother got up and went to open the kitchen closet. She picked up a broom and slowly started to sweep the shattered bits into a pile. Cristina cleared the leftover dishes from the table, while Peter ran upstairs. My father remained seated in his chair, gazing into the void like a drunkard.

*

These were my first life lessons:

That tragedy leaves a trail in its wake, which alters the order of things.

That fragility has the same velocity as strength.

That guilt is as powerful as sorrow.

That nothing can be taken for granted.

That everything good can disappear.

My big father had now become small. My mother spoke in whispers.

Walter pretended that everything was just the same.

Ben hardly spoke at all, because he said his mouth hurt when he did.

As for me, every night I dreamt of the sea. Of enormous waves engulfing me.

Of Lucie's startled green eyes, just before she went under.

*

After two weeks, Lucie's body still wasn't found.

Walter urged us to return to London. "I'll wait for her. They'll find her," he said, sounding remarkably composed. "Bodies don't just disappear at sea."

We left reluctantly, but not before my mother said she was putting our Dorset house on the market. It was cursed, she said, and we couldn't possibly keep a house with windows facing the same beach on which Lucie – not to mention the other girl – had died. "It will be bad for our psyches," she said. "And this beach is unsafe."

"It isn't," my father replied. "It was a fluke. A terrible one, but a fluke nonetheless. It's very unlikely to ever happen again. I'm not selling this house."

They began to fight, late into the night. It was his house, not hers. He had owned it for twenty years and loved it more than anything. She had no right. "This isn't about rights, but common sense!" she shouted. "What about the children, Leon? Ask Freud what he would say!"

"I don't give a shit about Freud!" my father shouted back. "I just care about my house!"

But in the end she won the battle. I suppose she convinced my defeated father that it was the right thing to do. "I'm tired of arguing with her," he later told us. "And perhaps she has a point. Perhaps she knows best."

Ben and I didn't contest it, because we didn't know best. All we knew was that it broke our hearts further, but we were too fraught to stop her.

So the house was sold. I couldn't bring myself to say goodbye to it – neither could Ben. The last standing witness to our childhood was now gone, and it only added yet another sense of loss on top of everything else.

But it was a house. Lucie was a person. Yet it was the same. Time splattered, like blood.

3

Walter rang one morning to say that he was in London for two days and that he'd like to come for dinner the following evening.

My mother stuffed a goose as if it were Christmas. "We're eating French food, in honour of Lucie," she announced.

She hadn't cooked in weeks and made up for it. She prepared roast potatoes and chestnuts, grilled vegetables and warm gravy. She served French cheeses and dark-chocolate mousse for pudding. She lit the whole room with candles and put on a Charles Aznavour record.

The adults ate heartily, as if everything were normal.

Ben and I picked at our food and pretended to be happy.

Walter appeared as he had always done: jovial, gentle, though perhaps less prone to playful banter. He also drank more. Everyone drank more. Lucie was only discussed at the end of the meal, when enough alcohol had been consumed. Walter insisted that nothing could have been done to prevent the incident, therefore there was no use in discussing it.

"She's dead," he said, "and I'll recover. We all have to. The only way to do that is to press forward and move on."

I noticed that his lips had turned purple, just like the wine.

"It can't be that simple," my mother said. "You can't just move on like that."

My father looked at her with disapprobation. "Anita…"

"It's the trauma talking, not him," my mother continued, pointing at Walter.

She was drunk. I could tell. She spoke in a strange way, as if her mouth had turned soft, like jelly.

"There's no trauma, just sadness," said Walter, who had never used such words in front of us before.

"Walter, sadness is the least of it," my mother continued, speaking too loudly. "Trauma is the word you're looking for. T.R.A.U.M.A."

"Anita!" my father barked. "Enough!"

My mother looked at him and sniggered. "Enough? Really?" she dabbed her lips with a napkin and glared at him with shiny eyes. "Enough is this, Leon: if you hadn't played that stupid dip-dip game, none of this would have happened. None of it, and—"

"And the children have always loved that game – and you know it, because you used to play it too. Or maybe you've forgotten?" my father snapped back.

"No, I haven't forgotten, but that's beside the point, isn't it? Isn't it!" she cried out. "It's true! If you hadn't chosen to go into the sea when you did, and play that game when you did, none of it would have happened, would it?"

"Anita, Leon, none of what happened is anybody's fault. None of it," Walter said, in a barely audible voice.

But my father wasn't listening to Walter. His whole face had begun to tremble. I had never seen him look that way, and it frightened me. When he spoke, his words were slow and filled with menace. "Are you blaming me, Anita? Is that what you're doing? Fucking blaming me for a rip current I couldn't fucking control?"

"I'm not blaming you, but I think that we all have responsibilities here," my mother answered, avoiding his gaze as she poured herself another glass of wine. She was nervous now, and tried to hide it.

"Yes," my father declared, his tone still dark and angry. "You're right. If you had remembered that Lucie was in the water – because let's face it, you forgot that she was there, having rescued your son – YOUR son, not HERS – she probably would have been found and saved, wouldn't she? Wouldn't she?" he repeated, shouting this time.

"Leon, Anita, please," Walter repeated, and when I looked at him, his cheeks were all red, and he looked as if he might cry. "She's gone, and there's nothing we can do about it," he added, in a hoarse voice.

I longed to flee. Run and flee and hide in my bedroom. They were spewing hot words like venom. Was it really my parents speaking? Or was it the helplessness of grief?

My father poured himself another glass of wine. My mother lit a cigarette and smoked it nervously. Ben had lowered his head so that it was nearly touching his plate, and his legs were twitching under the table; I could feel them rubbing against mine. I touched his knee and squeezed it gently. I felt that I needed to say something. Anything to remove the ugliness and tension hanging over us and restore some decency to the conversation.

"Lucie was the bravest of us all, and that's how we should remember her," I blurted out. "No other way."

There was a stony silence as the adults looked at me. Then my father spoke. "You're right, Hannah, that was very well put. You're absolutely right. She was the bravest of us all."

Ben now looked up at us. His face looked small and fragile.

"I should have drowned. Not her. So it's my fault. That's why you're all shouting."

My mother immediately stubbed out her cigarette, stood up and walked towards him. "Don't ever say or think that, my darling boy, never," she said, her voice quivering as she wrapped her arms around him.

"But it's true," Ben continued. "I was mean to her. I made fun of her. And she tried to save me anyway, even though I was horrible."

"You weren't horrible, Ben, she knew you were just being silly," Walter interjected, looking worried. "Please don't ever think she took it seriously."

"Yes, she did – and Hannah's right," Ben continued, looking disconsolate. "She was nicer and braver than all of us, and now she's dead," he added, before breaking into uncontrollable sobs. "She's dead, and I made fun of her."

My mother held him hard against her, but he pushed her away and darted upstairs.

"Nobody's allowed into my room – and I said nobody!" he shouted.

I followed him quickly, but he slammed the door before I could get to him, and I stood behind it for a long while, calling his name in vain.

That night, just before going to bed, I went into the kitchen to get myself a glass of water. As I was about to enter, I saw Walter talking to my mother.

She was leaning against the stove. He was standing close to her, and she was laughing, pushing him gently away. "Come on, Walter," I heard her say, followed by a few inaudible words.

He stopped in his tracks and looked suddenly sad. "Of course," he said. "Of course."

I must have made some noise, because the two of them looked up.

"Hannah, darling?" my mother said. She quickly moved away from Walter.

"I just wanted to get some water," I said.

My mother filled me a glass and handed it to me. I kissed her and Walter goodnight, and went upstairs to my room. I tried to fall asleep, but I couldn't. Something felt wrong. An intangible feeling, like slipping on ice.

*

Ben and I were sent to see a child psychologist whose office was on a leafy street in Hampstead. Dr Glass wore large glasses, and her grey hair was pulled back into a tight bun, which revealed her scalp; I found it intensely displeasing to look at, and it made me want to get up and run back home. But then she started to talk, and I quickly forgot about her hairline.

Dr Glass explained that what had happened wasn't a single occurrence, but was linked to other concomitant events (she explained the word "concomitant"). It was important, she said, that we understood the meaning of cause and effect. That there were such things as flukes, and this was one of them. "Not everything in life happens for a justifiable reason."

Lucie, Dr Glass continued, speaking very carefully, would have drowned no matter what. There was a rip current, and it would probably have ripped her away (hence its name), regardless of whether or not she had tried to save Ben. It wasn't our fault, Dr Glass stressed. It was very important we understood that. None of it was our fault. And the fact that Ben had made fun of her once or twice was neither here nor there.

She repeated that several times. "Neither here nor there."

"That's not true," Ben said in a small voice.

"Why not, Ben?"

"Because it's normal to feel bad when you're mean to people. And usually you have a chance to say sorry. I can't say sorry to Lucie, because she's dead."

Then he lowered his head in order to hide his tears. I clasped his small hand and held it in mine.

Dr Glass looked at Ben for a long time before speaking. "What you say is correct, Ben. And you're obviously a very sensitive and good person. But you see, I think that Lucie knew how sorry you felt from the start. I think that she forgave you immediately, because she could see it as clearly as I do: she knew that you didn't mean it. You're still young. Anyone would forgive you."

Ben looked up at Dr Glass with tears in his eyes. "But I don't forgive myself," he whispered, almost as if he didn't want us to hear him.

He said nothing else after that, and was quiet all the way home.

My mother decided that we should see Dr Glass a few more times.

We did. The sadness didn't go away. But its burdensome weight did, at least for me. And then, one morning, Walter rang to say that Lucie's body had been found on the Dorset coast, not far from where it had happened. Her body had washed ashore during the storm. A fisherman had found her.

"We can bury her now," he said.

I asked my mother what Lucie had looked like when she was found, but didn't get an answer. The main thing, she said, was that she had been found, and we could finally lay her to rest.

Lucie was buried in France.

My parents went to the funeral, and we stayed with my god-mother, Nancy, my mother's old friend. She was a painter and lived above a Thai restaurant in Covent Garden. The smell of

Thai food often wafted through the windows, but she didn't seem to mind.

She made us cookies and let us watch television until very late that night.

The next morning her daughter Anna, a fashion student who wore plaits and a large turquoise ring on her index finger, showed me how to bead necklaces. Then she put on a Supertramp record loudly, and we held hands and danced in the living room to 'Breakfast in America'.

Ben jumped up and down and laughed. There was hope, I thought. Everything was going to be all right from now on.

*

We moved to Notting Hill in December 1983, one day after the IRA bombed Harrods. It was an unfortunate coincidence, and my mother wanted to postpone the move so that we could honour the dead, but my father told her it was a ridiculous suggestion, that life couldn't stop for us just because it had for others.

So we moved.

Compared to our Hammersmith flat, there was something cavernous about this new house, a period building on Oxford Gardens. Our furniture looked suddenly small within the grandeur of the rooms, especially in the kitchen and the sitting room, which overlooked a beautiful secluded garden with a large pear tree and rosebushes. The bedrooms themselves, four in all, smelled of fresh paint. They had high ceilings and windows with wrought-iron bars. Some of them were in poor, dilapidated condition, as was a lot of the house, which needed a makeover. "We'll get to it eventually," my mother said. "And at least we've done it," she added. "We'll never forget what happened, but we can start anew," she repeated, in a confident voice. "With Walter," she added.

Walter still had a flat in Chelsea, but it felt empty without Lucie, he said. So increasingly, especially when he and my father had had too much to drink, he stayed over. "I'd rather not risk that drive," he would say. "Safer to stay put."

He stayed put a lot, and I was delighted; I loved his company.

Walter slept in the attic. It was a quiet room, with a slanting roof and a double bed with lions carved on its headpost. There was a small blue basin, which didn't work, a relic from the previous owner, and a mahogany chest of drawers that had once belonged to my grandfather. The room had a slight smell of hay, or something rural, and my mother joked that a farmer must have lived there before us. My father reminded her that an artist had lived there before – hardly a farmer – and she laughed, although I couldn't understand why it was funny. But at least they were laughing.

Two days after Christmas my father, who had slipped a disc as a result of "the accident", as my parents labelled it, was able to stand up straight again, and my mother said it was a sign. By January, she had taken up yoga and enrolled at the Open University. "I'm going to become a therapist," she announced. "I want to get an MA, open my own clinic and help people. Better than we were able to help ourselves," she added, smiling. Ben could not help himself – neither could we, seemingly, help him. We glossed over it, because none of us knew how to handle the problem. Still, I was relying on my mother to save him: she had to. That's what parents did, wasn't it?

Then in the middle of it all my grandfather Fredrik died.

My mother flew to Oslo for the funeral, alone. She didn't want my father to accompany her. When she returned, she seemed upset, which I hadn't expected her to be.

"I should have made peace with him," she said, sounding fragile. "But how could I? He betrayed my mother with another woman. And now there's Olav. He was at the funeral, you know. A beautiful little boy. He's one year old now. And my brother was there too, with his new wife. She's very nice. They promised to come and visit next time they're in London. They have a son your age, Ben."

I wasn't interested in my uncle, but in Olav. She had never mentioned his name before. We discussed the baby and my grandfather's "other woman". "A simple young woman who didn't really know what she was getting herself into. But now she does," my mother added. "Now she really does."

Hilde, my mother continued, wanted to help. She had forgiven her husband everything, including his mistress and child. She had always loved Fredrik.

I found that an odd concept to take in. From what I had seen of my grandfather, there wasn't much to love or to forgive. He had always looked old and unhappy. But aside from our trip to Norway a few years back, we hardly knew him. Perhaps there was a whole other side to him. A gentler, softer side. There must have been. Otherwise, why would a woman so young and so pretty fall in love with him?

So I found myself grieving for him. Not for the man I knew, but for the one I didn't. For the missed opportunities in my life. For the fact that, had I made an effort, or had my mother made peace with him, I might have grown to love my grandfather.

And had I spent more time with Lucie, I might have grown to love her as well.

*

Whenever he talked about that fateful day at the sea – which, as the years went by, became a rarity – Ben relived it. I could see it on his face, the way his voice became heated when he spoke. It was as if he were hiding behind Lucie again, making faces and wiggling his fingers. As if he were back in the sea, fighting the waves.

"I want you to be happy and annoying again," I said to him once. "I want my brother back. I miss you."

If those words touched him in any way, he didn't show it. By then, he showed very little of himself, except for anger.

My parents, on the other hand, showed more of themselves than I wanted to see. Whenever they relived the story, their words were fuelled by alcohol. Who had been responsible for the drowning became a regular topic of conversation. The result was a repeat of what I had witnessed that night when Walter had come for dinner. But by then Ben and I knew better than to remain seated, and left the two of them to their own devices, their inebriated squabbles echoing through the stairwell.

We grew up, Ben and I, and the squabbles diminished in their frequency. But when they flared up again, the results were always the same. It soon became apparent that no matter how many years went by, how many hours of therapy we had undergone, the final conclusion of who had ultimately been responsible for Lucie's plight would never be determined, at least not as far as my parents and Ben were concerned.

I felt differently. I blamed the sea and I still do. It was a fluke, one we had to learn to live with. Lucie's selfless gesture, the way she had dived in without a second thought, would never leave us, however far we fled. She had left invisible particles of herself behind, and although they were clearing with time, something of her would always remain. I was sure of it.

I had heard a program on the radio about trauma and how it affected families. The man interviewed, a psychologist from an eminent university, had discussed the "repercussions of trauma on the family unit". During the course of the interview, he had used the word "dysfunctional". That word, and his definition of it, struck a chord. Had we become such a family? Unable to read the signs, as he described it?

"The line between boundaries and blame will be harder to demarcate," the psychologist explained. In our case, both had been blurred. Blame covered our family like an invisible pall, and boundaries had become unenforceable. As painful as it was to hear an actual explanation of what I had, until then, deemed to be a temporary situation, it served to quell my anxieties and answered some of the questions I had been grappling with until then.

When I relayed the man's words to my mother, she refuted my theory with an overreaction I could only interpret as further proof that what I had heard was accurate. "There's a big difference between trauma and dysfunction," she snapped. "We're hardly dysfunctional. We're coping with the situation."

"No, we're not," I answered back.

"That's your opinion, not mine." she declared. "Think what you wish."

I don't know if she shared this information with my father; I suspect not.

The eminent psychologist had also talked about that: death and grief, how to cope with it and the importance of communication. He had mentioned how trauma can alter one's internal space, and how finding one's bearings again was a sign of recovery.

My parents hadn't found their bearings. They still argued over who had been responsible for the drowning in the first place. Until that was resolved, they would remain disoriented, searching for an internal space I was now certain they would never find again.

4

My father's play opened on a cold December evening. We left early, dragging a reluctant Ben with us. It was one of the only times I ever saw my mother threaten him. "This is a very important night in your father's career. If you don't make the effort and come with us, he will send you away. And I mean it. So you're coming, and that's all there is to it."

"Where will he send me away to?" Ben sniggered. "Prison?"

"A military boarding school," my mother retorted. "Where you'll be whipped into shape from dawn to dusk."

I smiled, and I saw Ben do the same. The chances of that happening were highly unlikely. But for once he didn't protest. He shrugged his shoulders and even took a shower, which he hadn't done for as long as I could remember. He came out of his bedroom wearing black jeans, a crumpled shirt and spray-painted trainers. But the fact that he was there at all was sufficient for my mother to refrain from commenting on his attire.

We jumped into a cab and arrived at the theatre to find a throng of people at the front entrance. My father, taller than most, waved at us from among the crowd. The play was advertised on a large poster: "A MONTH IN THE COUNTRY: IVAN TURGENEV DIRECTED BY LEON KARALIS". As he walked towards us, a journalist brandishing a large camera asked us to stand together, so that he could take a family photograph.

I still have it, among my old notebooks and paraphernalia. The four of us smiling at the camera, Ben standing behind us all, head lowered, shoulders hunched. The photographer had yelled "C'mon lad, show us your face!" to no avail.

He took the picture anyway, one of the last recorded memories I have of us standing in a room together.

We were ushered into a private area. A few people were congregating around my father. Walter, other family friends, acquaintances, members of the theatre. My father introduced us all proudly, his arm around Ben, who was struggling to retain his usually gloomy composure. For the first time in years, I heard him make small talk with Nancy and a man I didn't know. Then we were asked to come inside the hall and take our seats.

A man came on stage and talked a little bit about Turgenev, the actors, the theatre itself and my father. He then left the stage, the lights dimmed and the performance began.

It was unlike any of my father's usual minimalist, avant-garde plays. Here the lavish costumes, the setting and the acting were on a par with the best productions I had ever seen. I watched as Natalya fell in love with Alexei, and thought of my own relationship with Arun and what might happen if I were to meet another man.

The previous week, lying naked in bed, he had twiddled my hair and held a lock between his fingers. "Your hair is jet-black like Indian girls'," he said. "Beautiful." He paused and looked at me gently. "Could I have a lock to take home with me?"

"Yes," I nodded.

He stood up and retrieved a pair of small scissors from his jacket. "I brought them with me," he said, blushing.

He carefully cut off a small lock of my hair and placed it in his jacket pocket. "I've been wanting to ask for a while," he admitted, lying back next to me.

Was this his way of telling me that the end was near? I wondered.

Our relationship had changed. We had grown up during those two years, and although the love was still there, it burned less ardently than it had during our first few months together. We knew each other well now. We had had fights – shouting matches even – which often resulted in him hanging the phone up on me, leaving me incandescent with anger. Arun was stubborn, especially when it came to politics. He considered Rajiv Gandhi, the Indian Prime Minister, weak and ineffectual, and resented the notion of empire, and all it had done to India. "You may have built our railways, but you destroyed our people," he often ranted, his eyes flashing with anger, as if I had been personally responsible for India's ills. "Marxism is the only way out," he continued. "The only way our people will be freed from mass poverty, exploitation and social divisions."

I looked at him and scoffed. "So you're actually telling me that you would be happy living in India as a Marxist?"

"I certainly would," he retorted.

"And Cambridge?" He had not only gained a place, but a scholarship to boot. "The Mayfair apartment you live in? Your parents with all their talk of landed gentry and good marriages? Do you think Marxists live comfortably and talk about good marriages?"

"I'm different," Arun replied confidently. "I'm enlightened."

"Actually, I don't think you are," I said.

He took it badly and shouted at me. I walked away, and he ran after me down the street and begged me to forgive him. I did, half-heartedly. But in truth, something about him had changed. Arun had become more assertive, more confident. Tinges of modesty with flickers of hubris. Maybe I had outgrown him after all.

A sound next to me interrupted my thoughts. "Wow."

It was Ben. He was staring at the stage, his mouth open, his body hunched forward so as to take it all in. I wanted to squeeze his hand, but then decided against it: I didn't want to break the spell.

When the play was over, there was a standing ovation. For the actors and for my father, who was rushed to the stage, and who bowed to thunderous applause. My heart burst with unmitigated pride for him, and I joined my mother and Walter and shouted "Leon! Bravo Leon!" – our voices filled with muffled tears and emotion.

And then I turned to Ben. "What did you think?" I asked him.

"Not bad," he said, reducing the vigour of his applause.

"And the acting?"

He nodded. "Yes. The acting. That was good. I want to do that. I want to pretend to be someone else," he said, avoiding my gaze. "That's what I want to do."

And I knew then that my brother had found his vocation. He was going to take up the mantle Lucie had left in her wake.

*

It was a sunny Saturday, a June afternoon, two weeks after Arun and I had split up.

I was in my bedroom studying for my A levels, trying to concentrate on my history exam. My father was in Paris, and Ben had gone to stay with a friend. My mother had offered to take me shopping to cheer me up, but I had declined. I had to study, no matter how upset I was about our breakup. Every so often I would burst into tears at the thought of Arun, reaching for the box of tissues that sat on my desk. My parents had been comforting and supportive. The previous evening, my mother had cooked us a lamb stew, and we had gone to see a film together. Even Ben had accompanied us, although he later assured me that it was for the film and not because he felt sorry for me. "I don't want you to get any ideas," he said firmly. "I don't like that guy. He's a pretentious weirdo. I think it's actually great that you're not together any more."

"Shut up, Ben," I snapped.

I tried not to pay heed to Ben's comments, because he liked very few people, and had hardly exchanged a word with Arun.

But his words stung nonetheless.

A few weeks more and school would be over. The summer appeared in front of me, filled with possibilities. My parents had rented a house in France, in the Loire Valley. We were to spend some time there before I met up with a few friends, on a tour of Spain. I had been offered a place at Oxford and I was looking forward to it all. A new life was about to begin for me. I needed to get out of London in order to forget Arun; everything about the city reminded me of him: the streets we had walked on, the shops, the cafés, the school gate, the park bench where we had first kissed.

"Hang on to the stuff that really upsets you," my father had told me. "That way it will make the separation easier to cope with."

I did, and it worked. But then, something would remind me of Arun – a phrase, a song, an Indian accent – and all my anger would dissolve into an intense longing for him.

But I hung in there, as my father told me. I didn't call or write to him. I was stubborn that way, just as Arun was. And I knew that once I left London, everything would become much easier.

I had saved some money from tutoring lessons. My parents were buying my train ticket and, unbeknownst to them, Walter had slipped me two £50 notes that smelled of fresh ink. "Take these for an emergency and keep them to yourself," he had told me.

Walter still came to visit, though less often than he used to. He had sold the shop in Bridport and was opening a new one on the New King's Road. My mother was helping him set it up. She had cut down on her patients and was working three days a week, spending her spare time scouring for antiques with Walter. I could tell that she was enjoying it, that she wanted Walter to succeed and be happy again. That's what she often told us. "He needs to find happiness, perhaps with a new woman." He no longer slept late in the attic bedroom, as he often used to, when he and my father had shared too many whiskies. He had bought himself a small flat on Smith Street, in Chelsea. My mother had found it for him, and Walter seemed very grateful. So grateful that a few times I wondered whether he was secretly in love with her. Whenever she spoke, or when she was near him, he seemed acutely aware of her presence, so aware that he wouldn't move unless she did. It was as if his body was invisibly attached to hers. But of course that wasn't possible, because Walter was like family, and my mother loved my father, not him.

So I banished those thoughts from my mind and concentrated on what was important: Arun, my schoolwork, my friends. And now, everything was changing.

School was ending, I would begin Oxford in the autumn; Walter was running a shop again, and my parents were working hard.

Ben though was getting worse. He had turned fifteen and grown a few inches. Soon he would be nearly as tall as my father. But the similarity was purely physical. The two of them barely spoke to each other. The burst of pride Ben had felt during my father's opening night seemed to have evaporated, and I could understand why: the last term of school was ending, and no sixth form was willing to take him. Ben took this as a valid reason to come and go as he pleased, with predictable consequences. My parents imposed a curfew that involved my mother personally taking him to school every morning, and my father picking him up a few times a week.

But, even then, Ben managed to slip through the net.

At night, he smoked in our bathroom with the window open and played heavy metal at full volume. My parents shouted at him, at each other.

The atmosphere at home was proving increasingly unsustainable. The previous week, Ben had run away from home, and my father called the police. When Ben showed up the next morning, looking haggard and white as a sheet, my father slapped him so hard that Ben teetered under the blow and fell to the floor. A gush of blood came spouting from his nose, though it was unclear whether it resulted from the hit or from something unconnected. My mother clasped her hand to her mouth, and I screamed at my father: "What's your problem? Are you insane? Can't you speak to him instead of shouting and hitting him? How is that going to make him a better man?"

My father looked at me with angry eyes. "Don't you dare, Hannah," he hissed. "Don't you dare get involved. And I didn't hit him: I slapped him."

Ben stood up slowly, trembling, wiping the blood with the back of his hand. I ran towards him and hugged him. "I'm sorry, Ben, I'm sorry," I said, feeling like crying.

But Ben pushed me away. "Fuck you," he said. "Fuck you all."

I couldn't sleep that night. I decided to go downstairs and check up on Ben. As I reached his bedroom door, I heard him sobbing uncontrollably. I hadn't heard him cry in many years, and it broke my heart. "Ben," I whispered. "Let me in, Ben."

"Leave me alone," he said, in between his tears.

"No, you've got to let me in."

He paused, and I heard him get up. He opened the door, my tall and gangly brother, his face blotchy with tears. "I want to be alone," he repeated, pushing me away as I tried to hug him.

"I love you," I said to him.

"Me too," he answered, sounding small.

*

The doorbell rang downstairs. I heard my mother open the door to a man's voice; I hadn't even realized she had returned home.

I yawned and stretched my arms out. I put my pen down and stood up. I looked across the way at where Flora Dobbs had once lived. I often thought of her house, the things we had spoken about, the porcelain dolls lining her bathroom shelves. Was she still alive? Where had she gone? She had been such a mysterious figure. Had she returned to France after all those years in England? I thought about the way she had announced we could no longer see each other, how I had stood there, holding the lemon cake. I thought of my father's and Walter's conspiracy theories about her. Had they been right or plain mad?

Walter. He was the man downstairs. I could hear him speaking to my mother. I wondered why he was visiting in the middle of the afternoon. For some reason, I always associated Walter with night-time. But then I reasoned that perhaps he was there because of the shop; there was always something happening at the shop. I made my way downstairs. As I was about to reach the ground floor, I suddenly stopped in my tracks; I could no longer hear their voices, and the silence was laden with something ominous. Something worse than noise. I heard a shuffling sound and a sigh. What was happening?

I froze, unable to move, my heart pounding loudly.

But I had to find out.

I had barely reached the last step when I saw them.

My mother and Walter were lying in the middle of the sitting-room floor in a wild embrace. Walter's hand was underneath my mother's skirt and he was pressing against her, kissing her frantically. They had clearly forgotten I was home.

I shouted. I couldn't control myself. I shouted so loudly I could hear my own echo, like in a tunnel. I'm not sure how long it lasted. I was glued to the banister, watching the shock on their faces as they sprang up, Walter with his trousers undone, my mother with her unbuttoned shirt, her tousled hair. They rushed towards me and said something I couldn't understand. Or perhaps they didn't. My memory of that day is jumbled, out of kilter, as if the ground had been partially pulled from beneath my feet.

Walter disappeared and my mother began to cry.

Later she confessed all. Walter had been in love with her for a very long time. "We waited three years before giving in to each other," she said, as if that might lessen the blow. "And now that we have, I can no longer hide it."

"Hide what? What can't you hide?" I asked, with a trembling voice, although I already knew the answer.

"The fact that I don't love your father any more," she said, in a quivering voice. "I'm going to leave him, Hannah," she added, looking at me as if I were a friend rather than her own daughter.

"I don't want to know!" I shouted. "I don't want to know, and you can't do that to us! You can't break up the family!"

"We've been broken for a long time," she answered hoarsely. "A very long time. I'm so sorry, my darling." Her hand reached out for mine, but I pushed it away violently. "I love Walter," she continued, in a near-whisper. "I want to be with him. I don't want to lie any more. Especially not to you and Ben."

I rushed upstairs, grabbed my jacket, schoolbag and keys and rushed back down.

"Where are you going?" my mother asked, her voice now frantic. "Hannah, please, what are you doing?" She got up and attempted to stop me, but I pushed her away, opened the front door and slammed it hard behind me.

FLORA

9

It is August 1946, and I've returned to an empty Paris. The streets are deserted, the shops shut. A lot has happened since I've been away, and I don't understand much about France any more. The Vichy government has been dissolved, replaced by a provisional one. General Charles de Gaulle has temporarily resigned. There is the guilt of war and what it has done to its people. A new President of the Provisional Government has been elected, but I know little about him. Inflation is spreading throughout Europe; the USSR and USA have emerged as world powers. "As a result of France's wounds," says General de Gaulle, "the equilibrium of the world has been compromised."

The word "equilibrium" resonates with me. We have been knocked down, like skittles.

What the Parisians can't have in food, they make up for in babies. There are newborns everywhere and prams crowding the streets. Yet bread is still rationed – as is coffee, sugar and rice. The Métro stations have reopened, as have music halls. People talk of the Folies Bergère. But I'm not interested. I visit the Beaux-Arts studios. Many of the men sport beards. I haven't decided if I like it or not.

I'm modelling for painters again, and I also have a job working twice a week at Galignani, an English bookshop on the Rue de Rivoli. I like working there, meeting some of the writers who stop by, the fact that I can read at my leisure – and that litera-ture affords me solace. I no longer have any desire to write a novel, but I have an increased desire to read. I devour books, especially English ones, and I take notes. I'd like to resume teaching, and am practising my English. My plan is to leave for London as soon as I've mastered the language completely. Knowing I have a purpose has made life easier for me in Paris. At first, on returning from Palestine, I was numb with shock. Every morning I woke up in tears, as if I missed Ezra, which I certainly didn't: I felt utterly betrayed by him. Then I found myself missing Jerusalem terribly. I thought about my year there, before the darkness. Before the charred debris, the white dust, the people screaming and the corpses strewn on the hot rubble. I closed my eyes and felt the heat and saw the stones and smelled the jasmine and thought of the people I had encountered, and the food and the Café Atara and the parties at Lotta's, and the way everyone spoke to each other in such an easy manner. I had never been to such a place before, and I had a feeling that I would never visit one like it again.

I wrote to Ava and Mordechai. He told me that Ezra had committed suicide in his cell. He had chosen to die rather than confess. It made me hate him even more. How could he perform such a cowardly act? And then I changed my mind and accepted that the hatred was also tinged with grief. I had loved him, after all. But he was a murderer with blood on his hands, so I went back to hating him, especially as the image of Claire Betts came frequently into my mind. She often appeared unexpectedly, like a mirage, in the same way my parents did, the only difference being that my parents were dead and she wasn't – at least not that I knew of – so I didn't understand why the experience was so similar.

I told Catherine about my experience. I had never shared it with anyone beside Mordechai, and I thought she would understand.

I found her living in the same flat. After Roger's death, she had gone to stay with her sister in the Auvergne, because she wanted to get away from it all. Now she was back; she had aged a lot, and her brown curls had turned grey. Her only daughter never came to visit, she said, even though she now had a grandson. "She was always a complicated daughter," she said, and we talked about that, and my mother, for a while. It felt so good to speak about my mother that I didn't want to stop. Suddenly there she was again, speaking, laughing, hugging me the way she used to. It made me want to cry, but I held my tears back, especially as Catherine had now steered the conversation to Palestine and my time there.

We sat down at her kitchen table, the same one we had eaten our soup on the previous year. Roger's chair was still there, against the table. "It's shit without him," she confessed. "But at least I was able to mourn him before he died. I knew he was very ill. I was prepared. But it's still shit."

Her words hit me. I hadn't been prepared for my parents' death. I had had no time to mourn them. Everything had been so sudden. So fraught. I still didn't fully understand it.

"It wasn't the same for you, I know," Catherine said, looking at me. "I miss your parents. I can only imagine what you must feel. It must have been very hard."

I nodded. "It's all shit, whether one is prepared or not."

Catherine smiled at me. "You were always a wise one, Flore—"

"Flora. Thanks to Roger. I'm Flora now."

"Yes, of course. Flora. Much nicer."

Catherine was thinking of visiting her brother in Palestine. "Not much for me left in Paris," she said, speaking softly.

We spoke about Jerusalem and my time there. I explained why I had returned to France. Strangely, she didn't seem particularly moved by Claire Betts or by Ezra the Irgun fighter. If anything, she seemed to sympathize with him, which I hadn't expected.

"You can't blame him, can you?" she asked me, sounding surprised I would harbour such misgivings. "He was a Holocaust survivor. You should have forgiven him."

"But he killed people! Innocent civilians!" I exclaimed.

"He was a Holocaust survivor," she repeated. "He wanted his own country. I don't blame him." She paused and shrugged her shoulders. "I'm old; I'm tired of wars, of fighting. I'm tired of everything. I'm sure your Ezra was too."

I got up and told Catherine I had to be going. I had never heard anyone defend the Irgun before, and I wished I could scrub out her words, because hearing her defend Ezra made me falter for the briefest of moments, love him violently again for the briefest of moments, which I could never do, because I hated him and now he was dead.

I would and could never forgive him.

*

I live in the 4th Arrondissement, in a small flat which belongs to M. Bonnet's wife's sister. It is a sunlit room with a small kitchen, a washbasin and a view of the Place des Vosges. I sometimes invite friends over. Not my old ones from the Sorbonne, but people I have met at the Beaux-Arts. The other week I was able to squeeze four of us around my kitchen table and we ate bread with *saucisson* and cheese and drank too many carafes of red wine. It was very cold outside, and soon it began to snow and we all gazed as the flakes drifted in the wind. There was a man who tried to seduce me, but I'm not interested in meeting anyone new. I flee from love. I avoid men. And I need to leave Paris for London. Everything here is coated in a veneer of treachery and lies. The government didn't protect us. On the contrary. They shopped us to the enemy. They witnessed and facilitated the deportation of the Jews. They will spend the rest of their lives covering it up. Paris has become a stranger to me. I have become a stranger to me. The world as I knew it has vanished, as have my roots. *In nihilo.*

I feel denuded. I float in the shallows of the irreparable. I wonder if my emotions are transparent. I wouldn't want anyone to see through me.

"You don't smile much, do you?" a Beaux-Arts student remarks one day.

"I don't when I model, but otherwise I do," I assure her.

The student, a beautiful young American woman called Paulette, laughs.

"OK, I didn't mean it to sound, you know, upsetting."

"It didn't," I say.

"Come and have a coffee with me," she suggests.

I follow her, and we sit down on the terrace of a café, behind the Boulevard Saint-Michel. We order coffee and cake and spend the afternoon talking. She doesn't ask me many questions, but I don't mind. I prefer to listen anyway. Paulette studies painting, and she is not very good at it, but doesn't seem to mind much. "I'm just there for the experience, not to get better. And to have fun," she says, laughing.

Paulette has white teeth and long blond hair, and is very popular with men. She says that when she's done with her studies, she'd like to settle down and get married to a rich man. Money is important to her. She grew up rich. When she describes her background, it sounds like a foreign country.

Nothing I can relate to. But I listen anyway. And I find her entertaining.

A few weeks later, she takes me to the bar of the Ritz hotel. Many rich men go there, she says. I've never sat among such opulence before. Even the whispers sound polished, like silver. The walls are of panelled wood and the seats are made of leather. The lighting is dim, and I feel like I could be on a film set. The women wear cocktail dresses and the men suits and ties. I am underdressed. I am wearing a grey dress and bland loafers. Paulette says it doesn't matter. We're sitting in the Ritz, and that's all that matters. She tells me that Ernest Hemingway liberated the bar as the Nazis were retreating and then ordered champagne for everyone. She wishes she had been there. She wishes she had met Ernest Hemingway. I tell her that he stopped by Galignani one day, but I didn't get a chance to speak to him. Her eyes widen. "Oh my God, you're kidding?"

She'd like to find a husband like Ernest, she says. Rich and powerful, but also interesting. Her father is powerful in New York, where she grew up. Powerful and strict, she says, as if the two things were intrinsically linked. I stop listening. I don't like hearing about fathers. We sit at the bar and order martinis and smoke cigarettes.

I've never had martinis before. We laugh, and she orders us another drink. A man comes up to the bar and starts speaking to us. He's from Spain, he says. I think he's handsome, but Paulette doesn't. She asks him to leave us alone. Her tone is condescending. But I don't say anything. Then she starts speaking about her father again, and I tell her that I need to go home.

I see Paulette one more time. She's going with a group of friends to hear Yves Montand sing in a nightclub. I don't like groups, and am wary of her friends. But I would like to hear the great man sing, so I accept her invitation. Her friends, a smattering of rich Americans and a few students from the Beaux-Arts, are civil towards me, but not particularly friendly. Except for one, Patrick, a young man with gentle eyes, who recognizes me as the nude model from the Beaux-Arts and mentions something flattering about my body, then immediately retracts and says he hopes he didn't embarrass me. I find him endearing, and we spend the evening talking to each other and drinking kir royal until Yves Montand comes on stage. The singer is riveting. Patrick places his hand on my knee and attempts to kiss me in a clumsy fashion. I gently push him away, and he seems upset. After the concert, Paulette asks me to go backstage with her and I follow, my heart beating wildly. Montand is very kind and attentive to Paulette, and flirts with her. I try to speak to him, but he rudely brushes me aside. Still under the influence of a few too many kir royals, I snap at him. To this day, I cannot remember what I said to Yves Montand. All I know is that Paulette looked at me aghast and said "Leave us, Flora" – so I did. I found myself standing alone on the street, a woollen beret on my head. I asked a passer-by for a cigarette and smoked it quickly, standing still, shivering in the cold. A strong wind had picked up, and I buttoned my thin coat. I'm not sure how long I stood there. At one point I heard the sound of laughter and turned round. It was Yves Montand leaving the club with Paulette and two of her friends. Paulette's hair was blowing in the wind, and as they walked past she glanced at me. I'm not sure she recognized me with my beret on – or, if she did, she pretended not to. The click of her heels and the sound of their laughter lingered on in the night air until the street fell silent again.

*

I drifted around Paris for two more years. Through Catherine, I found myself a job as a librarian. It was a good job, and I needed the money.

But these were lonely years. I will not dwell on them, simply because there isn't much to say. I lived alone, I rarely went out. The centre of my world had shifted. I was lost, no doubt; but at the same time, I was lucid enough to know that I needed to regain my strength before leaving Paris. I couldn't arrive in England in my fragile state. I needed to rebuild myself. To remantle myself, if such a word exists. Not build, but remantle: little by little, step by step.

I spent time reading, writing in English. I read the *Concise Oxford Dictionary* and practised sounds, cracking consonants like nuts against my palate, letting this new voice settle inside me, become me. I wanted words to glue themselves on my skin. *Kilogram. Number. Nuclear. Require.* I saw films, the occasional play. Once, I nearly slept with a man, Louis, the director of the library. He had charm and a good sense of humour. He also knew a lot of poetry by heart, especially Gérard de Nerval, whom I particularly liked. I kissed Louis, but he smelled bad. I wondered if he ever washed. I was disgusted by him, and embarrassed by my disgust. I tried to convince him to be my friend instead, but he refused. "I want your body, not your friendship," he said, and I wasn't sure whether his words made me feel cheap or special.

And then one day, in the autumn of 1950, I received a letter. I was still living in that small apartment near the Place des Vosges. I seldom received any post, except for the occasional magazine, because I had cut ties with everyone I had known before the war, and didn't see many of those I had met afterwards either. So I was surprised when I opened my letterbox and found an envelope bearing my name.

The stamp was a Hebrew one, and the letter was from Lotta, in Jerusalem. She had found my address through Mordechai. She was aware that I might not be "particularly looking forward" to hearing from her, but she felt compelled to write nonetheless.

I was curious, so I began to read her letter, and found myself shaking as I did so. Not because it was her, but because it elicited in me an unexpected sense of elation at being reunited with a place I had loved and left behind. Ezra's face suddenly rose from the pages, and there I was, gazing at his hypnotic blue eyes, listening to his deep, confident voice, feeling the touch of his fingers on my skin – and for a short moment I forgot all about the horror of what he had done, of how he had died. All I could feel was the ineffable happiness I had once experienced at his side.

I closed my eyes and tried to distinguish the detailed features of his face, but they had become blurry. So I opened my eyes and continued to read.

Lotta wrote about David Ben-Gurion and the new-found independence of her country, "which you must have heard of" – yes I had, how could I not? – her life in Jerusalem, the people she still saw, "friends of Ezra's, you must remember them" – "Of course I remember them!" I shouted at the page. She then went on to describe at considerable length what Ezra's friends were up to, titbits of information I could have done without. Why was she telling me all of this, I wondered?

And then, as I read on, I understood.

Ezra, she wrote, had been very important to the two of us (I hated the way she did that, lumping me together with her in the same sentence). Although she had been older than him, eight years older, she had had very strong feelings for him, which she had kept to herself, because she didn't want to jeopardize our relationship. "Ezra loved you," Lotta wrote. "He liked me, he enjoyed my company very much, but he didn't love me as he did you. I knew that. You knew it too. And I respected you both, so I kept my feelings to myself."

So she said.

And yet, two weeks before the King David bombing, they had consummated their relationship. I had been at work that afternoon. It had been the only time, Lotta stressed, and Ezra felt terribly guilty about it. Soon after his arrest, she found out that she was pregnant. But she chose not to tell him.

The baby was born in 1947, and she named him Ezra Bernheim. "Calling him Radok was out of the question. It was too controversial. So I gave him my maiden name. He's now three years old and looks just like his father," Lotta concluded. "Ezra's flame lives on."

I didn't read the rest of the letter. Her words cut through me with such violent force that I threw myself on the sofa and began to howl, a searing howl which echoed through my every pore. I'm not sure how long I remained on that sofa. It may have been a few minutes or longer. Pain has the ability to blot out time.

Eventually I staggered to my feet and splashed cold water on my face. I had to collect myself and be strong. I had a duty to be strong. That's what my mother had once said: "You must be strong, Flore. Your duty is to show her how strong you are."

"My duty? But how?"

"Ignore her. Don't reply. Walk past her and ignore her. It will make you feel bigger, and will make her feel smaller."

That was my mother, sitting with me at the kitchen table, clutching a coffee cup – and here she was again. Her hair was pulled into a bun, and she was smiling. I was ten years old. A girl was being mean to me at school. I had a stomach ache every morning and wanted to stop going to school altogether. I didn't know how to defend myself, and those had been my mother's words of advice. I had paid heed. I still did. I applied it to my life. To grief, dressed like a woman. I walked past her every day, but ignored her. I needed to push forward, always forward, no pauses allowed, no backtracking for fear of falling.

But now I was falling, and I needed my mother to catch me. To comfort me. What should I do now? I wanted to ask her. I wanted her to tell me that everything was going to be all right. That I could still act big even if I felt small. I wanted to be a child. I wanted to rewind my life and start again as a child and pretend the war had never happened.

But it had happened, and there was no rewinding to be done. I was an adult, and I was alive. My parents were not. Ezra was not. Ezra, who could have been the father of my child and had ended up fathering one with Lotta. But he didn't know. My only consolation was that he didn't know.

There was one thing left for me to do: destroy the evidence that had catapulted me into this unwanted place.

I lit a match and spat on the letter before throwing it into my small fireplace. I watched as the flame engulfed Lotta's scalding words. I watched as they shrivelled into soot and died. I listened as my heartbeat slowed, as did my breathing.

Two days later, I packed my bags, said goodbye to my flat for the last time and booked myself a ticket on the night ferry bound for Dover.

10

I have found myself a one-bedroom furnished flat. It has a single bed, a tatty beige carpet and a Formica desk. I have few belongings aside from my books: some clothes and my father's porcelain dolls, which I had shipped from Paris and have placed on a shelf above the kitchen table. Sometimes, especially at night, I speak to them and brush their hair. I'm aware this is childish, but it provides me with an unexpected comfort, one I cannot seem to give up. I will one day, I imagine.

The estate agent who showed me the apartment described it as being "on the north side of Hyde Park". I love uttering those words. They sound evocative and mysterious, like the new woman I have become. Flora Baum, pronounced the Germanic way in English: *Bowm*. Flora Baum, the woman with the long black hair who now lives on the north side of Hyde Park. I have adapted quickly to my new land. Whatever sense of alienation I felt at the very beginning has turned into the thrill of the new. Everything here is crisp and fresh and crackles under my feet like fallen leaves, and so does my name. I'm finally getting to grips with the language. For all my valiant attempts to master English, I quickly realized, soon after my arrival, that I still had a lot to learn. I had spoken it at the Sorbonne, to myself, and with many of my friends in Palestine. But we were all foreigners there. Here in England it is different. I don't know any foreigners. The people I meet speak quickly, use words I've never heard before, and I have trouble keeping up. So I've enrolled in a class and have been learning fast. I have to: there is no one here to speak French with, and English is my only means of communication. It has become the language of my present, replacing the mists of my past. When I don't know a word, I translate it inside my head, and sometimes it doesn't come out as intended. *Faux amis*, the French call them. False friends. Words that look identical but differ significantly in meaning. I know because people look at me and smile politely when that happens. If I stay here long enough, which I fully intend to, I will have no false friends. My origins will be lost, and no one will ever know where it is I come from.

At night, when I cannot sleep, I think of my life. Of fate, and how one single decision can alter an entire destiny. Of the choices my family made. Of what might have happened if my cousin Sarah hadn't been sick that day.

If my mother hadn't taken her to the doctor.

If she hadn't walked down the Boulevard de Beaumarchais at the exact time when the French police happened to be walking there as well.

If she had waited a few more minutes before stepping out.

If she hadn't forgotten to sew Sarah's star on.

If I would have left for Palestine, had my parents been saved.

If I would still be living there if I hadn't met Ezra.

If I might have had a child with him, had he not chosen the path of vengeance.

The kitchen in my flat has a pine table and two chairs. There is a small stove and a pantry. I don't eat much, so it remains mostly empty. The sitting room overlooks the park. I find it magical. I take long walks there. I sit in cafés, read books and listen to music. I recently bought myself a record player, and music seems to fill a void which words cannot. But, most importantly, I have a job, for which I am paid fifteen shillings a week. The uniform is black and the hours are long, but I don't mind: I sell perfume at Selfridges, scent in coloured-glass bottles. Caron. Christian Dior. But also Guerlain: Vol de Nuit. Après l'Ondée. Shalimar. I spray and smell my mother everywhere.

On Saturdays, I model at the Slade School of Art. I had thought I would stop being a model, but something about it compels me to return: the smell of turpentine, how painted flesh comes alive with the stroke of a brush, or a pencil. My soul is prudish, but not my body. It speaks for itself, and I like that. I can be still for hours. When I pose, I let my thoughts drift to a faraway place. I sometimes forget where I am. I don't mind. I sit cross-legged, stand or recline. I am limbs and muscle, spine and skin. I am an anonymous person. No soul-baring, no storytelling. I remain still in silence. I like it, because stillness is like a cousin of death, as if my body has turned to stone, and stone covers where my parents lie.

I make friends at the school. My first real friends since Paris: artists and writers. One of them is called Vivian, and she is studying printmaking. She has a freckled face and red hair, and always looks clean. She wears dresses made out of parachute silk, seamless stockings and gloves. "Never leave home without gloves," Vivian says. In contrast, her boyfriend Declan dresses in shabby clothes and doesn't like to wash his hair. Vivian is entranced by him. Declan is a member of the pop-art movement and is seeking a new, post-war interpretation of art. "The idea of pop art," he tells us, "is to search for inspiration in the unknown rather than the familiar." Declan speaks of collages and consumer goods.

Of abstract expressionism and realism. Vivian and I follow him and his friends to bars in Soho and Chelsea. We listen to jazz and smoke cigarettes. One of them has fallen in love with me, a painter called Zak. His body is so pale it looks translucent. We make love once. I find out that he is Jewish. He mentions that he arrived in '38 as a Kindertransport, from Berlin. That his father died, but his mother survived. He asks me about France, about my past. I hesitate, because part of me would like to confide in him, but then I choose not to. If I'm going to have a man in my life, it's not going to be Zak. I find him difficult to talk to. Aside from an impressive knowledge of painting techniques and an unattractive self-confidence about his artistic abilities – "I'm just as good as Kandinsky" – he doesn't have much to say. And I do. My English is very good now. "You've only been here one year and you speak so well, almost like a native!" I'm told. "Isn't that unusual for a French person?"

"I don't know," I answer. "I no longer know what a usual French person is. I live here now."

I'm often asked about Paris. Why am I here, not there? Why am I not teaching French, for example?

I tried, but no one hired me, I explain. And I earn enough at Selfridges. Anyhow, I don't really care what I do, because I'm happy in London. I'll look for a teaching job again in due course.

But isn't everything more beautiful in Paris?

Not to me, it isn't. I cannot tell my friends. It might frighten them. And I can still feel the stigma of the Jew. I can still see myself sitting in that last Métro car, like a dangerous breed. So my answers remain as vague as my background. I find that rewriting my personal history is easier than having to explain it. I keep it nestled inside the lining of my skin, safe from outside interference.

My parents died in a car crash, is what I say.

"How awful!" is the usual response.

"Yes, it's awful," I say, nearly believing it myself.

My parents died in a car crash.

They weren't stripped naked and taken to the gas chambers and dumped into a pit together with hundreds of rotting corpses.

My parents died in a car crash, on their way to a Sunday lunch in the country. My mother was wearing her crocheted black dress and her pearl necklace. My father was wearing his light-brown suit and matching loafers.

They were driving through the countryside and took a wrong turn.

My parents died in a car crash.

*

I dress well, speak well. I surround myself with culture. My parents were shopkeepers. They weren't cultured. But they wanted the best for me. They would have been proud of me, had they seen me now.

My friends tell me I should work somewhere other than Selfridges. That I could do better. I could teach, or work in publishing. Perhaps I could. But I don't.

The shop promotes me to a managerial position. I take the job. I could do something different, but I take the job. I meet a man at the perfume counter, a physics teacher. He's looking for something for his mother. Something with a sweet smell, he says. He's kind and makes me laugh. He invites me for dinner. I accept. Then he asks me over to his house, but I decline. The following day he asks me to marry him. But I cannot marry him. I barely know him, and I don't love him.

I'm not sure I will find true love again. My friends worry about me. You must find a man, they say. "Old spinster," they must be thinking. But I cannot tell them about Ezra, or about Palestine. They wouldn't understand. And why would they?

There are many things about me I barely understand myself.

*

Vivian says she knows a man, Fletcher Schumann. Her older sister once worked with him. Vivian finds him attractive, and thinks I might too. If she weren't getting married herself, she would have considered him, she says. She is no longer with Declan. Her parents disapprove of artists, of the fact that their daughter chose to study art in the first place. "They said art was a phase, and that I would see the light, which I suppose I have," she tells me, with a hint of sadness in her voice. Vivian is now marrying a doctor, whom I find very uncharismatic. But I will never tell her that.

Fletcher, Vivian explains, is forty years old. He works in a bank and likes to read detective stories. He also loves classical music, and is a descendant of the composer Robert Schumann. She introduces me to him. A man of medium height, strong features, green eyes. He has a chipped front tooth. His thick lower lip looks soft, like a pin cushion. He asks me many questions about my life and tells me he finds me very beautiful. "I would like to get to know you," he tells me.

Fletcher bewitches me, and I become infatuated with him. A pounding, resounding infatuation. He is the great-great grandson of Robert Schumann. By associating with Fletcher I am associating with one of the most extraordinary composers of the Romantic period. I will be living love, just as I had with Ezra. Pleasure. Beauty. Music. Hope.

But Ezra was a murderer.

Fletcher asks me my age. I lie and tell him that I am thirty; thirty-five sounds too old. He is surprised that I haven't married yet.

*

I have lost my head to a married man. Fletcher has a wife and children. Vivian didn't know that. Two teenage boys. He won't tell me much about them, and I don't ask. He visits me in my small flat and takes me to hotels. To expensive restaurants. With Fletcher I eat my first lobster at L'Escargot, on Greek Street, where the tablecloths are decorated with snowflakes and one of the waiters brings us two glasses of champagne "on the house". He treats Fletcher as if he were a regular customer, which my lover – what a lovely word! – insists he isn't.

He tells me about Robert Schumann. His father owns some of his original scores. The piano concerto in A minor, the Kreisleriana and the Fantasy in C major. I can hardly believe it. I have never met anyone who has such relations. Schumann's music has seeped into his descendant's blood. It has made him special, he says. His whole family is special. Fletcher grew up in the countryside. His parents own a mansion. They're rich. His body is rich. His mind is rich. Everything about him sparkles.

Fletcher makes me feel female. Emboldened and female. Not like the young girl I was with Ezra, but a different sort of woman, a more decadent one.

Fletcher whispers dirty things to me in bed. He always wants to make love, and has a preference for kitchen floors and stairwells. He calls me his little French whore, and although I mind it at first, he quickly reassures me that it is only a figure of speech. He loves me, he says. He will leave his wife. He doesn't love her

any more. He loves me. Not Rosalind. I am beautiful, and he
wants me, only me, no longer her. I sleep badly at night. I want
him by my side. I want him for myself only. "I love you," I say
to him in English. The words ring false to me, but I cannot tell
whether it's because I've only uttered them in French before,
or because I'm trying to convince myself to believe them. But
I must believe them, because whenever I think of Fletcher my
cheeks glow. I look well, I'm told. I smile a lot and dream of
Fletcher. I wait for him to ring me, usually from the office. I
ask him where he works, and he is vague. Mayfair, he says. He
names a bank I don't know. Then again, I know very little about
banks. I would like to see where he works, but he won't let me.
Everywhere is dangerous, he says. Office and home. He cannot
ring from home. Rosalind will find out. That would not be a
good thing. Not yet. But he will tell her about me. Of course
he will. I must give him time. He will tell her.

*

I find out in October 1955 that I'm two months pregnant. We
weren't careful enough. Congratulations, says the doctor. He
asks about the father. I tell him that he's away. The doctor looks
uncomfortable. He asks me more questions. He wants to take
back the congratulations, I can tell. I leave his office. He doesn't
say goodbye. When I tell Fletcher, his lower-cushion lip trembles.
His face contorts into a strange grimace. I am shocked. He looks
like a different man. Then he tells me that I must get rid of the
child. I cannot have this child. He will not recognize it. It is not
the right time. I look at him and tell him that I do not understand. He was meant to leave his wife. He had promised. What
does he mean by the right time? So Fletcher's tone softens and he
embraces me. He will leave his wife, but I cannot keep the child.

He doesn't want another child. Not now. Later maybe, but not now. Also, what will people say? Am I aware of what it means in this country? Unmarried women don't have children alone. It is considered shameful. So he will help me find a doctor. It will be a straightforward intervention. I must not worry about anything.

I don't care what people will say. I will keep this child. I will not have an intervention. Fletcher says that in that case he cannot see me again. And that he no longer loves me.

I cannot live without him. I cannot function properly. I have lost everything in my life. I cannot lose him too. I cry for him. For my parents. For Paris. For who I was and who I have become. I have morning sickness. I am thirty-five years old, unmarried and I have morning sickness. The scent of perfume makes me ill. Shalimar especially. Every time I smell it, I have to rush to the loo. My supervisor is suspicious. She takes me aside and I confess. She is very upset. She mentions words like illegitimate. How could I. How did I. Who is he. Imagine what the others will think. Imagine what the child will think.

She fires me.

*

Fletcher is back in my life. I am four months pregnant with hardly anything to show for it. We smoke cigarettes in bed. He drinks whisky naked. We listen to Schumann. Fletcher has convinced me to give the child up for adoption. I must leave my flat and go somewhere else until the child is born. No one should know. No one. There is a good place, a mother-and-baby home. They will take good care of me. And he will come and visit. Once the child is born, he will leave Rosalind.

But I don't want to give the child up for adoption. I want to keep it. I want to tell Fletcher who I really am. That I'm not a French Catholic. That my parents died, that I'm a Jew. That I lived in Palestine. where the air smelled like pine. That I had a lover there. That I'm not who he thinks I am. That I want this child. But I want Fletcher too.

He tells me I must choose. Between him and the child. He will give me money to help me. He will pay the rent of the empty flat. But I must choose. He will leave his wife if I leave the child.

A vicar tells me I have committed a sin. Tells me it is unacceptable for a child to be raised without a father and mother. When he says the word "unacceptable", his voice rises. He has red lines on his nose and wears a signet ring. I confess to him that I am Jewish. I do not believe in sin. The vicar looks at me and says nothing more.

*

I tell my friends that I have to go to France. Something to do with my uncle. I will be gone for a few months. I don't explain, they don't ask questions.

A Church of England home takes me in, in Hackney. The women who work there are nuns. A matron interviews me. I lie and say I'm Protestant. She doesn't ask me for proof. "There is no bar to the kind of spiritual work we have always endeavoured to do for the patient," she says, in a voice she clearly reserves for all spiritual matters. "The hands of Jesus will reach us all with their healing powers."

When I visit the first time, all the pregnant women are smoking, busy talking to each other. There are about twenty of them in the home. Some are knitting clothes for their babies. I understand later that the knitting is a way of atoning for our sins. We've all been guilty of a terrible deed. Therefore by knitting clothes for our unborn baby, we are giving something back to society. No one seems to question it. Most of the women are younger than me. There is a chaplain there, and we have to attend Sunday services. During the day we have chores. Cleaning the stairwells, polishing the banisters. In the afternoons we're allowed out or have tea in the home. No one knows I'm here except for Vivian, who comes to visit at weekends. She swears she will never tell a soul, and I believe her. She assures me that the home is the right place to be. That society will not accept me if I keep the baby. That life will be very difficult for me.

Society means little to me, as do healing powers. But not for Vivian or Fletcher. He visits twice and seems very uncomfortable. Doesn't say much, except that I'm doing the right thing. Once he holds my hand. His palm feels warm. He speaks of the office, of his work. Says his sons are not doing well at school. I don't want to hear about his sons, and I tell him so. He gets up quickly. "I'll come back another time," he says, as if I had upset him. I apologize, although I'm not sure what for. Then one of the girls starts to shout, and we understand that her contractions have begun, and in the commotion Fletcher leaves without saying goodbye.

I have to share a room with eight other women. We sleep on bunk beds. We become friendly. But I feel desperate. I miss Fletcher, miss my books. No one here reads books. Except for one nun, Sylvia. She's a nice woman. When my waters break, she takes me to the Hackney Hospital. She assures me I will be fine, and then she's gone. From then on, nothing is fine. I can hear the other women screaming in the labour ward. We are separated by a thin curtain. The midwife is brutal. She knows why I'm here. "Your child will go to a deserving married couple," she says. I tell her my age. "I'm not a young girl," I think I answer, as if that matters. As if age has anything to do with being deserving. She doesn't flinch.

The contractions become unbearable. I scream with pain. I beg for pain relief. She ignores my cries. I think I tell her about my parents. How they died. I have never told anyone before. I'm not sure what she says. I don't remember much. All I know is that she wants to hurt me. But then he's born. Maurice. He has black hair and a tiny face. He screams loudly. I'm asked to sign a document on the dotted line. Dot-like Maurice. A dot of dreams. I don't want to sign, I cry. But a nurse tells me that I have to. So I do. *18th May 1956.*

Maurice Baum Schumann.

11

Maurice's adoption has been arranged privately, through the vicar with the signet ring. I am reminded that I cannot and will never see my child again. That I have to get on with my life. That's what girls in my situation do. Get on with their lives. I am told that I can keep Maurice for six weeks, until the couple come to collect him.

"This is not a collection," I cry out. "You're taking him away from me!" The vicar says nothing. Maybe he hasn't heard me. Or maybe he doesn't want to listen. I don't think he likes me. I take Maurice back with me from the hospital to the mother-and-baby home. I hold him against me and nurse him. He wears light-blue pyjamas, a cherished gift from one of the women in the home. There is also a simple white pair the hospital has given me. They smell of him, my son who never sleeps, as if he knows that he will have to leave. There are many other women there with their newborn babies. I don't remember much of them. All I remember is Maurice and how I lay awake looking at him and holding him in his light-blue pyjamas. I want Fletcher to see him, but he never comes. I send a note through Vivian, asking him to get in touch, but nothing happens. Then when the six weeks are up, one of the nuns tells me that the couple has arrived to take him away. I have to say goodbye. I hold Maurice in my arms one last time, and he smiles. His first smile. He focuses his dark eyes on me and smiles. I break down. I cannot do it. I cannot part with him. But it's too late. The nun says I have no choice. Now I can see the couple through the window. They are waiting, the nun says. I can see their shadows.

Maurice is taken from me and given to the shadows.

*

I pack a small bag and leave the home. I take the pyjamas with me. I say goodbye to no one. It is a sunny day. Crisp air, blue sky, warm sun. A beautiful day. Maurice is gone. I have lost a part of myself. That part which makes a woman whole. Without it, I will be diminished. An incomplete woman. But I have Fletcher. He is waiting for me at my flat. He will make me feel better. We can be together now. He has left his wife. We are free now. Free to start a new life.

*

I enter my flat. I drop the bag on the ground and call out Fletcher's name, but he isn't there. He hasn't left a note, and the flat looks immaculate, as if no one has set foot here in weeks. And yet, Fletcher said he would be waiting for me. "I'll be here for you when you return," he had said.

Perhaps it's because he's at work. Yes, that must be it. He'll be back later.

I walk into my bedroom and lie down on the bed. The pain I feel inside is close to unsustainable. I need Fletcher to come and rescue me.

I fall asleep. When I wake up, it is dark. There is still no Fletcher. No sign of him.

And so I understand. There will never be a Fletcher. He hasn't left his wife, and he never will. And I have no way of finding him. I don't know where he lives. Where he works. The bank name he has given me is a lie. Everything about him is a lie. I know nothing about him. I know nothing about anything any more. I am suddenly overcome by a terrifying thought: I can no longer see myself clearly. I can no longer see. The outside has dislocated from my inside. It has snapped in two, like a wire.

*

I am interned in a psychiatric ward. Someone takes me there. Was it Fletcher? Did he find me, lying on the ground? There was a pair of hands with slender fingers and clean nails. That is the only thing I can remember. Those slender fingers, then those nails and a hospital room. I am diagnosed with psychosis. Days blur into each other like a series of doors – opening, closing, opening, closing. Twice a week I am given electroconvulsive therapy. A rubber contraption is inserted into my mouth. Electrodes are placed on my temples, and I scream. The doctor says that he understands how I feel, but promises that it will cure me. I am too weak to protest. Too weak to tell him that I can feel that first jolt of electricity crack through me. I have terrible headaches afterwards, and drool like an old woman. I watch the burgeoning berries on the tree outside my window. I don't know what tree it is, but the berries look beautiful.

I barely eat, I see things, I hear people speak that aren't there. There is a multicoloured carpet in my bedroom. I distinguish shapes in it, like wings. I imagine what it would be like to fly out the window. But if I fly I might die. And I cannot die, because I have a son, Maurice. The top of his head smells like blossom.

My blossom boy.

Do I tell anyone about him? A doctor, perhaps? A man who wears a tie takes notes and prescribes me small white pills. I swallow the pills from a plastic glass. So do all the other patients. We always seem to be swallowing something. I share my room with a woman whose face is lopsided because of the treatment. We speak, the two of us. She is worse off than I am. She laughs to herself at night. She has entered the corridors of madness, whereas I stand on its threshold, trembling.

I am discharged on a rainy August day. I remember seeing myself in the mirror after I leave the ward. I feel and look like a different person. Strands of my hair have turned white. I have shed all my pregnancy weight and appear very thin. My skin is covered in small spots, which take years to fade. And when they do, scars remain, long and thin like threads of saffron. From that day on, I always appear much older than I am.

*

The days and months after my hospital stay all seemed alike. Stagnant. Hazy. I was given more pills, which helped me function. When my friends from the Slade tried to get in touch, I told them I had been ill in France and was still convalescing. They seemed concerned, and I told them I would be in touch as soon as I felt better. I don't know if they believed me; I didn't care whether they did or not. I cared only about hiding. But Vivian, loyal Vivian, decided otherwise. "We all miss you," she said. "There's no point in staying home alone. You need to come out with us again. Be strong again."

That Vivian regarded me as her closest friend I have no doubt. But guilt also played a significant part in her behaviour. She was the one who took me home after my stay in the ward, and I'll never forget the look on her face when she first saw me. She wanted to make amends. She felt responsible for introducing me to Fletcher. She never said so, but I knew.

And, to a certain extent, her forcing me out worked. I did see some of my friends again. They were too discreet to ask what illness I had contracted, although a painter I knew wondered if the spots on my face had something to do with it. I told her they did, and that seemed to satisfy her. And, unexpectedly, it satisfied me as well. Speaking about it, even in such vague terms, made a difference. For the first time in a long while I felt a tinge of relief slowly settle inside me.

I stopped using the pills the doctor had prescribed. I didn't feel I needed them any longer, and they had made me gain a lot of weight, which didn't suit me.

I had a bit of money left at first, but that soon ran out. It became clear that I needed to find myself a job. I could not return to Selfridges, so I thought about applying to another department store. Then I decided that I wanted to do something altogether different. I needed to challenge myself. Use my brain a bit more. Perhaps work in a bookshop, like in Paris, or a school. Something to do with words, possibly.

One Saturday morning, as I passed by a synagogue on St Petersburgh Place, I heard the sound of a familiar melody and stopped dead in my tracks. It was an Eastern European chant, intoned by a deep baritone voice, a cantor presumably. I had heard it before. When? Then I remembered. It was with my parents at a high-holiday service in 1941, at the synagogue on the Rue Pavée. I had accompanied them reluctantly. We had bickered on the way, because I had argued that I wasn't religious and found no solace in God, especially not in times of war. "It's not about God or the war, but duty," my father had replied tersely. "Duty comes before all else."

I had gone with them, but I was uncomfortable during the service, feeling that I didn't belong. And then, towards the end, the Rabbi had begun to sing. Three other men joined in. It was exquisitely beautiful, and I was transfixed.

A few weeks later, a bomb planted by the Germans exploded and destroyed the synagogue. Every time I walked past the ruins, I remembered that day, that song.

And now, here it was again. I still didn't know what the song was called, nor did I wish to find out. I stood and listened. It was very cold outside, and the sun shone a feeble, winter yellow. I could have sought shelter inside the warmth of the synagogue, but I didn't want to. It would have meant renewing ties with something I had long ago abandoned. It was enough to stand on the street and listen. The melody sounded as beautiful as it had in 1941. The notes were like drops of rain ringing. They rose and rang and burst inside me, and next thing I knew, I was sobbing. I hid in the doorway of a nearby building, hoping no one would see me, and went on crying. I couldn't stop. I had slipped into that small space where my heart seeped. I could feel the seepage releasing within every particle of my body, like a warm liquid.

But it wasn't an impression. There was a warm liquid. I was urinating all over myself. I was a thirty-seven-year-old woman who had urinated all over herself. I felt so humiliated that I stopped crying instantly. The urine had trickled through my underwear into my trousers. I could smell it. A rancid smell, like ammonia. I was sure others walking past me could smell it too, as if I were a tramp.

I rushed home. I didn't dare get into a taxi, so I ran, feeling the wetness against my skin. As soon as I reached my apartment, I tore off my clothes, threw them into a basin and scrubbed them viciously clean. I hung them out to dry and lit myself a cigarette, my hands shaking. Eventually, I calmed down and sat on my sofa in my underwear, smoking and looking at the tops of the trees outside my window. I stood up and put on some music – a Frank Sinatra song I think it was. Slowly I began to hum, then sing along. The feeling of humiliation evaporated. Instead, and this took me by surprise, I felt a sense of relief, or perhaps even elation, as if I had finally purged myself of something infectious, like a disease. What the disease was, I didn't know. Nor did I wish to. I strongly believe that some things in life are not worth investigating. And this was one of them.

That night, I jumped into a taxi and went out to a pub alone, something I had never done before. I knew the pub, the French House in Soho, because I had been there several times with Vivian and my friends from the Slade. Fletcher had never liked it. He deemed it too pretentious, because of all the artists and writers who frequented it, which was all the more reason for me to go there.

I wore a woollen skirt, a flattering blouse, black baby-doll pumps and a few dabs of Shalimar. I covered up the scars on my face with foundation cream, a habit I was to keep for many years. I sat at the bar and ordered a Tom Collins, then another. A man asked if he could join me. I said yes. He wore a dark suit and an expensive watch. He spoke English with a thick accent and turned out to be French. His face wasn't handsome, but it was confident and strong. I like strong faces. I pretended to be English, and he believed me. I told him that my parents were

Polish, but that I had been brought up here. He asked where in Poland, and I said Cracow. He was from Rouen, he explained, a manager at Colgate-Palmolive. At one point in the conversation he expressed surprise that I didn't want to know more about France. "Most of the ladies do," he volunteered. I told him that I had been there a couple of times, though never to Rouen, which was the truth. Then I asked him about his home town, and he appeared satisfied. I may even have betrayed my roots when I mentioned Flaubert, who had immortalized the region in *Madame Bovary*. "How do you know Flaubert is from Rouen?" he asked, looking surprised.

"I read books," I declared firmly. "And I love Flaubert."

We stayed in the pub talking and drinking until closing time. Then he walked me home. I spent the night with him. He was a very good lover. The last man I had made love with was Fletcher, three years back. But Fletcher wasn't a good lover. He just thought he was.

In the morning, the Frenchman was about to leave when he stopped in his tracks. He had noticed the books on my shelves. "Do you speak French?" he asked, in our native language.

"No," I answered back, in English. "The books are not mine. They belong to my roommate. She's French."

The man left and tried to contact me a few more times, but I declined to see him again.

*

By a strange coincidence, one of the teachers at the Slade wrote to me about a job she knew of, teaching French. The man who ran the school, Andrew Burr, was her cousin, and they were looking for teachers. Was I interested?

I went to meet Mr Burr and he hired me.

The school was a mediocre one for foreign students in Bloomsbury. The pay wasn't much, but it was better than nothing. I had never taught before, and I did so mechanically, as if the room were empty and I were talking to myself. I cannot recall what those students looked like or what they said. All I know is that after one month I was called into Mr Burr's office and told that I wasn't fit for the job. "The students say that you can teach all right, but you don't look at them when you give your classes and you don't speak to them," he told me. "It's like you're talking to yourself. Never heard anything like it," he added scratching his chin. "Anyway, Ms Baum, fact is, in our school we have standards to maintain. We believe in the *rapport*" – he stressed the word – "between teacher and student, that sort of thing. I'm sure you understand."

"Yes, of course."

Andrew Burr had a large face. When he smiled, it accentuated the small, pearl-like beads of sweat on his brow. He was coarse, but he was kind. "But because you're a friend of my cousin, I'm going to help you out here." He grabbed a mint from a tray and popped it into his mouth. "My colleague is looking for a researcher," he continued, sucking on his mint. "She's writing a book about some French writer, can't remember who. Some famous one, though. Would that interest you? And you can do all the daydreaming you want, because no one will be there to watch you," he chuckled.

And that's how I found my peace. Doing research for someone else, about Paul Valéry, as it turned out. The writer, an American woman who wore too much make-up, paid me handsomely for my work, which she declared "faultless". To this day, she doesn't know how grateful I am to her. How, by losing myself in another place and time, I was able to regain something I had lost: a modicum of dignity, of self-assurance. I began reading again, and listening to music, nineteenth-century pieces mostly. I wouldn't say that I was entirely cured by the time Vivian introduced me to Henry, but I wasn't far off. I nearly didn't go to hear him play, because I was feeling tired, but she insisted. "Henry Dobbs is a great pianist," she said. "And you're always tired."

So I made the effort and met Vivian at Wigmore Hall, and we took our seats in the third row. I looked at the programme. The first piece was *Fantaisie-Impromptu*, Op. 66, by Chopin. I knew the piece well. I listened to it often.

Henry Dobbs appeared on stage with a thick mop of white hair. He walked slowly towards the piano and sat down. Then he began to play, and his hands flew over the piano like small birds. I was transfixed.

The melody glided in and out, with crystal-clear dexterity and lightness of touch. In the middle section it slowed down and swelled, like a wave rising into a place of great beauty, then crashing and rising again, against all the odds, challenging everything I had believed possible until now.

I closed my eyes and began to cry.

His fingers were singing.

Later we went backstage, and Vivian introduced us. It was as if we had always known each other. That's what I felt when I met Henry. I didn't tell him, but I didn't need too. He admitted later that he had felt the same way: the irrefutable certitude that I was the one. That he had been waiting for me all his life.

"Your ship's come in," said Vivian.

12

Henry was fifteen years older than me. He had only been in love once, with a young violinist, Sonia, who left him a month before their wedding. "She fell in love with another man," said Henry. "It was a bit of a shock."

He devoted the next eight years to his musical career, and to the care of his ageing parents. There were few women during that time, "maybe one or two, nothing serious". When his parents died, he inherited their Chelsea house, where he now lived. "Now you've come along," said Henry, smiling at me. "And you've messed up all my tidy little plans."

Henry and I got married on a spring day, in a small ceremony at Chelsea Town Hall. I wore a white dress and flowers in my hair. Henry wore a suit. Aside from our witnesses and Henry's siblings, we had each invited four close friends. Afterwards we went to Claridge's for dinner. We drank several glasses of champagne, and Henry ordered caviar for everyone. Around midnight we excused ourselves and checked into our room. We made love all night, and Henry later admitted he had never experienced a night of passion before. "Sonia was not a passionate woman," he said.

The next morning, after breakfast, we returned to our new house in Chelsea, and Henry went back to practising the Mendelssohn piano trio he was to perform the following week.

In the middle of his practice he got up and came to find me. I was writing in this notebook. He stood in the doorway and looked at me tenderly.

"I want to tell you that I've never been happier than I am today," he said. "I am very lucky to have you in my life."

*

Luck. Henry brought me plenty of it. I lived a life I couldn't possibly have dreamt of before I met him. We travelled round the world, stayed in good hotels, had friends in high places. I never missed a performance of his, except for Israel and China. After China he got tired. He declared he would no longer play in public. He was nearly seventy and worn out. We had moved to our house in Notting Hill by then. Our fussier friends had disapproved. Why have you left Chelsea? Why in the world would you want to live anywhere else? "My wife likes 'else'," Henry chuckled. "And I like to do as my wife says."

We were happy in that house. Henry perhaps less so than me initially, but only because, as he was the first to admit, "I've never set foot outside a predictable neighbourhood."

Notting Hill's unpredictability caught him by surprise. If he found the adjustment difficult, which I suspect he did, he kept it mostly to himself, although he did complain about "those West Indian marauders". His priority, as he often reminded me, was to take care of me. "I never thought I would find love again," he once admitted. "Certainly not with a woman like you."

He showered me with gifts and compliments. He worried about my health, my state of mind. He was the most delicate and sensitive of men, and I honoured him for it.

If my love for him was more subdued than his for me, I made up for it by offering encouragement and praise. I admired Henry's talent. I was proud of being Mrs Dobbs. I kept nothing from him except for my past. I never told him about Maurice. I couldn't. My son's existence was part of an underworld no one could enter but me. And I feared Henry might judge me if he knew the truth. I couldn't take that risk, nor did I ever feel compelled to do so. But I did open up to him about my childhood and my parents, my time in Palestine. I think he found it intimidating, "too monumental", as he put it, so we seldom discussed it, although the subject of Ezra often came up. "Did you love him?" he wanted to know. I gave him an honest answer, but I could tell that it made him uncomfortable, so we agreed it was best to avoid the subject.

But after a few years Henry began asking questions again. He wanted to know more about my parents and their history. "I can't imagine what they must have gone through," he said. "And I can only guess how painful it must have been for you." We talked about it, but superficially. By then, I was the one who was reluctant. Many years had gone by, and although the pain hadn't diminished, the desire to discuss it had. So, after a while, Henry stopped asking altogether. He was good that way. And I was grateful for his understanding, even though I knew that he probably continued to conjecture. Another man might have insisted, but not Henry. Whatever he felt, he kept it to himself. He never lost his patience or his temper – at least not in front of me. Except once.

We were on our way to New York. He was to perform at Carnegie Hall. If I remember correctly, the programme was Mozart, Alban Berg and Shostakovich. The evening was sold out. I was happy and excited for him, but he was nervous. He always was before performances – especially when playing Shostakovich – and before flying.

The plane was leaving from Heathrow. Henry wanted to buy a good bottle of Scotch for our friends the Walhams, patrons of Henry's who lived in a sprawling apartment on Park Avenue. I had already been to the duty-free shop, so I told Henry I would wait for him in the First Class airport lounge. Henry never flew anything but first class, as befitted his status as a world-famous concert pianist. And I enjoyed every minute of it. Vivian had once asked me whether I didn't find it embarrassing, the notion that everything I had once stood for had gone out of the window when I met Henry. That I had become a "kept woman".

I confessed to being utterly bewildered by her comment. What did she mean by "what I had once stood for?" And what window and why should I be embarrassed? Henry worked hard, harder than anyone I knew. He was an astonishingly good pianist, and people paid lots of money to hear him play. If anything, I was proud. Deeply proud of him. "And surprised you would say such a thing," I added. "I'm as much a kept woman as he's a kept man. We keep each other happy."

Vivian looked upset. "You used to be like a hippy. You were an artists' model, a cool French girl with integrity."

"Until you introduced me to Fletcher," I snapped. "I didn't lose my integrity, but I lost something else."

"You cannot blame me for what happened between you and Fletcher," she said, looking upset.

"Well, don't accuse me of having lost my integrity, then," I answered coldly. "Let me enjoy my life as it is."

"Yes," she whispered, "yes, of course."

"And you married a doctor," I added. "You're hardly well placed to judge."

I didn't hear from Vivian after that.

Henry returned from the duty-free shop empty-handed and looking very distressed. His well-pressed trousers and polished shoes appeared to be covered in something. As he approached, I could see and smell what it was: vomit.

In all our years together, I had never seen him look so upset. He spoke heatedly as he recounted what had happened. He was queuing at the till, he said, waiting to pay for his Scotch. Ahead of him was a woman with a little girl. The woman looked harried and unhappy. The child must have been three or four. She was very pretty, the total opposite of her mother, who kept mentioning her name. "Stay still, Donna! Smile at the lady, Donna!" Donna had blond, curly hair and wore earrings, which marred the prettiness, he thought. She was dressed in pink and clutched a fur animal. She looked at Henry, and her face suddenly turned white. "My tummy," she whined.

The next thing Henry knew, Donna was vomiting all over the floor and on his trousers and shoes. A few women from the duty-free shop rushed to the scene with paper towels and kept asking Henry if he was all right. "I'm not bloody all right!" he shouted, as Donna's mother stood looking at him, saying nothing. Not even "I'm sorry". Nothing. "Vulgar, rude woman," said Henry, his voice quivering.

Donna began to cry and vomited again, and Henry fled the scene.

Now he was in the bathroom cleaning himself up. I waited outside for him to reappear. When he did, his trousers were all wet, and his shoes had regained their previous shine. But Henry was still cursing the woman and her daughter all the way to the aeroplane. "It was hardly the child's fault," I ventured, as we sat down in our seats. "Don't be so harsh on her."

"You're right," he admitted. "She was a sweet little girl. But you know about me. I've never liked children much. Thank goodness we didn't have a child – I don't think I could cope. I really don't. That vomit, Flora. All that vomit…"

Now it was my voice that began to quiver. "Adults get sick too sometimes, Henry. You can't blame the child. It was hardly her fault, " I repeated. "And for what it's worth, I think that children are lovely. I would have liked to have a child of my own."

I avoided his gaze, as I felt his boring into mine.

"We have each other," he said, grabbing my hand and squeezing it tightly. "We have each other, and I wouldn't want anything more."

*

We celebrated 1968 by going to the Royal Opera House to hear a performance of Strauss's *Elektra*. Henry and I had grand-tier seats. Expensive seats. I was wearing a black dress and a pearl necklace. During the interval, we went to the bar to get a glass of wine. It was very crowded. There was a flurry of fabric and a sweetness of scent. A woman next to me smelled of violets and tobacco. Another of tuberose: Fracas. I recognized it instantly. Then Dior. I had developed a nose at Selfridges.

There was a man jostling for the waiter's attention. I could see him from behind. The waiter placed a glass of wine in front of the man, who had grey hair and a plump neck, like uncooked roast beef. He was fumbling for his change. Then he turned round and I saw him: Fletcher Schumann. An overweight man with grey hair and weary eyes. Of the man I had once known, once loved, there were only vague traces, like the remaining foundations of a demolished building. And that man turned white when he saw me. That demolished building of a man turned ashen white. I thought he might faint. I wanted to do something to him. I wanted to squeeze his plump rump of a neck until he stopped breathing. I wanted to watch him die. I had never harboured such strong feelings of hatred towards anyone – not even Ezra. But towards Fletcher, I clearly did. I was about to say something when someone called out his name. I had time to see her, a woman wearing a pink dress and matching lipstick. She had to be his wife, Rosalind. And then Henry appeared. "There you are, darling," he said, handing me a glass of white wine.

I was momentarily distracted by Henry. By the wine. When I turned round again, Fletcher had disappeared. Vanished. That's all it took. A few seconds of distraction. And I was shaking and squeezing the glass so hard that it broke. A few onlookers stared at me as I stood there, holding pieces of shattered glass. A woman shouted and pointed. I looked at my hand. It was covered in blood, and drops of it were falling onto the dark carpet.

13

A new family has moved into Bert Moser's house. The date is 18th December 1983, a day after an IRA bomb injured 91 people outside Harrods. The nation is in shock, and I'm surprised anyone would choose to move on such a day. Then again, it would have been planned weeks before. Most moves are. I can almost hear Henry reprimanding me. "Come on, Flora, stop judging people. You're too harsh."

I enjoyed it, the way he used to call me "harsh". It was the last word I would have used to describe myself. Harsh. Then again, do I have an objective view of myself? Does anyone?

Henry.

He died in 1981, after a severe stroke. He was practising a Mozart sonata when suddenly I heard a loud thump and found him on the floor, unconscious. He died on the way to hospital.

I went to say goodbye to him in the morgue. That's when I told him the truth. About Fletcher and Maurice. I stood by his side, holding his stiff hand, and I told him everything, in a low voice. As I did so, my tears flowed, down my cheeks and onto the casket. I knelt, leant towards him and kissed him. "Forgive me, Henry," I whispered. "Forgive me. And thank you for the life you gave me."

Hundreds of people attended his funeral. He was a famous pianist after all. I don't remember much about that day. I felt incoherent, as if drunk. Poems and tributes were read. Henry's old and closest friend, Carlo, broke down as he recited Auden. I couldn't say anything. Something sharp became lodged inside me, like the tip of an arrow.

I can still feel it sometimes.

*

The family that has moved into Bert's house is good-looking. Both the parents and the two children. The wife is beautiful. Blond, slender, looks like a Scandinavian model. The husband is very tall. He has a beard and an interesting face, like the children. I see them nearly every morning on my way to the British Library, where I'm doing research on my book.

I like the girl. Skinny, black hair, alert eyes. She looks Mediterranean, like her father, and reminds me of my younger self. Same hair, same eyes. She always says hello. The brother doesn't. Sullen, angry boy. I never see him speak, but there is a bond between him and his sister. The father always says hello too. He's friendly. The mother tries to be. But I'm not sure about her.

A man often visits the new family. Dapper, very *comme il faut*. Sense of humour, generous man, not a great reader. I can tell. I know the type. Henry had friends like him. A delightful and entertaining façade, but often unhappy inside. But perhaps this man isn't unhappy. Perhaps I'm judging again.

I hear the daughter call after him once:

"Walter!"

Walter.

Mr Patel, the newspaper agent on Ladbroke Grove, has told me who they are. The man is Leon Karalis, the theatre director. He's well known. Mr Patel doesn't know anything about the wife. His son finds her beautiful, but Mr Patel doesn't.

"I don't like blonde ladies," he says. And the daughter is called Hannah.

The Karalises like visitors. Various men and women come and go. Fashionable types, like them. Though Walter seems to be there the most. Does he live with them? I've seen him in the room Bert Moser use to work in. I can see it from my bathroom. The small attic room with the blue basin. I wonder if it's still there. Bert was our friend. These people are not our friends.

I hear shouting at night. The Karalises fight a lot. Especially the son. "I hate you!" I can hear him shout across the rooftops.

It's a good thing Henry is not here to witness this. He did not like noise or being disturbed in any way when he practised. And the sound of a teenager screaming across the rooftops would have upset him greatly.

I miss Henry. But it is his piano-playing I miss even more. Now the house is always quiet. I keep the piano there to remind me of him, to break the quiet. Sometimes, when I close my eyes, I can hear him, his fingers gliding over the keyboard. There he is, head bent towards the piano keys, playing a Beethoven sonata, humming. There he is again with his flop of white hair, his smiling eyes, his hearty laugh, his love, his touch when we held each other, our fingers intertwined.

*

I was walking down Piccadilly the other day, having had a meeting with a woman Henry and I knew, the editor of a small publishing company. We had discussed the idea of my writing a book about Robert Schumann. She had been very receptive, and I was in high spirits as I bade her goodbye.

It was a beautiful spring day, and the street was crowded. A row of French children walked past me, holding hands. As I passed Fortnum & Mason, I heard an Italian man speaking to his wife. I turned round and saw that he was carrying his small daughter on his shoulders. She was laughing, and when I caught her eye she said something to me in Italian. I wish I could have understood what she said. Italian is a language I would like to have learnt. Henry spoke a few words, though his accent was terrible. I didn't tease him about it, because Henry was not a man who enjoyed being teased. There was a certain earnestness about him, a trait he shared with many of his musician friends. "We live for our music while the world passes us by," he used to say.

Henry would have been happy to know that my meeting with the editor had gone well. He had always encouraged me to pursue my writing, or anything else for that matter. He believed in me. He might not have known everything about my life, but that wasn't important; most of us retain a certain element of mystery about our past. Although in Henry's case his candour excluded the possibility of mystery. As far as I knew, he had never hidden anything from me. Or had he? Perhaps there were elements of him that had escaped me? I wondered, as a couple walked past. The woman was beautiful, and the man had his arm tightly wrapped around her waist. How much did they know about each other? Probably little. They were only starting to find out, and every revelation would further deepen their infatuation for each other. There was a youthful abandon about them, a concept which seemed to belong to a distant part of my life. I was no longer youthful, and abandon had become a dirty word. Behind the couple was an older woman who, from afar, looked vaguely familiar. She must have been my age, in her seventies, with grey hair and a small, heavy frame. She was carrying a bag and looking around her, as if uncertain of her whereabouts. As she came closer, I stopped suddenly in the middle of the pavement. "Hey, watch out!" a man said, nearly bumping into me. I didn't move. I couldn't. Because it was her. I was nearly sure of it. Claire Betts. Her face bore the traces of the young woman she had once been. I could see those traces in among the wrinkles of her older cheeks. The eyes hadn't changed. They were still hers, those eyes I had first seen in the heat of that day, forty years before, and kept with me ever since. As she was about to walk past me, I let out a cry and grabbed her arm. I will never know why I did that – grab her arm rather than say her name, or approach her more gently – but that is what I did. My brusque gesture led her to push me away, as if she had just encountered a lunatic. "Keep your hands off me!" she shouted, looking frightened. I tried to say something, to explain myself, but it was too late. She scrambled into a cab and was gone. I stood on the pavement, trembling from head to toe. "Are you OK?" someone asked. I didn't answer. I slowly regained my composure and managed to hail a cab. The driver tried to make conversation with me, but I was too fraught to answer. I was still trembling when I arrived home. It was as if the image I had preserved of Claire Betts had been sullied, our mutual history obliterated. Or perhaps I was the one who had changed. She hadn't recognized me, after all. As far as Claire was concerned, I was the crazy woman who had grabbed her arm in the middle of the street. Not the young Frenchwoman who had seen her kiss her husband a last goodbye.

Later on, when I felt better, I decided that for my own sanity I needed to put this incident aside. To forget it had happened. For all I knew, I could have made a mistake. She could have been a woman who looked like Claire Betts, but wasn't her. Or perhaps it was Claire and I had genuinely frightened her. Whatever the truth was, I didn't want to know. I wanted to carry on living with the 1946 image I had of Claire Betts. The woman I had sought to comfort, not the one I had frightened away.

With time, the image began to fade, but not the words she had shouted. I could hear them, replaying in my mind: "Keep your hands off me!" – and every time I did, I shuddered.

*

Three years have passed, and the family is still living in Bert Moser's house. The children have grown. The boy is nearly as tall as his father. A child's face on a man's body. The daughter has become very pretty. I often see them in the morning, brother and sister, walking to the Tube station together. Their step is steady, synchronous. It is a comforting sight.

This morning, the girl was alone. I wondered whether her brother was sick. Later on I went to buy some vegetables on the Portobello Road, and there he was, loafing around in Vernon Yard with two hippy-looking men. It was a school day and he shouldn't have been there. He wasn't sick at all, but smoking marijuana. I know the smell from my days at the Slade. The hippies looked like vagrants. One of them laughed, and he sounded like an engine revving. Hannah's brother looked in my direction, but I don't think he recognized me. He was high on drugs. I felt bad for the family. I wonder if they know what their son is up to. He cannot be more than thirteen or fourteen. Too young to be so lost.

About a week later, I met Hannah Karalis. We had tea together. Lovely, intelligent girl. She knocked on my door in the freezing cold. When she stepped into the house she brought in something warm: youth, hope and curiosity. I was struck, once again, by the way she looked and spoke. It reminded me of the young girl I once was, walking in the streets of Paris, *circa* 1936, when life burned with promise and expectation.

Hannah told me a bit about herself. That she was sixteen and wanted to become a writer. She told me who her parents were, where she went to school. She wanted me to be interested in her parents. But I wasn't. I couldn't tell her, but I wasn't. It was her I was interested in. She mentioned French books, and when I told her I was from Paris, her face glowed. She mentioned that she had read *The Lover* by Marguerite Duras, which surprised me. She seems too young to read such books, or perhaps I'm just old-fashioned. At one point, she said something about an accident, and I could tell that she was referring to something painful. She didn't say anything, but I could tell. It was shaping who she would later become. I could almost feel the shaping.

Hannah said she liked Victorians authors. George Eliot, in particular. She was about to tell me why when her father arrived. I like the way she expressed herself and took everything in. There was also a certain shyness to her, despite her volubility. I will invite her again. I would like to see her again. I felt something akin to happiness in her presence. I could have had a daughter like her. Henry and I tried to have children, but it didn't happen. Hannah asked about that. Children. Or perhaps she didn't and I think that she did. She looked at my bookshelves and asked if I was a writer. I told her that I was writing a book about Robert Schumann. I'm not sure she knew who he was, so I didn't pursue it. I didn't tell her that I have unearthed previously unseen documents about Robert and Clara. That I am writing these words for my son, Maurice. He might want to know some day. Who were his parents? Why did his mother leave him? These words are for him. To know how great and illustrious his pedigree is. The power of Robert's music lives on and always will. Nothing will live on of Fletcher, except for his son. If Robert were still alive, he'd be appalled by his descendant's behaviour.

But it isn't Maurice's fault that his father was a worthless, filthy scoundrel. It isn't his fault I abandoned him. But it is my fault that I believed every word that filthy Fletcher uttered.

And for this, I shall never forgive myself.

Every day of my life begins with Maurice. Every night of my life ends with Maurice. Every day I hope for a letter from him. And every night I go to sleep, thinking that it might come tomorrow.

*

I was combing my hair in the bathroom when I saw Walter in Bert Moser's room. He was standing by the window. There was someone with him. Her. The mother. She wore a white blouse. She was moving towards him with her long hair and her white blouse. Walter turned round and kissed her. A passionate embrace. I saw it all. How she removed her blouse and exposed her breasts. How he cupped them. How they disappeared onto the bed. They had done this before. I could see it clearly. They had done it before and they would do it again.

I can never see Hannah again. I cannot speak to her again. Some may deem it too rash a decision, but I am a rash woman. And I know too much that Hannah doesn't. I cannot bear the thought. It is too painful. Best that I cut off ties immediately. Because I know what will happen next. There will come a time when Leon will find out. Perhaps not soon, but one day. Someone will make a mistake and Leon will find out. It is generally mistakes that betray the sinner. Not honesty.

Leon will pack up his belongings and leave the house. I do not want to witness it. I do not want to see his belongings stuffed into cardboard boxes. Nor do I want to witness the girl's pain. I'm no good at comforting people.

I'm no good at pain.

*

She knocked at my door. It was a sunny day. She knocked at my door, and there she was with a cake her mother had baked for me. She was all smiles and youth and gentleness, and I was so distraught I nearly cried for her. For her goodness and the way she held the cake, with expectation and friendship and everything I should have given her but couldn't.

I think she confused my distress with rudeness. I didn't mean to be rude. On the contrary. I wanted to say it. I wanted to tell her that her mother was cheating on her father and that her family would soon implode. It was inevitable. Her father would find out, it was only a matter of time. And I liked him. I knew that he wanted to lure me into his house like a mouse into a trap. I knew it when he blasted Henry's music from his open window, wooing me with his Schubert impromptus. It made me smile, but it didn't tempt me in, mostly because of the mother. I had never liked her, and now I knew why. She was a narcissist. I could smell a narcissist from miles away. Everything was about her, and that would never change, even after the implosion. Life has taught me a few of its secrets, and human psychology is one of them.

I stood by my door and tried to say the right thing, but nothing was right and everything was wrong, because it didn't make sense – of course it didn't. Hannah looked very hurt, very confused: I could see it on her face, in the way her cheeks flushed red; it was all I could do not to hug her. But I remained firm and explained, as gently as I could, that this was about me, not her.

I don't think she understood. Why would she?

I closed the door between us, holding the cake in between my trembling fingers. I wondered whether I hadn't made a terrible mistake. I began to feel that same constriction of the throat I had experienced years back in Paris, as if I were choking on splinters. But these were splinters of shame, not sadness. Pointy splinters of shame, sharp as a scalpel.

14

I have sold my house in Oxford Gardens. "Don't stay here when I'm gone," Henry had said, as if he knew that he would die before me. "Move back to Chelsea."

Fortuitously a flat came up for rent, which belonged to a friend of Carlo's. "She's looking for a responsible tenant," he said. I accepted. I wanted to rent, not buy, and I couldn't stand being in Notting Hill any longer, especially given what had happened. And so I moved. I chose a rainy Sunday morning, during half-term, when I knew that the street would be empty. I had seen the Karalises leave with a few suitcases the previous day; it was unlikely their return would coincide with my departure.

I left my house without saying goodbye. I shut the door behind me and climbed into a taxi. I didn't look back. I couldn't. I wasn't sure what might happen if I did.

*

The flat is in a mansion block on Tedworth Square. My neighbours are different from the ones in Notting Hill. Richer. More tanned. The woman who lives next door has a Jack Russell that barks too much. I should complain, but I don't. I pass the time reading books, writing a little. People come and visit me, especially Carlo. His wife died of cancer in the '80s; he tells me he still thinks of her every day.

I miss the girl, Hannah. I miss the conversations we never had. I miss seeing her from my bathroom window. I curse my lack of courage. I should have been braver. But I wasn't. I didn't have it in me. I must accept that I didn't have it in me. I can only do one thing to redeem myself. I will entrust this notebook to her. I might also leave her some of my books. Because from the moment she stumbled into my life, I knew there was something different about her, like an old soul in a young heart.

What I didn't know was that there would be no further meetings between us; I'm sorry I never got the chance to tell her why. I made the wrong decision. The mistake was entirely mine, and I wish I had done it differently. Sometimes it is hard to know why we act as we do.

Now is my chance to explain, alongside everything else about me, because by the time Hannah reads this, I will be dead.

It has been nineteen years since she first appeared in my life. Hannah is an adult now. She is probably married, possibly with children. She is still as special as the day I met her. I am sure of it.

I know a man who says her mother still lives on the same street. It won't be difficult to locate her daughter's whereabouts, the man assured me.

Once, shortly before leaving, I caught a glimpse of her. She was in her bedroom, studying, just as I used to study at her age. I could see her long black hair, the way it parted in the middle, falling below her shoulders. I waved at her after I had drawn the curtains.

Goodbye, Hannah.

Goodbye.

A woman I know once asked me if my life had been a happy one. I told her the truth. That it has been fulfilling. I have done everything I ever wanted to do. I have loved and been loved. I have more money than I need. My book on Robert Schumann was published by a small press and garnered good reviews. I have become an expert on the composer's life, but not my own. Despite good fortune in my later years, that feeling of having left a part of myself behind never went away. The hole of Maurice's absence was never filled. I'm eighty-three years old, yet I still hope that my son will appear one day.

If he does, I will feel complete and die happy.

Part II

HANNAH

1

I live in North London now. I bought myself a small house in Green Lanes, overlooking the river. I had stumbled upon it by pure chance, when visiting my old friend Sheila who lived nearby. She had taken me to a local shop to stock up on some vegetables. "The area's nicknamed Little Cyprus," she said.

I had never been to that part of London before and was intrigued. As we walked down the street, the shops signs became Greek and Turkish. A cornucopia of gloriously colourful fruit-and-vegetable shops vied for space with restaurants and jewellers: through one window, I saw heated barter taking place over a thick and shiny necklace. In a restaurant, women wearing hairnets were rolling out traditional *gözleme* crêpes. A bakery was filled from floor to ceiling with cakes and baklavas. A young bride wearing a sparkling wedding dress was having her hair done in one of the many hairdressers lining the street.

For all I knew, I had been transported into a poorer suburb of Istanbul, where Az and I had just spent a few days. And I loved it. I had the strange sensation that this was the place I had been looking for all along: close enough to what I needed, and far enough from what I knew – namely my mother. However hard I tried, and despite the years having gone by, our relationship was still tangled, like a skein of yarn. At least to me it was. I'm not sure how my mother viewed it. We pretended the problem wasn't there, but I knew better. This is how I had come to view my mother throughout the years. My love hadn't receded, but my trust in her had. And having her live in close proximity to me, in Notting Hill, hadn't made matters easier.

Here in N4, a few miles away from West London, everything appeared different. I stood on Green Lanes and watched an elderly Mediterranean couple argue in front of a shop, Yaser Halim, in a foreign language (Turkish? Kurdish?). The woman's bright-yellow headscarf matched her gold front teeth, and her husband smoked an unfiltered cigarette, his features weathered like a Dardanelles fisherman. He smiled at me as he caught me staring, and I smiled back. The way he stood and spoke to his wife made me want to hug him. I told Sheila I wanted to find out more about the neighbourhood, perhaps look at a few houses next time I came to visit. "Forget next time," Sheila said. She dragged me to an estate agent she knew, and one hour later I was staring at a three-bedroom Edwardian house on Cavendish Road. It needed work, and the garden was a forest of bramble bushes and ivy. There was a bedsit across the way, "about to be closed down", I was assured. "But the neighbours are really friendly, and the area is gentrifying quickly," the estate agent added, as if I needed to be reassured. But I didn't, because the house was exactly what I was looking for. Peaceful, filled with light, much bigger than the cramped apartments I had seen for the same price. And, most importantly, it faced a river. The New River. I could see the afternoon light sparkle on the water from what would become my bedroom window. My sitting-room window. My study window.

I made an offer, and by the next morning the house was mine.

Az and I moved in a few months later. We varnished the wooden floor and polished the doors a deep mahogany. We decorated the house with eclectic furniture and rugs which my mother had stored away after selling the house in Bridport. Our neighbours, a Greek Cypriot and her husband, took to dropping by with homemade cakes and figs from their tree. Further up the road, another neighbour, Bo, a slightly downtrodden woman who wore enormous glasses and boasted of an illustrious past as a costume designer, took to knocking on our door for no apparent reason other than to say hello.

We quickly understood that we had to adopt a sterner approach or not answer the door at all. Bo took it badly and left small pots of dead flowers on our doorstep. We confronted her and she became defensive. "Why would I ever do such a thing?" she said, her unsteady eyes peering at us from behind her enormous frames.

Early one morning, we were awakened by the sound of her kicking our door with unexpected might. "I know you're home!" she shouted, at which point I wanted to call the police. Az dissuaded me. "She's crazy, that's all. Totally crazy. She'll stop soon enough."

Az tried to reason with her through the window, but in vain. Bo kept on screaming and kicking at our door. "I'm calling the police!" I shouted.

"Sure, why don't you!" Bo shouted back.

But Az didn't like the police. I learnt that quickly. Where he came from, it was associated with trouble. I had to accept it. I hadn't grown up as he had. I knew nothing about Oran or the Algerian War, or the Pieds-Noirs, the FLN and the OAS, the right-wing secret armed organization which operated at the time. I became familiar with those acronyms as Az told me about his childhood, the death of his father when Az was still a small boy, which prompted his mother to leave for France. They eventually settled in the sink estate of Aubervilliers, outside Paris, where Az spent the first fifteen years of his life.

So we didn't call the police, but someone did it for us as the shouting increased in its volume. Two officers showed up, and Bo was taken away. We only saw her once more, standing next to a young man as movers loaded her belongings onto a truck. After that, we took to recounting the incident with near-melancholia, as if we had actually cared about this woman who had made our life difficult for a while.

Az's daughter Stéphanie came to stay with us at weekends. Her English wasn't very good, and at first she was shy around me. She had auburn hair and big, grey, slightly worried eleven-year-old eyes. I took an immediate liking to her. I had never felt such a connection to a child before. She looked as if she needed protection, and I wanted to give it to her. But it took time to woo her. She was visibly wary around me, until one evening when Az was out and we watched a film together, one she had brought with her because she loved it. It was called *Les Choristes* and was about a school for difficult boys in 1950s France. I cried and laughed, and so did she, and by the time Az came home we were sitting on the sofa and eating homemade ice cream, and Stéphanie was making fun of my broken French. There was no looking back for either of us after that day, although her mother Agnès didn't seem particularly enchanted by me or where we lived. I heard her and Az argue outside on the street. "*T'aurais pas pu choisir un endroit moins loin et moins dégueulasse? Tu la vois prendre le métro toute seule ici jusqu'au lycée? Moi non.*"

Az translated for me. "Couldn't you have chosen to live less far away and in less of a shithole? Do you think I'm going to let her take the Tube alone to school from here?"

"I'll walk her to the Tube. I'll take her to school."

"It's in South Kensington."

"So it is."

Az kissed me. "You're a good woman. You don't have to do it, and you're a good woman. Just like my mother. No wonder she loved you. She couldn't stand Agnès, but she immediately loved you."

"It's reciprocal," I told him.

"If my father were alive, he would have felt the same," he continued. "Even though I hardly knew him, I'm sure of it. We Algerians recognize good when we see it."

"You don't need to be Algerian to recognize goodness, Az," I said, smiling.

Nuria had come to visit us a few weeks back – a small woman with deep brown eyes, skin like an old walnut, a wide-open smile. Az's mother spoke no English, so we communicated in my passable French. She was simple, she was affectionate and she was wise. I understood that immediately, despite the cultural barrier. And she must have understood something about me too – namely that I needed a presence like hers in my life. Someone simple. In my family, we didn't do simple. We didn't think simple. Even my father had been complicated. But Az and Nuria awoke something in me which until then had been left unattended, like a plot of fallow land.

*

Ben, visiting from Los Angeles, had come to stay with us after having spent a few days with my mother. He arrived on a rainy evening, carrying his suitcase and a medium-sized, rather heavy cardboard box which he handed to me as he came in. "It's for you," he said, kissing me on both cheeks. "It was dropped off at Mum's this morning."

"What is it?"

"See for yourself," said Ben, as he hung his coat on a peg. "I'm not saying anything."

I carried it into the kitchen and placed it on the counter as Ben wheeled in his suitcase. The cardboard was damp. My name and address were written on the top flap in dark-blue felt-tip letters. There was a rip on the side of the box, through which I could distinguish the spine of a book.

I grabbed a kitchen knife and tore the box open. Crumpled newspaper met my eye. I glanced at a page. 12th December 2004. Four months back. What was this? Who had sent this to me?

Ben looked at me. "It's from Flora Dobbs," he said. "Remember her? The old lady from Oxford Gardens? She died and left this for you in her will. Don't ask me why, I have no clue. A man showed up at the house yesterday, wanted to make sure you still lived here, said he would drop it off this morning – and he did. Mum asked me to bring it over."

"What?" I gasped. "But why me?"

Ben shrugged his shoulders. "I dunno. Mum says Flora left the street like nineteen years ago. So yeah, it's weird. Like what the fuck?"

"Like yeah."

I started looking through the box. I searched for a note or a letter, something personal, but found nothing.

Instead, there were books. Eight of them to be precise. I removed them carefully and glanced at them, one by one. Saul Bellow, Muriel Spark, Elizabeth Jane Howard. There were also Victorian novels: used and possibly rare hardback editions of Trollope, Dickens, Charlotte Brontë, George Eliot and Thomas Hardy – the books from Flora Dobbs's library. It had to be them. Some covers were green or red cloth, with gilded spines. *Silas Marner* looked as if it had never been opened. As for Charlotte Brönte and Dickens, they were Oxford University Press hardcovers from the 1960s – well-read ones at that, judging from their crumpled, stained pages.

So she had remembered our brief conversation then. Of course she would have. She wanted to leave me her books as a reminder of that moment we had shared. But she must also have felt some sort of guilt. She had, after all, cut me out of her life just as abruptly as she had allowed me in. Was this her way of apologizing?

If it was, I accepted the apology. There had clearly been something preoccupying her at the time that had made her behave as she had. And what had stayed with me most was not so much the way she had disappeared, but the feeling, despite the short time we had spent together, that this woman had gained an insight into my character, possibly more than my parents could at the time. "She could become my French lady friend," I had told my father.

The memory of that cold, rainy afternoon came back to me. The way she had opened her door and handed me a towel. The baby grand piano. The Monet poster on her bathroom door. The way her dolls were dressed and how they sat. The way she sipped her tea and listened as I spoke. The way I had shown up at her house with my mother's lemon cake, and how Flora had closed the door for ever behind me.

And now she was dead.

"Hey," said Ben. "Can I see?"

"It's just books," I said.

Ben's phone rang, and he answered it quickly. "Mum wants to talk to you," he said, handing me his handset.

"Hi Mum," I said, grabbing it from him. "So I'm here with Flora Dobbs in a box."

"Yes, I know," she answered quickly. "I should have warned you this was coming. A man – her solicitor, I think – showed up yesterday. I meant to call you but I forgot. It's been such a crazy few days."

"OK. What did the man say?"

"That she had died and been buried last week. I think he said she was eighty-three years old. She gave specific instructions in her will for the contents of this box to be left for you. Books, I think? Or did he say notebooks?"

"Yes, books.

"It is a bit ironic, isn't it," she said softly. "Your father banged on for so long about Flora Dobbs and next thing you know she's leaving you her books as a goodbye gift."

"Yes," I conceded, remembering how much time my father had spent speculating about her true identity. We both laughed, though her laughter was tinged with sadness.

Anything to do with my father's memory was tinged with sadness.

He had suffered a cardiac arrest in 2002. It happened in broad daylight, as he was walking to the theatre. I had cooked him dinner the night before. He had been unwell, with some heart trouble he had dismissed as silly. But I knew better. No heart problem was silly. He just wanted to keep it from me. When pressed for details, he had been so vague about it that I eventually gave up. "I need to take some pills, is the gist of it," is all he volunteered, despite my insistence. He had never been good at being ill, and was hardly going to change at the age of sixty-six.

It was his Irish girlfriend, Ailis, who rang me that night to tell me. "He's gone," she repeated, her voice faltering. "He's gone."

*

I went to see him in the morgue. I didn't recognize him. It was as if his insides had been drained out. His face was white and still, like a wax statue. His hands were clasped together. I wondered whether he had died in that position. My mighty father. Now the shell of a king.

We buried him in Highgate Cemetery. Six feet under, surrounded by cold earth and forgotten bones.

"I wish I could be there with you both, right now," my mother said, her voice interrupting my thoughts. And something in her tone made my throat tighten.

I could picture her, sitting at the kitchen table, gazing out of the window. She was still beautiful, but something had changed in her face, as if all her happiness had been sapped, leaving a hollowness in its stead.

She suffered, and it showed. She had destroyed her marriage and would never forgive herself. She didn't say so, but I knew it. I had to be gentler with her. More forgiving. Now that I had Az in my life, it was time to turn over a new leaf. I had punished her enough. And so had my brother, in his own way: years of diving in and out of a dark place, a place populated by people who lived on the fringes of society and who, like him, mistook recklessness for character.

"You'll never understand," Ben would say, as if we were the ones to blame.

And he was right: we didn't understand my seventeen-year-old brother. The fact was that none of us was sufficiently prescient to interpret his behaviour as a cry for help.

We found out later, when he confessed, its full extent: how he stole from my father, then my mother. How All Saints Road became his second home until his skunk dealer was arrested.

How he bribed Hairy Mary to supply him with alcohol, and how he eventually got beaten up by her pimp. How he drank on his way to school, stuffing small vodka bottles into his satchel, finishing them by the time he got home, steadily progressing to a level of alcoholism which was increasingly hard to sustain.

"It's safer than heroin," he once quipped, as if the lesser evil were worthy of a compliment.

Eventually, he ended up in a rehabilitation centre. As soon as he came out, he enrolled in acting classes. "This is what I'm meant to do," he told us.

His talent became quickly apparent, and after two years got a small part in a Royal Court production. The suddenness of it all took us by surprise. "Vodka and poppers have been replaced by Miller and Pinter," said my father, greeting this transformation with cautious enthusiasm. But we were happy for Ben. An American agent happened to be in the audience the night before the play closed. After the performance, he went backstage and introduced himself to Ben. There was a casting for a television series, he told him. It was for an important role.

Ben went to the audition and won the part. By the following year, he was flitting between London and Los Angeles, and had become one of the lead actors in the television series, which, although it was met with a lukewarm reception, convinced him that Los Angeles was where he wanted to be.

My parents watched and worried. Surely he wouldn't be able to sustain this? And how was he going to support himself? California was expensive. And treacherous. He might relapse, fall in with the wrong crowd again. But their concerns proved unfounded.

Today, although he still hasn't found stardom, Ben seems to have settled into his Californian life. Despite promises of acting jobs which haven't materialized, he hasn't given up hope. "I'll get there," he told me. "I've found a part-time job, modelling swimwear. You never know. And I have a good agent. Watch this space."

I'm still watching, and I worry. Fame has no mercy on the broken ones.

"So, what sort of books?" My mother's voice came piping through the phone.

"Victorian novels, beautiful editions. Some more recent ones too, but mainly Victorian. They look valuable," I added, as I removed the newspaper from the last book: *Jude the Obscure* stared at me in gilded lettering.

"Did she leave you a note?" my mother asked.

"Not that I can see. I think that her books are meant to be the note."

"To each his own," my mother remarked. "I would have left a note. Any normal person would have."

"I know," I concurred. "But I'm not sure how normal she was."

We hung up. I made a mental note to check up on my mother the following day. Az hurried me. We were going to have dinner with some friends of his, in Kensal Rise. Ben was accompanying us. Traffic was bad, we needed to change and leave shortly. "What's that?" Az asked, pointing at the box.

"I'll tell you in the car," I said. "It's a long story."

I lifted the box and took it upstairs, to my study. I placed it on my desk, glanced at it again and went into my bedroom to get ready.

2

I met Az in 2003, at a dinner party in Islington. I was cooking
for Valerie, a well-known architect I had met through Nancy.
Valerie had short black hair, wore flares and white shirts. She
wasn't known for her sense of humour, and my godmother called
her husband "the poodle", because he did whatever she asked of
him. "He's terrified of Valerie, and so am I. But please do this
for me, because she and the poodle have become collectors of
my paintings. I'd like them to become even bigger ones. Blow
them away with your chocolate fondant."

"All right," I promised.

As soon as I arrived at her modernist glass house and was
exposed to her sharp, slightly condescending manner, I quickly
understood that Valerie was not the type to be blown away by
anything. But that didn't matter, because I had an ulterior motive
for being there. The dinner was in honour of Aziz Lascar, the
photographer. I had been a fan of his work for a while. A show
was opening at the Rouge Gallery, and I had read a fascinating
interview with the photographer, where he recalled his childhood
in the sink estates outside Paris and the source of his inspiration:
"I'm fascinated by the unseen. I don't like generic photography.
I like to capture the transience of things. The ephemeral. Water,
leaves, clouds. I work in shadows, not clarity."

Later on that day I heard him being interviewed on Radio 4.
He had a soft French accent and a gravelly voice, and when he
spoke it was as if colours and textures floated from his lips, and

it made me want to kiss him. He was gravitas and sensuality in one. I wondered whether the looks would match the words.

Now I was in the kitchen, adding last-minute touches to a gratin of aubergine and *chèvre*, and the man of colours and textures was about to arrive. I could hear the doorbell ring and guests coming in. I found that I was nervous, as if I too were a friend about to be introduced to the guest of honour, not the hired help with fingers coated in crushed garlic and goat's cheese. Because there were no two ways about it: by cooking for others I had become hired help. Until now I hadn't given it a thought. After finishing Oxford, I had abandoned academia in favour of gastronomy. It had been an agonizing decision, but I had done it. I had left my job as an English teacher and returned the advance I had been given on a book about the Victorian novelist George Moore, which I had barely started writing. I never regretted my decision. The world of food, just as it had for my mother, provided me with a pro-found happiness. Except that this particular evening I felt a tinge of self-consciousness – or perhaps was it frustration? – because I would have rather been mingling with Aziz Lascar, just for a few minutes, enough time to meet him and exchange a few words with him. Perhaps even tell him that I had always loved his work.

Or perhaps not, I grumbled, as the leftover contents of my choco-late pudding dropped on the floor and all over my white apron.

At the same moment, Valerie came into the kitchen looking frazzled, because the guest of honour was very late and everyone was getting hungry, and she asked if I could swiftly come up with something small to feed them in the mean time – "I'm sure you'll figure it out," she blurted out before running off again, leaving me cursing her under my breath – "No, I won't figure it out" – and then the doorbell rang again, and by the various oohs and aahs that followed I could tell it was him.

Since swapping Victorian novels for osso bucco, I had barely stopped working. A three-month stint in a Covent Garden restaurant as a sous-chef led to more jobs in other restaurants. Then, a friend asked me to cook for her engagement party. It was an unexpected success. Word of mouth spread, and my future as a private chef was sealed, so much so that I was able to give up my restaurant shifts and concentrate fully on private work. I made up my own recipes. I was paid to cook them for strangers and a small group of fans which grew swiftly in size and took me to unlikely and exciting places.

I spent time on a cruise ship and in imposing homes. I cooked a seated lunch for the family members of a polygamous African dictator. I became a favourite of a Hollywood film director who took me with him on set, and with whom I had a brief affair. I cooked for yummy mummies and their husbands, for Italian aristocrats and indolent children, for vegetarians, vegans and halal eaters, in a retirement home and a French chateau. My mind was filled with recipes. *Saltimbocca alla romana.* Pan-fried scallops with roasted squash. Double-baked cheese and courgette soufflé. Paupiette of monkfish and *gratin dau-phinois.* Chocolate fondant and strawberry coulis. Increasing my clientele. Scouring corner shops and farmers' markets. Sourcing fresh vegetables and organic ingredients. The tenderest meat. The ripest tomato. Perfecting my craft. I was enveloped in a swathe of gustatory experiments and delights, and had little space for anything else. If sometimes I felt lonely, I put it aside, as if loneliness, like one of my dishes, was something that could be sampled and assessed at a later time.

Now I was thirty-four and unmarried. I had had a fair share of men in my life, but aside from a violinist, Alexander, with whom

I had lived in my early twenties, there was no one special. A few brief affairs, but not love. I blamed it mostly on the nature of my work: I never had time. When I did, I saw family and friends and sometimes accompanied them on holiday, where I would inevitably end up cooking for them. If I occasionally minded it, I kept it to myself. Then, one by one, my friends got married or had children. I became godmother several times, possibly too many. Ben seldom visited, and my mother threatened to sink into a depression. "I can't stand Ben being away from us, when he was always so present, such a beam of light," she said, as if she had entirely forgotten what had happened during Ben's childhood.

And that was when my father died.

My brother came to live with me for a short while. I was worried he might relapse into a spiral of substance abuse and the modus operandi of his adolescence. We cried and laughed and talked about our father, our childhood. Their relationship had always been fraught. "But we made up. We made our peace. We reached our Higher Power," Ben said wistfully. "If we hadn't – man, I wouldn't have been able to speak to him again. He had been such a prick. So was I, I guess… But we bonded, and that was awesome." He paused. "It all started after we met up for breakfast that time, after the shit hit the fan, with Mum and Walter. Remember?"

"Of course I do."

Ben and I had gone to a coffee shop in Notting Hill, where we had had our first meaningful conversation in years. He had admitted to having had suspicions about Walter the entire time. "All I know is that I don't want to see Mum again," he had said, in his fifteen-year-old drawl. "Or that little pisshead Walter. I always knew he had the hots for her. Not when I was small, but later. I saw them kiss once, in the upstairs bedroom. Mum kept telling me I was inventing things, but I'm no moron. I know what I saw."

I had been taken aback by his confession, and we had discussed it for a long time. I couldn't tell what had most struck me: the fact that he knew, or the clarity of his words. "The question is why?" Ben kept repeating. In the end, we had both come to the conclusion that we had no firm answer.

It would be fifteen years before we discussed it again, on our way back from my father's funeral. My brother admitted that he had seen Walter, "standing alone and looking older", but had refused to speak to him. "I probably should have," he said, "but I couldn't bring myself to do it."

"Maybe next time." I ventured.

"I don't think there'll be a next time."

I didn't have the heart to tell him that I had been touch with Walter. He was remarried, had twin girls. We had met up a few times. Somehow I had found it easier to forgive him: he had been weak, distraught – which my mother was not.

"So why do you think she did it?" I asked him instead. Ben had always been defensive about my mother, and it was unlikely that had changed.

"Do you think she really did love Walter? Or was she trying to get back at Dad?"

"I dunno… I think she was lonely and just wanted sex, that's all. She probably wasn't getting much of it with Dad in the end."

"I never thought of it that way… yuck."

We both laughed.

The anger of Ben's youth had given way to a new softness, a strong desire to, as he put it, "do good for the world". If his banter sometimes veered towards the earnest, and if his jargon was peppered with American lingo, I didn't mind. He hadn't touched alcohol in five years and "without those AA meetings

I'd be fucked", he admitted. His only vice was cigarettes and the occasional joint. And even though his acting career hadn't turned out as planned, he was convinced it wouldn't be long before his talent was recognized. "I know I'm good. And at least my agent's getting me auditions. Everything's going to be cool," he said, the morning of his departure. We were standing at the entrance to Heathrow's security. We had just eaten a sandwich in a noisy café. A family of stroppy teenagers had argued in front of us. It had made Ben smile. "To think that was me once," he remarked. "And that those days are long gone. Thank fuck for that."

I hugged him hard, my tall and handsome brother. "One thing Mum and Dad have always been happy about is that we get along," I told him.

"I know," he said. He had seen my mother. She had taken my father's death very badly. I was due to visit her that day. Ben was worried about her. "You've got to be patient and nice to her," he said. "Don't freak out on her. Not this time."

"Of course not. '

"Remember. The Walter thing was about loneliness. Loss. All of it. Forgive her."

"I already have," I said, nearly believing it.

"See ya!" He walked away. I saw him queuing at security, then he was gone. There, then gone.

Unlike my father, I was going to see Ben again. But the memory of his presence moments before was nearly as painful as the death of my father who would never return: I could have hugged the sliver of space where Ben had just stood and still have felt him. I didn't want him to leave.

I didn't want to be alone with that sliver.

On my way back home, I suddenly remembered something else.

It was 1987. My parents had rented a house in the Pyrenees. Ben had finagled his way out of it. So we had gone the three of us. It rained the whole time, and I was lonely. I had wanted my brother to come with us. I liked knowing he was around, even if he was being intolerable. But he wasn't there, and I was the one who ended up behaving uncharacteristically tetchily.

The night before our departure, my mother had switched on the television. "Maybe there'll be something good on," she had said. "Like an old French film or something."

She flicked through the channels: the evening news, a cartoon, an advertisement for soap, a film showing a man and a woman dressed in Victorian garb. "Stop!" said my father. "Wait!"

"Why?" she asked.

He didn't need to answer, because we saw it for ourselves. The film was *L'Arrivée du mendiant*, and the woman was none other than Lucie. She was wearing a white dress and speaking animatedly to a handsome actor, the one I recognized from the poster in Walter's shop. It was night-time, and the actors were standing outside, against the backdrop of an illuminated castle. Lucie's voice sounded different, lower than I remembered. My French was not good enough to understand everything she said, but that hardly mattered. What mattered was that she was there, alive and well, laughing in the full moon.

We watched the film for a short while, and then I suddenly couldn't take it any more. "Turn it off! I don't want to hear her voice – please turn it off!"

My parents looked at each other, then at me. "Of course, darling," said my mother gently. "We understand."

But understanding was not what I was looking for. I wanted to see Lucie beside me, sitting in a chair. I wanted to grab her from the television screen and speak to her. Thank her for saving my brother. Touch her, hug her. Her features, which had become indistinct with time, had just been resurrected. It was a painful sensation.

"Do you want to watch something else?" my mother had asked demurely.

"No. I want to go to bed."

I rushed upstairs to my small bedroom. I changed into my night-gown, slid beneath the cold sheets and burst into tears. Something had been unleashed inside me, but for the first time in my adolescent life I couldn't tell whether it had all been made worse or better.

*

I cut down my work schedule to four days a week from six. And, for the first time, I started thinking about children. Until now, broodiness hadn't caught up with me. A combination of family history and my work schedule had ensured motherhood wasn't on my radar. But even if I had given it some thought, the reality was that becoming a mother frightened me. The fear that I might reproduce the same scenario I had watched unfold at home was too much of a gamble.

But the death of my father made me aware of my own mortality. I wanted something of him to be transmitted to the next genera-tion, and unless I overcame my fears that would never happen.

I had to stop being so wary. So worried about being infected by the virus of my own history. I wasn't like my mother or father. I had no desire to emulate them in any way. I was my own person with my own quirks and patterns and desires. I needed to be braver. It didn't follow that because my mother had destroyed our family unit I would too. On the contrary: I would do everything I could to preserve it. Wasn't that the way it worked? Ensuring that the pattern would not repeat itself?

I had recently read a book in which the main character mentioned that everything in life was a rehearsal for something later. I couldn't tell where I stood. Still in rehearsal, or had I reached the later stage? And if so, what stage was it?

Still in rehearsal, I decided, as Aziz Lascar walked into Valerie's kitchen. He was on his way out of the loo and had taken the wrong turn. "This house is too big for dyslexic people," he grinned. "Which way is the dining room?" I pointed him in the right direction. He looked at me, and I hoped he wouldn't notice my stained apron – then again, how could he not? It was covered in chocolate.

He smiled and introduced himself. "I love your work," I gushed, then wished I hadn't.

"Thank you," he smiled again. "What's for supper?"

He was short, shorter than me. His hair was dark, streaked with grey. His eyes had flecks of green, the colour of moss. His face was strong. Not handsome, but seductive. Sexy. There was something slightly coarse and earthy about his chiselled features that reminded me of waves crashing onto rocks. He was older than I thought. Then I remembered that he was ten years older than me. I had looked him up. He had no idea how much I knew about him. It was embarrassing, really.

I listed the menu. "Aubergine-and-goat's-cheese gratin. Salt-baked sea bass with sweet-potato mash and grilled fennel. Chocolate fondant for pudding. See my apron for details," I added, pointing at the smudge.

He smiled. "Sounds delicious. Including the apron," he added.

We began to talk. He told me about his Algerian mother, who was a great cook. When I asked him how come his English was so good, he explained that he had moved to London fifteen years ago and did not intend to return to Paris. He had a daughter here, he said, who lived in Kensington with her mother. They were no longer together, he added, as if he wanted me to know.

"How old is she?"

"Eleven. Stéphanie."

I wanted to pry further, but didn't dare. He asked me about my background and how I had become a chef. We discussed his upcoming exhibition, which featured droplets of water and butterfly chrysalides, as well as a series of people seen through windows. "It's the title of the show," Aziz said. "*Behind Windows*. I use a special technique, so everything looks like it's floating in space. I love that effect."

He added that his work featured people, but also what they leave behind. "The interaction of memory, time, forgotten objects, nature."

"Really?" I said. "That's very interesting." I stopped myself from elaborating further.

Ever since that afternoon at the beach, when my mother and I had stood on the pebbly shore waiting for the lifeguards to find Lucie, I observed nature differently, searching for ancient clues in the quiet of its beauty, but also in the untamed bosom of the natural world. In a furious wind. In the orange glow of a harvest moon.

After my father left the house, the search spread beyond ancient landscapes to synchronicity: the connection between occurrences. Messages waiting to be deciphered. I paid exaggerated attention to coincidences, to dreams and unexpected encounters. As a child, the outside world had seemed tantalizingly larger than my inner one. I longed to understand its secrets, but an invisible barrier restricted my movements. After Lucie died, that barrier crumbled, as did its protective layer, and pain altered the world as I knew it. I understood that in order to move forward I had to set my own parameters. But I was not going to share those thoughts with Aziz Lascar. So all I ventured was that I was interested in why and how things happen.

"Like chance encounters?" He smiled. "Come to my opening tomorrow evening," he added. "And come to the dinner too. We can discuss it further."

"I'd love to," I answered, trying to keep my voice steady. "I heard you on the radio this morning," I added. "Describing the show. It sounds great."

Then I suddenly remembered: Ailis, my father's last girl-friend, and probably his greatest love since my mother, owned a photograph of his. We had even discussed it when I had gone to visit her. How could I have forgotten? A portrait of a couple somewhere in South America, holding hands in a café.

I mentioned it to Aziz. "I don't know Ailis. But Leon Karalis was your father? I loved the man, he was a great director. I wish I had met him."

My eyes welled with unexpected tears. Why? I barely knew Aziz, and it was hardly the first time since his death that my father's name had been invoked with love. And yet, the connection reverberated somewhere inside me.

Then Valerie walked in. "Az? Oh, there you are. Hannah, is everything all right?"

"Yes, sure, we were talking. Let me know when you're ready for the first course."

"We've been ready for a while," she stated.

"You should have told me—"

"It's my fault," Aziz interrupted, placing his hand on Valerie's shoulder. "Entirely my fault for distracting her. We were talking about her father."

"He was a good director," said Valerie. "And his daughter's a good chef." She smiled at both of us – a coy smile. His to her was colder.

Before he walked away, Aziz slipped me his card. "Call me Az, and see you tomorrow," he said. "Please come."

His opening was so crowded that I couldn't find him. I had barely slept the night before, my mind filled with images of our meeting. Would this lead to anything? I wondered. I could hardly believe it would.

I walked around and focused on his photographs, which were mounted in enormous frames. Blurred faces behind windows, babies under water, superimposed tree trunks, a miniature chrysalis set against a black cloud. His work was stunning. I was able to forget about the heat, the noise, the people pushing me, the bright lights. And suddenly there was Az. His face broke into a smile when he saw me. "Thank you for coming," he said, holding my hand. "It's a bit crazy in here."

"The show is beautiful," I said.

"Yes it is, Az," a woman interjected. She looked Asian. She was very pretty and wore a sparkly white dress. Her perfume was too strong. "Hi Mona," said Az, greeting her warmly. He knew her well. How well? I wondered. He introduced us, "Mona, Hannah," then was interrupted again, by a man who must have been his dealer, as he was waving at him frantically with a sheet of paper in his hand and mouthing something incomprehensible.

"So how do you know Az?" Mona asked, as if she cared.

"I don't," I answered. "I only met him last night."

I wanted to go home. I felt out of place and underdressed. Everyone around me was dressed up. Why wasn't I? I had worn a simple pair of trousers and a white cardigan for the occasion. As if I had already decided that I wouldn't attend the dinner.

I couldn't face him in a crowd. If I were to get to know him better, it had to be alone. Not at a formal dinner. Anyway, he had clearly forgotten he had invited me. Otherwise he would have said something, wouldn't he? Something like "See you at the dinner?" Yes, of course he would have.

So I left without saying goodbye and with my heart beating quickly, and got on the Tube and wondered, for perhaps a split second, if I wasn't doing something foolish, then decided that I wasn't. He would have said something about the dinner if he really expected me there. It was probably one of those seated events with many bigwigs and artists and socialites – after all, I cooked for those sorts of people, I should know. And I also knew that I hardly counted as one of them. Yes, he looked happy to see me, but he looked equally happy to see Mona – whoever she was. This was obviously a very busy night for him: he had other more important things on his mind than the dark-haired woman with the stained apron he had only met the previous evening.

I sat down in a near-empty Tube carriage. A man was slouched in the seat opposite. He looked drunk and was mumbling to himself. I got off at Manor House and walked hurriedly home. I felt uncomfortable, as if I had done something wrong. Should I have stayed at the gallery? Had I misinterpreted Az? Why was I going home exactly?

As soon as I walked through the front door, the phone rang. It was Ben. "I've met this woman, Melody. She's gorgeous. A pop star, really talented. Just wanted to tell you about it," he said as my mobile began to ring. A number I didn't recognize appeared on the screen. "Hold on," I said to Ben.

I picked up the call: "Hannah, hi, it's Az. Took a while to find your number…"

"Oh, Az—"

"Listen," he said, speaking quickly, "we'll be sitting down for dinner shortly. A woman I met last night is supposed to be seated on my right and she's not here."

I was so shocked that for a very short while I said nothing. He had seated me next to him? I was a fool. A downright, idiotic fool. He would never forgive me or want to see me again. That much was clear. Unless I went back there immediately.

"I'm so sorry, Az, something came up," I said, feeling my cheeks burn. "I should have told you. But the place was so crowded that I couldn't find you to tell you."

That was a lie. I had seen him, but he was surrounded by people, and I hadn't dared barge in again when we had said hello only a few minutes before.

"Is this your way of saying that you're not coming? I need to know."

His tone was hurried, snappy. I pressed the phone against my ear. I had to think quickly. Rationally. If I didn't go, I might never see him again. And I had to see him again. Hoxton was a long way. But it didn't matter. I could take a cab. "I just got home," I said. "I could jump into a cab and be there in thirty minutes."

"That sounds like a good idea," he said, sounding relieved. "Looking forward to seeing you," He hung up quickly.

"Hello?" I heard Ben shout in the landline receiver. Are you there?"

"Sorry Ben," I said, breathlessly, "but I've got to go. I'll call you later."

"Yeah, sure, whatever, always a pleasure," he grumbled.

I changed into a black skirt and matching velvet blouse, slipped on a pair of high- heeled shoes. I added some make-up, a few dabs of perfume, clasped an amethyst necklace shut and decided that the time had come for me to pay more attention to my appearance.

I arrived just as the guests were sitting down. When Az saw me, he smiled in appreciation and beckoned me to my seat. There were speeches – "Aziz Lascar, master of the forgotten daguerreotype, you have enchanted us once again" etc. – many toasts and an attempt at conversation with the man on my left, a friend of Az's from Paris who spoke incomprehensible English, kept getting up to smoke cigarettes on the adjacent balcony and made movies everyone seemed to know about but me. "My impression is that when you're a chef you barely have time for anything else," said the American woman seated opposite me, who was called Strawberry. "I have a friend, and she works so hard that her children, who like never see her, thought she was the nanny." Strawberry's platinum hair was pulled back in a bun, and there was a diamond stud in her nose. Everyone laughed, but I didn't. I wasn't sure how to interpret her comment. Was this her way of empathizing with me or a covert way of criticizing the fact that I didn't know who the French director was? She fancied him, I could tell. Strawberry should have been the one seated next to him, not me.

"I don't have children, so I wouldn't know," I said instead.

"That's cool. I don't have children either," she retorted.

I could have said more. That I read books. I was educated. I was seated next to the guest of honour. I did more than just chop vegetables. I had time now. More than I used to. Still, there was no doubt that I had some catching up to do; but I didn't need Strawberry to tell me.

Az and I tried to talk to each other, but were constantly interrupted. "Let's go out for a drink afterwards," he leant over to tell me. "As soon as this is over."

"Are you sure that's a good idea?" I whispered. "Aren't they expecting you to stay until the end?

"I've done my bit," he said, smiling at me. "I think I could be forgiven for leaving when I choose to."

We slipped out right after pudding, and before he was about to be hounded again. We jumped into a cab and ended up at a pub in Shoreditch. We ordered a bottle of wine and began to talk. We couldn't stop. The more we spoke, the more attracted to him I became. We exchanged our views on life, on art, on the world. We discussed my childhood, Lucie's drowning, my work, my father. There was no doubt that Az was someone my father would have loved. "I meant to tell you that I met this man," I could imagine him saying. "I think you'd like each other."

Now this man was here, sitting in front of me, with his chiselled face and gravelly voice, telling me about his childhood, his ex-partner – who sounded awful – and their daughter. He saw Stéphanie every other weekend, he said, and on Wednesdays, when he picked her up at school. He missed her, wished he saw her more. But her mother was stubborn and difficult, and he didn't want to rock the boat. She worked in fashion. A tough woman. "Fashion is not my sort of world," he added.

But am I your sort of world? I wondered, as the wine went to my head.

I couldn't remember when I had last met someone like him. He seemed to know exactly what he wanted. Most of the men I had met or been with were prone to existential crises and bouts of insecurity. I could tell that Az was the polar opposite. If anything, his confidence might have been interpreted as smugness. Except that it wasn't. It was anything but.

The pub manager told us they were closing. Az offered to drop me off at home. "I probably should get some sleep anyway; it's been a very long day – and night," he added, smiling.

"Of course," I said. "I'm amazed you're still standing..."

I didn't want the conversation to end. I wanted it to continue. I wanted him to touch me. To kiss me. But I made a rule never to kiss on a first date. Kissing could lead to more and I wasn't ready for more. I liked to take things slowly. But I didn't go on many dates these days. So perhaps it was time to rethink my rules.

Az got out of the cab, asked the driver to wait for him and walked me to my front door. "We have a whole life to catch up on," he whispered, as he kissed me on the cheek.

Then he stepped back and waved at me. "To be continued," he said, before disappearing.

I closed the door behind me half-wishing he'd come back. *To be continued*. I was already half in love with him. I listened to the sound of his steps, the revving of the taxi engine. But I couldn't hear anything other than a few voices on the street. Was something wrong? Then there were footsteps outside again and a knock on my front door. I opened it and there he was: "I'm sorry, and this may not be the correct protocol, but I can't go home. I can't leave you," he said, his French accent sounding stronger than it had before.

"I don't usually follow protocol," I said, smiling.

"I'm very pleased to hear it."

He followed me inside and closed the door behind me. He gently leant me against the door frame and kissed me. I could feel his tongue inside my mouth, searching for me. I would have kissed him all night.

Then he stepped back and looked at me. He brushed a strand of hair away from my face and curled it behind my ear. He placed the cool palm of his hand on my collarbone. He slowly unbuttoned my shirt, unclasped my necklace. I tried to avoid his gaze, but couldn't. There was something about him which defeated me entirely.

"You're beautiful," he said.

He removed my shirt and threw it on a chair. He unzipped my skirt and let it fall to the floor. He ran his finger up my bare leg, until he reached the inside of my thigh. But then he stopped. He stepped back and looked at me, standing in my white-lace lingerie. "You take my breath away," he whispered. "You did as soon as I saw you in Valerie's house."

He removed my bra and underwear. I started to tremble. From head to toe. It had never happened to me before. It was a shiver of longing, of impending love as well as gratitude that he had chosen me. That the man who lived in shadows had chosen me. That we seemed to understand each other even though we barely knew each other. That even though things were moving fast, there was a slowness within the fastness as he drew me closer towards him. He took in the smell of my skin, my hair. He caressed my erect nipples and placed his lips against mine again. Tentative, then urgent. His fingers settled between my legs as my breathing became heavier. His lips slid down towards my neck, my breasts, my thighs, between my legs. I yielded to him in a way I hadn't yielded to anyone in a long time.

We lay down together on the carpet. He murmured my name, I whispered his. My legs opened beneath him, and I brought him towards me, inside me, sinking, floating.

We made love until dawn and then fell asleep. When we awoke, it was late morning. I got out of bed and opened my shutters.

Outside the sun hung high, like a gold medallion.

FLORA

15TH FEBRUARY 2005

It happened before yesterday. I was unconscious for twenty-four hours. Carlo is the one who found me. We were due to have tea, but I didn't answer the doorbell. After a few failed attempts to reach me on the house phone – which he could hear ringing as he tried my number from behind the closed door – he knew something was wrong. We see each other every Sunday for tea, a ritual we both look forward to which often stretches on into the evening. "This was very unlike you," Carlo said.

He called the police, who broke through the front door and found me lying in the kitchen with a broken teapot at my side and tea all over the floor. They think I must have slipped while I was preparing it. I landed on my head, I am told. A bad landing. I fell on my head. Cracked it like the broken teapot on my kitchen floor. It's a miracle I'm still alive. A real miracle, says Carlo.

I do not remember any of it – the tea, the fall, the blood, the doctor, Carlo, the ambulance and paramedics who came to rescue me. All I do know is that I woke up in a room at the Chelsea and Westminster Hospital. My arm was attached to a drip. There was a smell of antiseptic in the air. A man was speaking to a nurse, who was taking notes. "Yes, Dr Svelic," she said.

Dr Svelic was very tall. So tall that his head nearly reached the ceiling. Or perhaps it was me who felt small. I wanted to ask him where he came from. The Balkans? Czechoslovakia? Henry knew a Czech flautist with the same name. Perhaps it was his brother. Or his cousin. Or neither. Henry. I suddenly missed Henry. I wanted him by my side. I felt tears welling in my eyes. But now was not the moment. Later. I would cry later, if at all. I could feel the motions inside, which was unusual. I seldom cry. I don't like my face getting wet. I only cried in front of Henry once, and that was a mistake. He had caught me in the act, crying about Maurice. I had blamed it on something else, of course. Then he had hugged me. I could feel him now, hugging me. Except that he wasn't there. I was alone in a strange room. My head hurt. The doctor smiled at me. There was a gap between his two front teeth. "Hello there," he said pleasantly. "How are you feeling?" He then proceeded to sit down and ask me questions, as if I were a child. "What's your name? What is the date today? Hold up two fingers for me please."

"I might have fallen on my head, but I haven't lost my mind, you know," I retorted.

"Of course not, Mrs Dobbs," he smiled. "But this is standard procedure after any sort of head injury."

The nurse who was with him began to check my pulse, then adjusted the drip on the IV bag. Dr Svelic scribbled something down. There were strands of grey in his black hair. His eyebrows were thick, like wool. I felt tired. I wanted to go back to sleep. Then I heard a voice outside, and there was Carlo. He introduced himself to the doctor as he was leaving. Carlo grabbed a chair and came to sit next to me. He held my hand and told me that he had spent most of the night in the room with me, and was so relieved that I had regained consciousness. He tightened his grip and told me that he had been very worried – and that, once I was discharged, which hopefully should be in a few days, I was to come and live with him. He had an extra room, a lovely one facing Onslow Gardens. "It is not an option. I will not let you return to that flat," he said, sounding stern. "I owe it to

Henry to look after you. And I owe it to myself as well," he added, smiling at me.

I smiled feebly back. I was glad and reassured to see him. I was alive, and he was here to look after me.

I asked him whether he knew for sure that I would be discharged in a few days. He hesitated. No, he didn't know for sure, but it seemed obvious to him. "I'll speak to the doctor, find out what's happening and let you know."

Carlo stood up and brushed some invisible dust off his elegant coat. "I'm going home now, but I'll be back this afternoon. Is there anything you'd like me to bring you from your flat?"

Yes, there was. My nightdress, some clothes, a toothbrush and perfume. "The Shalimar bottle in my bathroom," I told him. "And there's a notebook too, in the third drawer of my desk. Please put it in a bag for me and bring it as soon as you can."

"I will," Carlo said, kissing my hand.

I didn't need to tell Carlo that the notebook was confidential. I knew that I could trust him implicitly.

Later, Dr Svelic returned and explained that my fall was serious, and that it was important I stay in hospital for a few days. He drew my skull on a piece of paper, using strange words like "pterion" and "axons", and mentioned something about burst arteries. "We may have to operate," he said.

I told him I'd rather die than have him operate on my skull. I didn't mention the ECT I went through years ago. No one knows. And no one shall ever go near my head again.

Dr Svelic said he'd be back that evening. "We will discuss it then," he said. "No we won't," I replied, and he said nothing. He didn't come back. Or did he? I cannot remember. Suddenly I was impossibly tired. I couldn't open my eyes. I could hear Carlo's voice in the room, or perhaps I was imagining it. I wanted to speak to him, to say thank you for being so caring, but I couldn't. I felt very weak. I heard another voice, which sounded like Henry's. Then I fell asleep.

I woke up in the middle of the night in great pain. My skull felt as if someone had hammered it open. Had they operated on me without telling me? No, no, of course they hadn't. I called for a nurse, who came in promptly and injected me with some morphine. It took an excruciatingly long time to kick in. And I was aware that my mind was becoming jumbled. I couldn't remember where I was. Everything was spinning. I gripped the bars on either side of my bed to slow myself down. I called out Carlo's name, but he wasn't there. I may have called out other names too. Someone came in and gave me a pill to swallow. I fell asleep, and this morning it was all gone – the pain as well as the spinning. A miracle. I sat upright in bed feeling strong. I saw that Carlo had brought my notebook, a pen, the Shalimar bottle.

I asked for a nurse and said I wanted to take a shower. I was told someone would be in shortly. I also asked for some breakfast. I was hungry. I telephoned Carlo, and he seemed very surprised to hear me sound so alert. "You're like a new woman!" he exclaimed. "So strong! I'll be there in thirty minutes."

Carlo is right. I am a strong woman. I could go home now. The worst is over. I need to speak to the doctor. The nurse mentioned that he ordered some tests. "He's not still thinking about brain surgery, is he?" I snapped. "I'm fine, can't you see?"

She didn't know, she replied. She was just a nurse. Breakfast was on its way, she added. It was important I eat something.

So I did. Just now. Passable coffee, dreary white bread. I've never liked white bread. Henry did. There were many things Henry liked which I didn't, and vice versa. But we had a good marriage. A stable marriage. He loved me very much. More than

I loved him. But it didn't matter. I pretended to be in love with him because it felt like the right thing to do. And it was an easy thing to do. He made me happy. He didn't fill my soul like Ezra had done, but he made me happy. He took good care of me. I'm not sure Ezra would have taken good care of me. He was too busy fighting for a cause. A terrible cause. He loved me with all his heart, but he also loved politics just as much. That was his downfall. Still, I've always known he was my one true love. I've always known it. He was a murderer. I loved a murderer. A murderer who betrayed me and had a child with someone else. Except that he didn't know about the child, so I had to forgive him on that score. I could have gone to visit his son (I often wondered what he might look like) when Henry and I were in Israel. But that would have meant facing Lotta – and that I couldn't do. I couldn't bear the thought of seeing her. And the truth is that I wish I had been the one to carry Ezra's child, not that horrible woman. But life is what it is.

And of course there was that phone call, in the mid-Nineties. How he found my number, I have no idea. Or perhaps he did tell me and I don't remember. All I know is that one summer morning the phone rang and a man with a thick accent asked to speak to me. It was a vaguely familiar accent, but I couldn't place it. The man introduced himself as Ezra Bernheim.

"I'm not sure I know you," I said.

"You knew my father. I'm Ezra Radok's son," he replied.

When I heard the name, I froze. I was speechless. I heard him say, "Hello? Are you there?" a few times, and finally I regained my composure and asked him why he was calling me. I must have sounded cold, or disagreeable, because he stammered a bit when he answered. He explained that his mother had told him a lot about me. He also said that he was a writer, just like his father. He had published a few books in Israel, and his last novel was about to come out in England, published under the name "Ezra Bernheim". Could we meet? he asked. He was going to be in London for a few days. I hesitated. Then I lied and told him I was going to be out of the country. I was sorry. He didn't ask me where I was going and said that he was sorry too. "I know that you and my father were close. It would have been enlightening to meet you."

Enlightening. Of course it would have been enlightening for him. What was I thinking? Why had I lied about my being away? I found myself trembling. I muttered a few words, wished him luck and hung up.

Almost immediately I realized, just as I had done with Hannah, that I had made the wrong decision. That I should have met him. And there was still time to atone for my mistake. A few months later his book came out, to mixed reviews. It was a thriller entitled *Out There*. I had no desire to read it, although I did contemplate writing to his publisher. But I didn't know how to start the letter.

There were pictures of Ezra Bernheim in the paper, a man with curly hair, sharp cheekbones, melancholic eyes. I saw nothing and everything of Ezra in him.

But I never got in touch.

Throughout the years, I often wondered why I acted as I did. Was I self-destructive? Was I afraid? Was something wrong with me?

I think it is probably more complicated than that. Ultimately, nothing mattered enough. I managed to live life as though it did, but I was, in essence, living a lie. A comfortable one, but a lie nonetheless. The only thing that mattered was Maurice. The truth, the only truth, was that my newborn son had been wrenched away from me. His existence had become another mother's reality. Not mine.

The only physical reminder I had left of Maurice was his pair of light-blue pyjamas. I kept them with me all those years, hidden among jumpers in my wardrobe. In the early years, I would take them out just to smell him. I would press the fabric to my face and inhale it deeply, desperately trying to retrieve what no longer belonged to me. Eventually, when the smell faded (or perhaps it never faded), I folded the pyjamas neatly and took them out only a few times a year, just to look at them. To caress them.

Henry never knew, never saw. Would he have understood? I'm not sure. But I know that Ezra would have. I always felt that he understood me better than I understood myself. I wish we had met when we were both older and wiser. But such is fate. We spoke of that a lot, Ezra and I. Fate. He often talked of Confucius and his teachings: "The pull of experience is about breaking through the barrier of what we know so that we can change and grow." Ezra followed the pull blindly. He followed everything blindly. He didn't understand that some of those barriers were there for a reason. That some things were best left unexplored. He wouldn't hear of it when I told him so. "You're such a prude," he once told me. "A French prude."

And now the French prude is old. Bent, shrivelled, ill and old. I wonder whether my secret is what caused my demise. I've kept the image of my son's newborn face, his very existence, cloistered inside me for forty-nine years. I have never spoken his name. I have thought it and breathed it, but I couldn't speak it. My old limbs have wrapped themselves around that newborn face and mummified it. My internal equilibrium can no longer withstand the pressure of silence. I am quietly rotting.

What does Maurice look like today? *Mon fils*. Why didn't I ever tell Henry about my son? Why didn't my son come searching for me? Did his parents not tell him he was adopted? Maurice, can you hear me? What colour are your eyes? *Tes yeux*. Did you love your adopted mother? *Je suis ta mère*. Did you ever wonder about me? Someone has to find you. Hannah. Yes. Hannah. Why didn't I ever contact her again? My head hurts. A voice in the room. "Did you want a little wash, Mrs Dobbs?"

All is still. I must stop writing. Sinking. *Mon fils. Viens me trouver*. My head hurts, bursts. I must—

HANNAH

1

My mother rang me to say that Claire Plendon, formerly known as Claire Betts, had died. She had slowly been going blind, but wouldn't admit to it. On the previous Monday morning, she had chosen to go shopping on her own and got hit by a car. By Monday afternoon she was dead. The event was reported in the local newspaper. How she lay in the middle of the road, surrounded by the contents of her shopping trolley. A few apples and grapes. A pint of milk. A bag of potatoes. *The Daily Mail*. "A death that could have been avoided," my mother said. "She made it to the shop, but didn't make it back."

"And Peter?"

"He's taken it better than we feared. But that's maybe because the circumstances of his life have changed so much."

Peter and Cristina were divorced now, had been for years. After a successful exhibition in London, Cristina decided that she no longer wanted to live in the countryside – neither did she want to live with Peter any more. She admitted that she had wanted to leave him for a while. "I'm tired of his politics," she told my father. "It was fun in the beginning, but now it's become repetitive. I lost count of what we were supposed to be angry about. Turns out it was pretty much everything. And Israel? Is it really that evil? The owner of my gallery is Jewish, and he's very nice. Handsome too. He's got family there in Israel. He couldn't believe the things that were coming out of my mouth. And to tell you the truth? Neither can I. Oh, and one more thing: I no longer want to be a Labour supporter. I'm voting Tory from now on. I've had it with the Left. And I've had it with my husband."

I'm not sure she phrased her disillusion quite so explicitly to Peter. All I know is that he cried when we next saw him. I had never seen a man cry before, and I found it unsettling. "She's all I have," he kept repeating, as my father tried to console him. "Without Cristina I'm nothing, Leon, nothing. What have I done to deserve this? I love her, I've always loved her. And the children? What about the children?" He was sobbing, like a child. "I love her," he repeated. I'll never stop loving her. I don't understand Leon, I don't understand."

"There's nothing to understand," my father said gently. "It's one of those things in life which are beyond our control. You must not and cannot ever blame yourself for this. You know that, don't you?"

He shook his head. "No, I don't know that, Leon. I really don't."

Neither did I. I didn't believe my father. Cristina had had it with her husband, and that was all there was to it. Although I later learnt that there was an ulterior motive to her restlessness: the nice Jewish owner of the gallery had become her boyfriend. By the time Peter found out, he was already undergoing treatment for a depression which was to afflict him on and off for years to come. The children eventually distanced themselves from him too. They were still young, in their early teens, and could not reconcile the image of their once combative and zealous father with the broken, defeated man that he had become.

By then, my parents had separated as well. Everything was changing around me. Life as I knew it was unrecognizable. Peter's internal battles were left for others to untangle. A Dutch woman took responsibility. Peter fell in love with her, moved to a village outside Rotterdam and gave up politics. "He's opened a flower shop in Rotterdam," is what my mother told me. "Instead of distributing pamphlets about racism and Zionism, he sells flowers. Peonies have replaced politics."

It was an extraordinary concept, one I had trouble reconciling with the Peter of my youth. I remembered the way his eyes used to burn with political fervour. The folder of photographs and articles about the King David Hotel, and how heated he would become when we discussed his father's death and the struggle of the early days with his mother, in their cramped flat, somewhere near the Kentish coast.

Now that Claire was dead, perhaps that circle had finally closed for Peter. There was no battle left to fight. No memory to honour. The path was cleared for him to begin a new life. A new circle of life.

Just as I had.

*

On our way to the dinner in Kensal Rise, I told Az about Flora Dobbs. Ben added his own recollections from the back seat, and by the time we had arrived at our destination we all agreed that something was amiss: it was unlikely she would have left no note, no personal explanation. Mrs Dobbs may have been eccentric, but she didn't seem careless. And there was something careless about sending me a box without specific instructions. Was it possible that I hadn't looked carefully enough?

"As soon as we get home we'll give it another look," said Az. "I bet you she left you a letter and it's sitting at the bottom of the box."

The dinner was drawn out. I was longing to get home. To look inside that box again. Az was right: there probably was a letter, sitting at the bottom of that box, explaining everything: what Flora had become. Where she had gone to live. What had made her decide to leave me her books.

Ben was the object of much attention on the part of a budding and very pretty actress. His youthful beauty had given way to a manlier one: stronger cheekbones, thicker lips, broader shoulders – a beauty that hurts, a girlfriend had once said of him.

I watched as the actress spoke to him animatedly, with quiet expectation, while he responded politely, unmoved.

California suited Ben, as did his new relationship with Melody. He had mentioned earlier that a Spanish director, a friend of hers, had asked him to audition for a feature film. He was still modelling for the swimwear company and making some money. "It's not exactly Calvin Klein, but hey, it's still a few quid, right? And if this audition works out, I can quit."

He sounded hopeful, determined. Perhaps, I reasoned, my worries about Ben had more to do with my own anxieties than his. Perhaps it was time I put them aside once and for all.

We managed to leave the dinner as soon as pudding was served. "I'm so sorry, but we have to go. I have an early-morning meeting," Az explained to our hosts, who were too drunk to care. The night was cold. We ran to the car and drove off. Ben was tired, still jet-lagged, he said. Az drove quickly, his hand on the steering wheel. "That girl, the actress, was pretty, wasn't she, Ben?" he ventured, eyeing him through the rear-view mirror.

"She was all right. Not a patch on Melody though."

"Yes, Hannah showed me a picture. She's beautiful. Hope we get to meet her *un de ces jours*."

"Sure, yeah that would be nice."

As soon as we arrived Ben bade us goodnight and went to bed.

Az and I carried the box to the sitting room. We opened it and took the books out one by one. We found more newspaper at the bottom, then something small, a notebook. Black, 5x5, wire-bound.

I didn't think much of it. I was looking for a letter, not a notebook. But then I opened it. The first page was blank. On the second one there was a dedication – "*To Hannah*" – and a signature: "Flora Baum".

"Oh my God," I gasped.

So that had been her name, then. And this is what she had left me. Not a letter, but a notebook.

"This is it!" I exclaimed. I turned the page and found a folded piece of paper. I opened it quickly: it was a birth certificate. A name was written in red letters:

"Maurice Baum Schumann. Date of birth: 18th May 1956, Hackney Hospital. Signed: Flore Baum, 18th May 1956."

"God, Az, look at this," I said, handing it to him. My heart was beating quickly.

"Who was Maurice? Her son? Did she have a son?"

Az put on his glasses and looked at it carefully. "There's only one way of finding out," he said, pointing at the notebook.

Its pages were filled with meticulous writing – black ink, single-spaced, tightly fitting between the margins, in cursive French handwriting.

I sat down on the sofa and leafed quickly through it. It looked like a memoir of sorts. Given that the notebook stated that it was ninety-five pages long, I reckoned she had filled approximately seventy. Perhaps she had said all she needed to. Or perhaps she had run out of time.

"Can I see?" Az asked, peering over my shoulder.

I handed it to him, and he looked through it attentively. "Is it a diary?"

"No, I think it's the story of her life."

He gave it back to me. Would you read from the first page?" he asked, taking a seat next to me on the sofa.

I opened it and began to read:

"Jean is my first boyfriend. We are nineteen years old, students at the Sorbonne. In our spare time, we ride bicycles along the Seine and discuss literature. We both want to become writers and change the world. 'I could become the next Proust,' he tells me."

My hands were shaking. Az looked at me gently. "Continue," he said. "I want to hear it all."

"All of it?"

"Yes. The night is young. Read on. Read it all."

2

To say that I was moved by the content of that notebook would be an understatement. It floored me. It dumbfounded me. It ripped through me and left me breathless. I didn't know where or how to begin looking. The truth was there, bare as a bone: Flora had endured unimaginable suffering. She had lost her loved ones, including her child. She had escaped evil in the shape of war, only to run straight back into it in the guise of love. First with Ezra, then blindly with Fletcher, woefully unaware of its murky underside. And there was a son. Another Ezra. The fact that she had chosen not to meet him left me flabbergasted. How? Why? There was so much to take in I didn't know where to start. But at least she had found Henry. He had been her saviour. She had found her peace with him. Or had she? This notebook, her memoir, was the only witness of her life and death. "I must" she had written before drawing her last breath. What had she wanted to say? The arm of the letter "t" sloped downward, and every time I looked at it, I trembled.

Then of course there had been that fortuitous meeting with Claire Betts, in Palestine. To think that Flora had met Claire. To think that all that time we had lived across the street from the last person, aside from his wife, who had seen James Betts alive – and we had no idea.

For all I knew, she had probably crossed paths with Peter and Cristina when they came to visit. They might have exchanged a glance or a smile before she entered her house and they entered ours. Or perhaps a few words, about the weather. What if Flora had found out? I wondered. Could they have struck up a friendship? Would Flora have still moved away?

I rang Peter in Holland to tell him. He answered the phone and seemed surprised to hear from me. "How are you, Hannah?" as if I were part of a life he had long forgotten.

I didn't waste any time. I told him everything. "She saw your father, Peter. She was, with your mother, the last one to see him alive. They hugged each other, the two of them. She never forgot Claire, and I'm sure it's the same for your mother."

Peter was very quiet. Then he cleared his throat. "Will you show me that notebook when I next come to London? I would really like to see it."

"I could send you the pages in question," I offered.

"Yes, please," he answered. His voice sounded hoarse. I knew that if he wasn't crying, he was about to. "You see, my mum told me about that lady. She was young, like her. Pretty. She helped my mum when my dad was dying. It's like you said. She held Claire and told her things. She comforted her. And no, Mum never forgot her either," he added. "And now she's dead, so I'll never be able to tell her that I found the lady with the French accent. That's what she used to call her. She had forgotten her name. So she called her 'the lady with the French accent'. She would have liked to know that. That you had found her. The last person besides Mum to see my father alive."

"You never mentioned her before," I remarked. "Of all the information you kept in that folder, you never told us about the lady with the French accent..."

"I guess not," he answered. "It didn't seem as important as all the rest."

"But it was..."

"To you maybe. Not to me," he said abruptly.

We hung up. He was too distraught to continue the conversation. And in truth, so was I. All of it beggared belief, including that Flora had sold her house because of me. There was no other reason. She had moved away because she could not stand knowing something which I didn't. She had understood me before I had even understood myself. "Pain was shaping who she would later become." She feared seeing me get hurt. She had chosen to cut me out of her life rather than witness the undoing of my family. But why? Couldn't she have withheld the truth from me? Couldn't we have continued to see each other as friends? Wasn't there a middle ground? No, of course there wasn't. Flora didn't do middle grounds. *Vincit omnia veritas*. Truth conquers all. No white lies for Flora Baum. She was too pure, too virtuous. And impetuous. She followed her emotions. She didn't compromise. I couldn't blame her. She had a deep-rooted fear of abandonment. Of treachery. So she chose to flee rather than face me. I understood her. I wish she had trusted me, but I understood. Of course I did. I could forgive her anything. And I had to forgive myself too, for those presumptions I, as well as my family, had made about her. Had any of us discovered the truth, we would have been horrified.

Now it had been revealed. And it was up to me to find her son. She hadn't formulated it as such, but the message was quite clear. And I wouldn't give up until I had found him.

*

A friend from my Oxford years, a woman who had been adopted, put me in touch with Harry Yeovil. He had once been employed in an intermediary adoption agency, and now worked alone.

"He's a bit like a private investigator," she had explained. "And because of the complexity of your case, I strongly urge you to go to him, not a conventional agency."

My friend had used Harry to trace her birth mother, and had warned me that, as I wasn't a relative, my quest was going to be nigh on impossible. "Unless the impossible is circumvented," she had added. "Which is where Harry Yeovil comes in."

He had echoed her sentiments. Having looked at my case, he thought I had a chance, "though much is conspiring against you", he admitted. "Then again, two things are on your side: the fact that the adoption was done privately, which means that no records have been held, and the horrors of history. Sorry to say it, but it's true. The fact that Flora lost her parents in the Holocaust will make your case stronger, only because there's no way they can trace her roots – and that includes yours."

Harry explained that my relationship to the deceased required some further "tweaking". I would have to be upgraded from neighbour to relative. "You'll be closer to her that way," he said.

Anything that brought me closer was good. I urged Harry to cut as many corners as he could, and he promised to do his best. "But not all corners are cuttable," he added, in his mellifluous voice, launching into a long diatribe about data protection and various UK adoption acts. "There are always more formalities than one thinks," he concluded. "But let's worry about that later."

Harry had had sent off a copy of Maurice's birth certificate to the General Registry Office. He had warned me that the search might take some time, anywhere from a few weeks to a year, information I had baulked at, but he had urged me to trust him – and I did.

Harry was a thoughtful, studious man in his early thirties. He wore his hair parted on the side, and had a penchant for pastel-coloured clothing. He was vague about his background and family. I suspected that he had been adopted as well, and not in the happiest of circumstances. He was equally vague about his sexuality, mentioning "my friend" at various times. But professionally, there was something strong and determined about Harry, which was what I needed. Someone with bravura. I could not, under any circumstances, let Flora down. I was not going to be satisfied until I had found Maurice – or whatever he was now called. Harry had explained that his name had most probably been changed. And while Harry worked at his end, Az and I had both agreed that we would do our own fieldwork, starting with Fletcher Schumann. "He's probably dead – likewise the wife. But his children shouldn't be too hard to find," I had ventured.

Az and I had trawled through the internet and yellow pages. There were a few Schumanns, though no Fletchers. I tried all the ones I could find, as far as Scotland. None of them had heard of a Rosalind or a Fletcher. There was one name left, a Simon Schumann, with an address in Battersea. I had tried ringing, but no one had answered. I had tried so many times that I knew the phone number by heart. I had decided that if no one answered by the following day I would show up at the house. And then I got lucky: just as I was about to hang up, a man's voice answered.

"Who is this?" It was a gruff voice. I introduced myself, explained that I was looking for Fletcher or Rosalind Schumann. "Would you happen to be a relation?" I asked, in a friendly tone.

I could hear the sound of a television in the background. "Maybe. Why do you want to know?"

"A friend of mine, an older lady, knew Fletcher," I said. "She's just died. There're a few things I wanted to discuss. Would it be possible to speak to your parents?"

Simon paused again. "My father died ten years ago. My mother's in a home."

"I see," I said slowly. "I don't suppose I could visit her, could I? Or perhaps visit you?"

"You need to tell me what this is about. Otherwise, I won't be able to help." Given the supposed pedigree of the family, I had expected a more educated voice. His was snarky. "Are you a journalist or something?"

"No, not at all." I took a deep breath. "I think it might be easier if I spoke to your mother. It's rather confidential."

Simon laughed. A raucous, unpleasant laugh. "My mother doesn't do confidential. She's got Alzheimer's disease."

I cleared my throat. "I see. Sorry about that. All right then, I'll try to explain."

Was it worth going into detail over the phone? Wouldn't it be better to meet him? What if he hung up on me?

"This might be a bit upsetting for you," I ventured cautiously. "Perhaps it would be better to meet somewhere."

"No, it wouldn't. I work all day. Tell me what this is about. I don't get upset easily."

"OK." I sat down and spoke slowly. "How much did your father tell you about Robert Schumann?"

"Who?"

"Robert Schumann, the classical composer? Nineteenth-century?"

"Oh, him! I don't know much about his music. I'm more of a jazzer myself," he confessed, his voice sounding chirpier.

"I understand. Well, what did he tell you about Robert?"

"Nothing really, apart from that we had the same surname."

"He never told you that you were related? That his father held some of his scores in his house in the country?"

This time, Simon burst out laughing. "House in the country? Scores? What exactly are you trying to say?"

"Your father revealed certain things to my friend, a woman I knew called Flora," I explained. "He told her that he had grown up in a mansion, that his father owned some of Schumann's scores and that Robert was a relation of yours."

"Well, either she didn't hear him right or my father was lying. And he was no liar."

"No, of course not. Could you tell me then what you think he meant by that?"

"How would I know? I'm not my father," he snapped, his tone gruff again.

"No, but you may have an idea? I mean, where did he grow up? Do you know a bit about his background?"

"He was from Slough. His father was an insurance broker, his mother a nurse. No sodding country mansion. No money. No Robert in the family that I ever knew of. The Schumann we were related to was some German pharmacist from Bavaria." He paused. "Who was this Flora anyway?"

I hesitated before answering. "A friend of his. A woman he had an affair with, a very long time ago."

There was another silence at the other end of the line. "I see. Why do I need to know this?"

"Because Flora believed your father about Robert Schumann, and I wanted to confirm that what she believed was the truth. I now see that it wasn't."

"No," Simon corroborated. "It wasn't." He paused again. "My father had a few Floras in his life. But that didn't make him a liar."

"Of course not." I wanted to add more, but held myself back. "Thank you for your time," I said instead.

"That's all right." He paused again. There was no longer a sound in the background; he had switched the television off.

"Was she keen on my father, this Flora?" Simon asked, with some hesitation in his voice.

"Yes," I answered. "She was. He broke her heart."

"I'm sorry." His voice dropped. "He broke my mother's heart too."

Then he hung up without saying goodbye.

*

In the middle of it all, a French fashion designer asked me to provide catering for her daughter's wedding. It was a major booking, and I couldn't afford to turn it down. The wedding was in August, so I had time to prepare.

But my head was in a different place. For the first time in many years, food had been supplanted by something else: Flora. What she wrote, how she wrote and what she sounded like. Because I could hear her speaking to me again, her low and faintly accented voice rising from her crowded, cursive writing.

The neatness of her flowery letters belied the urgency of her tone. Had it been me, my handwriting would have been scruffy and quasi-illegible. But Flora's suggested a woman who could distance herself from her emotions. A woman who, despite what she had undergone in her life, understood that even despair requires a modicum of self-control. That sinking further would only defeat her purpose.

Ben, who had read the memoir during his subsequent visit, was in a similar state of excitement. "Bloody hell," he kept repeating. "And how she had to give her baby up – man, that must have hurt," Ben continued heatedly, pacing back and forth. "And what about that Israeli writer dude? Do you know anything about him?"

"No," I answered, "but I looked him up. He's a very good-looking guy, like his father was, I imagine. I've written to his agent, hope I'll hear back quickly. From what I gather he writes thrillers, mostly. I want to meet him or talk to him at least. It could be interesting."

I poured myself a glass of white wine, handing Ben a Diet Coke. He took a few sips and replaced the glass on the counter. "Listen," he said, sounding serious. "I want to help you find him. I want to come and help you search for Maurice. Or whatever his name is."

"Do you really? That would be great."

I explained what I had been doing with Harry. How he had warned me that the administrative side of things might take some time. "I'm not related to her, so we're going to have to lie and pretend that I am."

"Of course," said Ben. "There's no other way. I'm a strong believer in bullshit when it comes to getting immediate action."

I laughed. "I'm honest. I tend to play by the rules."

He paused and smirked. "You won't this time, if you want any answers."

*

Harry had good news. "Things are moving along swiftly," he said, crossing his fingers. "That's why I called you in to see me."

"Really? How swiftly?" I asked.

"I found him," he said slowly. "I found Flora's son and I spoke to him. But there're a few issues which I need to discuss with you."

"But that's fantastic!" I exclaimed. "Where is he? What's his name?"

"I can't give you that information yet. All I can tell you is that his name is not Maurice. But one thing at a time," Harry cautioned me. "There's one more hurdle before we're done. And then I can put you in touch."

"Hurdle?"

"Well, it's not really a hurdle," he backtracked. "The agency I'm dealing with would like to meet you," he stated, sounding nervous.

"What kind of an agency?" I was worried.

"A government-registered adoption agency. It's part of the procedure. As you saw in the document I sent you, you're required to sign a declaration certifying that you and Flora are related."

I gasped. "What document? You never sent me anything! How am I going to certify it if it's a lie?"

Harry spoke slowly. "I sent you a document which I send to all my clients. It's called 'Different stages in the intermediary process'. If you didn't read it, I'm sorry."

"So am I," I mumbled.

"The document in question," Harry continued, "explains what the process of tracing a relative entails. Now – and please listen carefully…" he added, speaking firmly.

"I am."

"You have become Flora's cousin, thrice-removed, on her father Maurice's side."

"Have I?"

"Yes. Maurice's brother's son, David, had a daughter, Anna, who later married your grandfather."

I was flummoxed. "Yes, Anna was my grandmother. How did you know that? How did you figure this out?"

"I did a bit of research. So for the time being, Anna was as Jewish as you have now become."

"Fine."

"And as your father's history is equally murky," he continued, "that makes you a lucky woman. But you still have to sign that paper," he added.

I squirmed in my seat. "I'm a law-abiding citizen, Harry, I cannot lie in front of an official, can I?"

"Official is a big word, and you'll be all right," he reassured me. "I understand why you're nervous. But it isn't entirely a lie, either. Stop seeing it as one." He paused. "You do want to meet him, don't you?"

"Yes of course!"

"Well, then you're going to have play the game. And in any case," he continued, "Flora mentioned in her memoir that you could have been her daughter, right? In a way, given what you've inherited from her, it wouldn't be that far-fetched to say you're related."

"I guess," I answered. "But what if they ask me to show, I don't know, my father's birth certificate? I don't even know if I have it!"

Harry spoke calmly. "They're not going to ask you for your father's birth certificate. He doesn't really matter to them. What matters is you and Flora. That's the link they want on paper, which they're not going to get. All we have is the birth certificate, which is a big plus. It indicates some sort of filial connection, because otherwise, why would you have it?"

"That's true. And the memoir?"

He hesitated. "I would keep it as a last resort. Bring it to the meeting and only pull it out if you think you really need to."

*

I received a reply from Ezra Bernheim. He thanked me for getting in touch. My email had taken him by surprise, he wrote, because few people knew who his father really was. Ever since he was a child, his mother had maintained that Ezra had been a soldier, killed on the battlefield. A hero whom she had loved very much. Then, when Ezra turned eighteen, she finally told him the truth. That yes, they had loved each other very much, but to some people he was a traitor – although to Lotta, and others as well, he would always be a hero. "It was a hard one to digest," he admitted. "And I'm still digesting it. What happened that day in 1946 divided the nation."

He went on to tell me that his mother had moved to Berlin in the '80s. She had remarried – a prominent German journalist. She seldom came back to visit. "Too much baggage, I guess," he said. But Ezra had stayed in Israel. One of the ways of confronting his demons, he explained, was to write books. Another way was to find out as much as he could about who his father really was. "Which is why I was so interested in hearing from you. I want to hear from anyone who knew him, aside from his Irgun sidekicks, whom I've already spoken to. How much do you know about Flora and Ezra? How did you meet Flora?"

I explained. I didn't elaborate on any details, only mentioning that I had met Flora when she lived in Notting Hill. She had told me about her days in Palestine and her relationship with Ezra. I didn't tell him about the memoir, as it seemed too personal. He had never met Flora after all, so why tell him more than was needed?

Ezra's emails became more heated. He admitted that he had been very upset after Flora had declined to meet him. "I knew she was lying," he wrote, "and that she wasn't leaving the country at all. She obviously didn't want anything to do

with me, or my father. He was a terrorist, so I understand.
But still. From what my mother told me, they had been in love
with each other."

I explained. That indeed, his father had been the only love of
Flora's life. That although she had branded him a murderer, I
didn't think she had ever stopped loving him. But that finding
out about his son's birth had upset her. "I think she would have
liked to have had a child with him," I wrote. Then I immediately
wished I hadn't. But it was too late. Ezra asked me to ring him,
and I did.

We spoke for a long time. His English was very good, despite
an Israeli accent. He asked me several times how come I knew
so much about Flora, but however much I wanted to tell him
the truth, I couldn't. Flora had asked me to find her son. Not
Ezra's. I needed to safeguard her privacy, and so I did. I told
Ezra that she had confided in me a few times, but then she had
moved and I hadn't heard her name mentioned for many years,
except to find out that she had died.

"Listen, I don't understand," he said, speaking quickly. "Why
did you get in touch with me now, after so many years? Why
not before? Something must have made you do it. I'm a writer.
I know these things," he added.

"I read about you and your book in the paper," I blurted out.
"I saw the name, the title, and I knew it was you. I wanted to
get in touch. I was curious."

"Did you buy my book?"

"Yes I did," I said. "But I haven't read it yet."

"OK. Fine. But listen," Ezra was saying. "How did you know
it was me, since my name isn't the same?"

I breathed in deeply. How indeed? "Because Flora told me
about you. She knew. Your mother wrote to her. And I never

forgot your name when I heard it," I added, pre-empting further prodding.

"What?" Ezra exclaimed. "My mother wrote to her? She never told me!" He paused, and I heard him light a cigarette. "What else do you know?" he asked. I could hear him blowing the smoke into the receiver.

"Not much," I answered simply. "Just that your father and Flora had loved each other and she was devastated when she boarded that boat back to France."

"Yes, I can imagine. What happened was terrible."

"I'm sorry I didn't stay in touch with Flora," I continued. "She was fascinating."

"Yes," Ezra said softly. "My mother said that she was great. But she also said their relationship was a complicated one. It would have been, of course."

I froze. "Why?"

"My mother and Ezra had been together before Flora came on the scene. She never told you that?"

"No…"

"That's interesting. Well, my father left Lotta for Flora. My mother was broken-hearted. It was terrible for her."

"I don't remember Flora mentioning that," I said, dumbfounded by the news.

Was this true? Something told me it wasn't. Lotta's letter had stipulated that it had only happened once. So she had to have made this up in order to protect her son. To make him feel wanted by mother and father alike. No one likes to know they're the result of a one-night stand. She had concocted the story that she and Ezra had been a couple. That they had loved each other. And then Flora had come along, breaking up their affair. But that couldn't have happened. Relationships such as those are never kept secret. Flora would have been bound to find out one way or another, and she would have written about it. Therefore I didn't believe what Lotta had told her son. What she had shared with Flora was the truth. A cruel truth, but then again Lotta had always been jealous of Flora; that much was clear. She wanted to ensure she could dig that knife in one more time before closing the Ezra-and-Flora chapter.

And it was certainly not my place to interfere with her son's version.

My head was spinning. I needed to find out more. I needed to speak to Lotta. She was the only one who could lift the lid on Flora's younger years. No matter how jealous she had been, surely enough time had now elapsed since those events of 1946. But how could I ask Ezra without appearing suspicious? There was no reason for me to speak to Lotta, unless I knew something he didn't.

Then I stopped myself. Did it matter? Why was I becoming so embroiled in this dead woman's life? Shouldn't I be concentrating on Maurice exclusively?

The answer came to me immediately. Everything about Flora Baum mattered. Her past, her present, her future.

Everything.

I took my courage in both hands and asked Ezra if he might give me his mother's email address. I explained that I wanted to find out more about Flora and her time in Palestine.

"OK. But you're not related to Flora, so why are you so interested in this woman?"

"I've always been interested in her," I declared.

"But why do you want to speak to my mother?" he insisted. "What can she tell you that I can't?

"She knew Flora. You didn't."

Ezra paused. "Yes, that is correct. But listen, I don't know you. I know nothing about you. And there's something about this story that doesn't add up. I think you're keeping information from me. I could be wrong, but I don't think so."

"You're wrong," I replied firmly. "Like I said, I'm just very interested in the whole story, in Palestine and in Flora."

"I don't believe you," Ezra declared. "I repeat, I think you're keeping information from me."

"I'm not," I repeated, less firmly than before. "But if you'd rather we left it, then let's do that. Thank you for your time."

"Yes," he said. "Let's leave it." He paused. "And you should read my book. I believe you'll find it interesting."

He hung up before I could say anything more.

*

A lanky woman from the adoption agency was the one who interviewed me. She had highlighted hair and thin lips. She wasn't sympathetic, but neither was she antagonistic. It was hard to determine her age – late thirties, early forties – but it was easy to see that she was efficient. Despite her dulcet tones, the nature of her questions and her requests for me to elaborate on some of my answers demonstrated an ability to read between the lines which made me feel uncomfortable.

"So why now?" was one of the first questions Pauline asked. "What made you decide to come and look for your cousin now?"

I hesitated and she saw it. "I inherited a box of books from Flora. In one of the books there was her son's birth certificate. I had heard a lot about him from my father, but never did much about it. This made me want to do more."

"I see. So you weren't interested in finding out about him before?"

"Yes, of course I was! But I didn't know enough about him. There's much more urgency now that Flora's dead. And I didn't really know how to go about it," I added. "I didn't know who to contact, until I saw that birth certificate…"

Pauline's eyes rested on mine. "Tell me a bit more about what you know of the adoption. What circumstances was Flora in when she gave the baby up for adoption? Do you know any of her family members?"

I told her everything I knew and she listened carefully. "Everyone on my father's side is dead," I concluded. "Flora's son is the only one left. So here I am, searching for answers."

Pauline nodded slowly. "Yes, I can see that. But you see, Hannah, a moment ago you mentioned that your father used to tell you a lot about Flora and her son. Then you said that you didn't really know about him. I'm confused. Help me out here." She twiddled her pencil between her fingers as she awaited my answer. I felt hot, and my mouth was dry. I had meant to bring some water with me. But I couldn't ask for it now. It would betray the sense of anxiety that was now permeating my very bones.

"OK," I said, looking at her and trying to keep my voice steady. "I'm going to give you the answer."

I opened my bag and pulled out the notebook. I placed it in front of her and explained. "Flora left me her books, but she also left me her handwritten memoir. It recounts her terrible years in the war, how she lost her family in a concentration camp and how she was forced to give Maurice – or whatever his name is now – up for adoption." I paused. "What I read was so harrowing I felt that I had to do something and do it now. I thought Flora's son might want to know where his birth mother comes from and might want to meet his cousins."

"Yes," Pauline said, "yes, that makes sense. But why didn't you mention the memoir before?"

"It's a very private document," I replied. "And a private story."

"But this is our job," Pauline said, leaning towards me. "Private stories are our job," she added. "What can be more private than an adoption? You should have mentioned it before."

"Yes, yes, I can see that." I was getting nervous again. But then I quickly realized that there was no reason to. Pauline thumbed quickly through the memoir, then produced the declaration, which I duly signed, managing to steady my shaking hand. "Good luck with your cousin," she said, smiling. "We don't get many war stories like yours around here."

*

I cooked Az and Stéphanie supper that night. Beef stew with roast potatoes, my mother's signature dish. I added chopped minted courgettes and made a tarte Tatin for Stéphanie. We drank a lot of wine, possibly too much wine, and played a raucous game of Scrabble with Stéphanie. Az took pictures of the two of us – of me drinking a glass of wine, Stéphanie lying on the sofa, the two of us laughing.

Az was happy whenever Stéphanie stayed with us. And he was thrilled we got along so well. She was slowly opening up to me, and a few times I had gone to pick her up at school. I had never had such an immediate rapport with any child before, and I could feel the newness of it, the excitement of it, like spice on the tip of my tongue.

"You're nice," Stéphanie told me one day, as we were walking towards the Tube from the Lycée.

I nearly cried when she said it. I nearly told her I loved her, but that would have been premature. So we walked into a French bakery on Harrington Road, and I bought us both two large chocolate éclairs instead, and we sat around a little wrought-iron table outside and ate them with sticky fingers.

I was ready for a child, for marriage, for everything, and I told Az as much, after Stéphanie had gone to bed.

At first we spoke about us: our plans for the future. A baby, a wedding. We had discussed it before, but now we made more concrete plans. A summer or autumn wedding. Somewhere by the sea? Or here in London? Perhaps I might be pregnant then? We had been trying; a week more and I would find out. If I wasn't pregnant, we would start again. And if that didn't work, said Az, we would adopt a baby. "Algerian," we added in unison, then laughed.

The conversation turned to Flora and Maurice. I told him about Pauline, about the administrative red tape I had managed to circumvent. And this is where Az caught me off guard. "You could have easily avoided that red tape completely, by not going on this crazy search for Flora's son. You chose to do it, but you didn't have to."

"But of course I did!" I exclaimed. "Come on, Az, don't you remember? You were just as shocked as I was! You found Flora's story just as harrowing as Ben and I did!"

"I suppose I did, yes," he admitted. "But I didn't think you'd actually go to the trouble of finding him. And Ezra's son? Why would you get in touch with him? Flora's past with Ezra has nothing to do with her story with Maurice."

"I don't think that's true," I replied. "One led to the other."

He held my hand. "OK, maybe. But she's dead, *mon amour*. You don't owe her anything. You don't need to investigate this connection. *Pas besoin de donner un coup de pied dans la fourmillière*, as we would say. No need to kick the hornet's nest. You could just leave it be."

"I certainly couldn't. I owe it to her and her memory."

"That's one way of looking at it," he said. "But it's not the approach she chose."

"What do you mean?" I released myself from his grasp.

"I mean that Flora didn't come looking for you. She could have said something after she moved away, sent you a note of explanation about her behaviour. But she chose to keep it to herself for nineteen years and do nothing about it during all that time, even though her conscience urged her to."

"OK, but in the end she did, right? She left me her memoir. It may have taken nineteen years, but at least she did it. Are you saying that I should hold a grudge against her? Is that what you're saying?"

"No," he answered calmly. "But you were young, vulnerable. It reveals something about her. I know that she felt very bad about leaving without saying anything to you. And I know that it was done with the best of intentions. But she didn't do anything to rectify the situation."

"OK but we're not dealing with an ordinary woman here," I answered, slightly shaken. "You read what she went through. It's a miracle she came out sane at all. Her whole life was one of loss. And she was trying to protect me, because she knew loss was coming my way. She even admitted that she had made a mistake. You read what she said about things not mattering enough. So I forgive her everything. I love her. She was a good woman, an extraordinary woman."

"Yes," Az agreed. "But she should have known better."

"I totally disagree and I don't think that anything in this case is about knowing better. It's about survival."

"OK, OK. You're upset."

"Yes," I said. "I'm upset."

He pulled me back towards him. "I'm going to tell you a story. Are you ready for it?"

I was still upset. "No."

"Well I'm going to tell you anyway."

"If you must," I mumbled.

"I don't. But I think you're going to like it," he said. "I promise."

"OK. But what does it have to do with Flora?"

"You'll see. It's about my mother and Oran and a poster."

"All right, go ahead," I sighed. It was hard to resist Az. Whenever I sulked, he knew how to make me snap out of it. Except for this time. This was more than a sulk. I felt that he completely misunderstood the situation. And it bothered me; but he didn't seem to care.

"As you know," he began, "after my father was killed, we fled to France and moved to a dingy one-bedroom apartment in Aubervilliers. Horrible, dismal place. My mother, who had been a teacher in Oran, took a job as a cleaner. She could find nothing else. Every night I would come home and I could smell the detergent on her fingers. It was shit, really, and the only thing we wanted to do was go back to Algeria. But there was a civil war going on. So my mother found an alternative. She got us a poster she had found somewhere, not sure where. It was a large poster of Oran, and she hung it in our small kitchen. It took up the entire wall, but we didn't mind. We looked at it every morning before I set off for school. The turquoise sea, the white rooftops, the orange trees. 'This is what we will return to as soon as the war is over,' she used to promise me, and it gave me hope. The squalor we lived in now couldn't last. It was only temporary, right?"

"Right."

"But then the years went by, and my mother continued to clean houses, and a rich family decided to employ her full-time. Eventually, we moved to Paris. We found a furnished and very ugly small flat in the 12th Arrondissement, but I loved it. To me it was magical. Beautiful. A new beginning. But my mother didn't think so. She still kept talking about how we would return home. She would point at the Oran poster which hung once again in our new kitchen. 'This is where we belong, not here,' she would repeat.

"But things had changed for me. By then, that image of Oran had stopped being a symbol of hope, and became one of resentment. I didn't want to return anywhere. I was happy in Paris, at my school, with my new friends. I had also begun to take pictures with a second-hand camera my mother had bought me. I had found my vocation. I wanted to photograph the present, not the past. Now I ignored the poster of Oran glaring at me from the kitchen wall. I had become French and felt French. Oran was a vestige of a land we had passed through on the way to somewhere else. When I told my mother, she went crazy. She threw a plate against the wall and screamed. Then she tore the poster off the wall and began to rip it to pieces. I tried to stop her, but she pushed me away and screamed again and again until I was so distraught that I began to cry, and then my mother broke down too and cried with me and we clutched each other, the two of us, standing in the middle of our small, ugly kitchen, strewn with bits of paper, and gazed at the wall: it was nearly empty except for a tiny slice of turquoise, where the sea had once sparkled."

We were both quiet for a while. "It's a very touching story, Az," I finally said. "But what does it have to do with Flora?"

He turned his face towards me. I could distinguish his features in the dark. "It has to do with the fact that my mother knew I was right. We couldn't go back, and chances were we never would. There's an Arab saying: 'What is coming is better than what is gone'. If we returned, it wouldn't be what we expected. We had changed. We had become aliens in both countries. We knew it was best to move forward. To focus on what was coming and not look back."

"So you're saying that I shouldn't go looking for Flora's son…"

"Yes. I think it's best you keep the story as it is. A wonderful one, written by someone you vaguely knew. No more, no less. Don't go looking for answers."

"But why?"

"Because this shouldn't become your story. If it does, it may carry you into a place you might regret visiting."

"How do you know?"

"I don't," Az said, after a brief pause. "I just feel it."

"Well, I still want to find him," I answered softly. "I don't expect anything. I'm ready for any eventuality. And you're too late: the story became mine as soon as I started reading it."

I had become so intrinsically linked to Flora that I had to remind myself that I wasn't, in fact, related to her. I didn't tell Az, but it was the truth. I had read her memoir so many times, I felt as if I really knew her. I could see her as a young girl, walking the streets of Paris. I could picture her mother, standing that day in the sunshine, before she disappeared. I could smell the musty odour in her father's shop. I could feel the hot stones of Jerusalem and imagine Ezra and Flora mingling among the refined crowd of the King David Hotel. I could see her as a young woman working behind that perfume counter at Selfridges.

I even bought Shalimar perfume in order to feel closer, still, to her as well as to her mother. I could feel her despair, after her baby was handed over. Her utter, gut-wrenching despair, the opening of a black void. And I had pictures of her in that psychiatric ward, shackled to a bed as a doctor pressed a button that sent shock waves through her. It was a miracle she hadn't suffered more long-term problems. Then again, how was I to know that she hadn't?

And then there were her days as a model. There was a contradiction there: she was a very private person, yet she had no qualms about stripping naked for painters. "My soul is prudish, but not my body. My body speaks for itself, and I like that," she had written. Her body was her language, and she stripped it bare.

Who was Flora Baum? Her flesh served as a canvas for the words she couldn't speak. But where were those paintings? Those drawings? I had made a visit to the Slade School and enquired about their records, anything that could provide me with additional information about her. "Every Saturday in 1955" was the only clue I had. But Flora hadn't been a student. There was no mention of her anywhere. As for portraits of her, it was impossible to know. Perhaps I could track down one of her fellow students, the archivist had suggested. There had to be someone left from that time. Did I want her to look into it?

I tried finding Vivian, but I didn't know her surname, or any of the other friends Flora had mentioned. I thought about getting in touch with Lotta anyway, despite her son's wishes. But I couldn't find a listing for her, even though I searched everywhere.

I looked for Flora's book on Robert Schumann, but the publisher had gone out of business. I visited a few libraries, hoping to find a copy of it, to no avail.

Claire Betts was now dead, though she had still been alive the week before Ben delivered the box.

When it came to Flora Baum, there was nothing and no one to track down. All I had for reference was a scribbled notebook of A5 paper I had found at the bottom of an old cardboard carton, my name highlighted in dark-blue felt-tip letters.

3

His name was Derek Casmin, Harry said. He had just turned fifty and lived in Canterbury. He was married with one daughter and two grandchildren. Harry had written to him, explaining who I was. We had exchanged two emails. His tone was dry and curt, not particularly polite. Yet he agreed to meet me at an appointed time, one week later.

Harry confessed that Derek had only expressed a mild interest in meeting me, until he had let slip that his mother had been French and that I was a private chef. That had made Derek curious. "He likes France and he likes food," said Harry. "I didn't get much else from him. Which doesn't necessarily mean there isn't much else. And by the way," he warned me, "don't get your hopes up. He's probably not what you expect. It rarely works out that way. You may be lucky, but be prepared for any eventuality."

"I am."

I needed to meet Derek in person before I would allow myself to form any sort of impression of him. Whatever had been transmitted through email was surely not an accurate reflection of his personality. He was being cautious, understandably taken aback by the revelation that an unknown family member had tracked him down. I had wanted to mention the memoir to him, but Harry had dissuaded me. "Don't give him too much too soon. Take your time," he had suggested. "I wouldn't mention it until the second or third meeting, if there is one." He had also urged me to stick to the cousin scenario until further notice.

"What you do after that is entirely in your hands. But I would break the news very slowly. You don't want to scare him off."

*

Ben rang to say that he had auditioned for the feature film, but hadn't got the part. "Although they led me to believe that I would get it. But hey, these things happen," he said, his voice sounding strained.

"I'm sorry, Ben."

"Yeah, me too." He spoke quickly, brusquely. But not all was lost, he added. He had been cast in a low-budget movie, to be shot in Latvia. He didn't know much about the director, but he wanted to give it a try. "Could be interesting," he said.

Something about my brother broke my heart. It always had, ever since that day at the beach, when his childish innocence was shattered into little pieces. But the shattering had fuelled his talent. It was raw, real. There was fire inside that darkness. Surely he deserved a break? Or perhaps it wasn't about merit, just luck. Somehow, that always seemed to bypass him. Was there a reason, or was it purely providence? All I could do was offer support. But he didn't seem interested. "I need action, not support."

"And it *will* happen," I said, wanting to believe it. "Remember that most artists struggle before they make it. 'He can who thinks he can, and he can't who thinks he can't.' Picasso said that, by the way."

"Picasso said many things," Ben declared. "And it's more complicated than that. It doesn't always work out that way."

"But it could."

"I'll keep you posted about next week," he said. "You know I want to be there."

"I know."

The reality was that I was starting to worry about meeting Derek on my own. My confidence was slowly crumbling. Perhaps Az had been right, after all. Perhaps I shouldn't have gone searching for him. What if it all went wrong? What if Derek discovered the truth? That we were, in fact, not related at all? His mother and I had met for no more than an hour. Until I read her memoir I knew next to nothing about her. What had I got myself into?

*

The day of our meeting, I picked Ben up at the airport. He was wearing a baseball cap and dark glasses. I squeezed his hand. "It's good to see you. I'm so glad you were able to pull it off."

He lifted his sunglasses. "I had to push a bit. But it worked."

"Are you all right?" He looked pale. Worn out.

"Not really. I didn't get much sleep last night. I partied too much on set. Not booze, if that's what you're thinking," he added quickly.

"It's not," I reassured him. "And I've got us a minicab to get us to Canterbury. Az arranged it all.

"Cool, thank you." He put his sunglasses back on. "Something's up with Melody," he said. "She's being fucking weird. She's not taking my calls."

"Maybe you need to have a good conversation, the two of you…"

"We did." He looked worried. "She doesn't like me shooting this crappy flick. Says it's porn. Which it's not. Well, not technically, anyway. It's just crap, that's all. Though some of the actors are nice. But there's more, I can tell. Something else is going on."

"Ben, I feel bad. I feel like I should hug you. Can I hug you?"

"Yeah, sure, whatever."

We embraced awkwardly. "I'm sorry. I never should have agreed to this," I said, releasing my grasp. "I shouldn't have insisted."

Ben looked at me. "You never insisted – and stop being sorry all the time – it's boring."

I smiled. "OK. I'll stop. I've just spotted the minicab driver. Let's go."

*

The Queen's Head pub, two o'clock, outside, Derek had said. The cab driver had parked nearby. "I'll be right here, if you need me," he told us.

We arrived at the pub early. It stood on an unattractive street, on the outskirts of the city centre. REAL ALES BAR FOOD was written on the front of the dirty white building in black letters. The rain had turned into a drizzle, interrupted by streams of light, moving in uneven patches. Two men were smoking outside. I wondered whether one of them was Derek. I had no idea what he looked like. I had described myself, and had, the previous day, informed him that I would be bringing my brother, his other cousin, along. I didn't expect, or receive, a reply. Now, though, I was suddenly worried it might have put him off altogether.

Ben lit a cigarette and paced around. He was wearing his black jeans and a matching jacket, and hadn't removed the baseball cap. We waited for ten minutes, and I was about to go inside and use the loo when a man appeared. He was of medium height, with pale skin and salt-and-pepper hair. He looked younger than his fifty years – an ordinary, rough-hewn sort of man who, in any other circumstances, I wouldn't even have noticed. His dark eyes rested momentarily on mine, then on Ben's. Scrutinizing eyes, with long dark lashes. He wore a striped grey suit and a creased white shirt. His smile was awkward, but I attributed it to nerves. We were all nervous. "I'm Derek Casmin," he said.

"Hello, it's very good to meet you. I'm Hannah," I said, shaking his hand.

"And I'm Ben," said my brother.

"OK," Derek said, his eyes resting on Ben's for a while longer. "Let's go inside."

We followed him, and I ran to the loo. My stomach was in knots. When I returned, Ben was ordering a Coca-Cola, Derek a beer. He knew the barman, a bearded man with a tattooed neck, and exchanged a few words with him. "These your friends?" the barman asked Derek.

"Nah. Londoners," Derek answered. "They're Londoners."

I ordered myself a mineral water, and we sat down. The pub was dark and dingy. It was daylight outside, but one wouldn't have known it. There was a smell of dank grease. Stains on the pale-red carpet. A man and a woman were playing pool in the next room. I could see their moving cues through the open door. There was the noise of a television in the background, a few men were shouting at a football match on the screen. I could hear them, but I couldn't see them.

Derek asked us where we lived in London.

"I live in North London," I answered.

"And I live in Notting Hill," Ben said.

"Notting Hill, like the movie?"

"Yes," Ben answered. "Like the movie."

"So you're rich?"

"No, not particularly," I answered. Ben said nothing. He was looking nervous.

"I thought you had to be rich to live there," Derek said, taking a few sips of his beer.

"Not necessarily," Ben answered.

"I used to work in London for a while. Oxford Street. In the 1980s," Derek continued. His accent was coarse. Since speaking to Simon, I had suspected Fletcher's must have been too, but Flora hadn't been enough of a native to detect it, and was consequently not in a position to question the tales of his pedigree.

"So, what work were you doing there?" Ben asked, in a friendly voice.

Derek nodded. "I sold shoes. That's my business. Shoes. I have a shop in Sittingbourne: Casmin's footwear. I have a partner. We sell international shoes."

"Nice," said Ben. "What kind of international shoes? I like shoes."

He displayed his white Nike trainers from underneath the table. "I stick to trainers, though. I don't have many proper shoes."

"Is that right? Well, come by my shop, then. I got plenty of proper ones."

Did Derek mean that or was he pretending? It was hard to tell.

"And you're a restaurant chef, is that right?" Derek asked, turning towards me.

"A chef, yes. But not for restaurants, private stuff. Catering."

"That's a good job," Derek declared. "I like good food. French food, especially. There's a new restaurant opened up here recently. The chef is from the south of France. Me and the wife like to go there. To the restaurant I mean, yeah?"

"Sounds nice."

"What about you?" he asked Ben, tapping his fingers against his glass. "What's your line of work?"

"Journalist," said Ben, without missing a beat. We had agreed that mentioning the word "actor" might prove counterproductive.

"Telly?" Derek asked, sounding hopeful.

"Sometimes. Mostly newspapers, but I've done some telly."

"I knew it," said Derek, leaning back on his chair. "I've seen your face before."

Ben mumbled something unintelligible. There was a slight lull in the conversation, and I decided to dive in.

"Derek," I said slowly, "I'd like to thank you for agreeing to see us today."

"Bloody right you should. I didn't know telly man was coming too," Derek retorted, pointing towards Ben. "You kind of threw that one into the pot, didn't you?"

"No, not at all!" I exclaimed. "It's just that… Ben really wanted to meet you too, but we didn't know if you'd mind, so you know…"

"No, I don't know, and yeah I mind," Derek retorted, drinking his beer quickly. "I never went looking for my birth mother. Never was interested. I got on fine with my family. Why would I go looking? My mum was a good woman. A hard worker. She died a few years ago."

"Sorry for your loss," said Ben. "And I agree. Why would you go looking if you don't want to? It's my sister who started this," he added, pointing at me. "She's been obsessed with Flora for a long time. And then she died."

"Who's Flora?"

"Your birth mother. Her name was Flora."

What was Ben up to now?

Derek pinched his lips nervously. "So she was French, yeah?"

"Yes. Flora was from Paris."

This seemed to pique Derek's interest. "From Paris?"

"Yes. She was an only child. Her father owned a toyshop."

Derek's eyes widened. "Really?"

"Yes. Why?"

"I used to like toys. I worked as an apprentice in a toyshop once. But that was a long time ago," he added gruffly.

"That's really interesting," Ben said. "That you liked toys too."

Derek looked at him. "Maybe. Maybe not." His tone had hardened. "So when did she come to London?"

"In the 1950s," I answered. "She had an affair with a man she loved. Your father. Then he left her."

"Why? Because she was a bitch, right?"

"No," I replied, stunned, but pretending not to be. "Because your father was married. So she had to give you up for adoption. And it broke her heart."

I nearly mentioned Simon Schumann, then remembered Harry's words of caution.

Derek began to laugh. "It broke her heart? Don't give me that shit. We all know that she abandoned me in a church. She left me wrapped in a fucking blanket in the doorway of the Salvation Army in Hackney, London, 1956. It's a miracle my parents happened to be on that same street at the same moment."

"Who told you that?" I asked, in a hoarse voice.

"My mother told me that. And she wouldn't lie."

I couldn't find the right words. I was in shock. Luckily, Ben could.

"Listen, mate, it's not true. I got proof that it's not true."

Derek laughed again. "What proof?"

"She told us stuff, and she also wrote a memoir. The story of her life. She left it to Hannah in her will."

"Oh yeah? Let me see it, then," he snapped.

"We didn't bring it," I said, speaking haltingly. "But we can tell you what it says and bring it to you next time."

"Next time?" He sniggered. "Why didn't you bring it today?" Derek stood up and pushed his chair back. "I would have liked to see it today."

"We didn't know whether you'd be interested," said Ben.

"I'm going to get myself another drink," said Derek. He got up, and Ben followed suit. "Where are you going?" I faltered.

"I'm gonna get a drink too," Ben said, avoiding my gaze. "I've been wanting one for the past three days. My career is going down the pan and Melody is playing mind games with me. And this piece of shit here isn't making things easier."

"But Ben, you can't!" I cried out, as he walked away. "You don't drink any more!"

Derek turned around and looked at me from the bar. I had spoken too loudly. Did it matter? In any case, Ben hadn't reacted. I could see my brother at the bar and the barman preparing him a drink. Something strong. He reappeared with a gin-and-tonic and sat back down. He drank quickly. His lips were wet. "That's nice," he said, as Derek returned to his seat. His phone rang. "The wife," he said, looking at the screen. "I'll call her later."

"What's your wife called?" I asked.

"Tracy. We have a daughter, Leanne, and two grandchildren. Nice children."

He took a sip of his drink, and I noticed that his hands were shaking.

"What does she do? Your wife, I mean," Ben asked.

"She's a beautician," Derek answered. "Works in a salon by the train station."

"Yes, we saw the train station. I think we even saw a salon," I said.

"Which station did you get off at?" Derek asked. "We got two Canterbury stations."

I hesitated. "We drove. My brother here wanted to drive."

"Oh yeah?" Derek took a few more sips of his beer, and he looked at the two of us. "Remind me how we're related again? The way Harry said it I couldn't understand a bloody thing."

I explained as best I could. "We're not first cousins or anything, but we're cousins three times removed."

"OK." This seemed to appease Derek. "So you never knew that Flora lady."

"Yes, we did," Ben said. "She lived near us in Notting Hill."

"You knew her?"

"Yes. She was a very nice woman. She was married to a concert pianist."

"A what?"

"A pianist who played classical music."

"I wasn't related to him too, was I?" Derek asked, looking worried.

"No, not at all," I reassured him. "But he was famous. A famous pianist."

"Yeah? I don't know much about that kind of music. Or about famous people."

"Fair enough, neither do I," said Ben, who had practically finished his gin-and-tonic.

Derek looked at him, then at me. "OK. So if she didn't abandon me, then what the fuck happened?"

I took a sip of my water. I could feel my knees shaking underneath the table. "She lost her parents during the war. They died."

"Yeah? How?"

"They were Jews," Ben stated slowly. "They were Jews and they were sent to a concentration camp."

Derek's face turned pale. "What? What did you say?"

Ben repeated the exact same words. Derek looked stunned. For a brief moment, he rocked in his chair and a cold shadow passed across his eyes. "They weren't Jews. They couldn't have been bloody Jews."

"Why not?" I asked, feeling my stomach tighten up.

Derek pushed his chair back again. "I need another beer."

I didn't dare look at Ben. I knew what he would do next. He had finished his drink, and he would have another. Five dry years and now this. He couldn't stop himself. I couldn't stop him. I was the one to blame. He had wanted to come on this trip with me to keep me company. I shouldn't have agreed. The timing couldn't have been worse. I could hear myself breathing loudly, breathlessly. "This isn't good," I whispered to Ben. "We should go."

Ben laughed. "Oh no. I'm starting to enjoy this. I want to hear what he has to say about the Jews."

"I don't. We should go."

"Not yet."

Ben stood up, walked to the bar and returned with a replenished glass. He sat down and finished his gin-and-tonic quickly, eagerly. I said nothing. What was there to say? He had fallen through the cracks, into a place I couldn't reach. But he would recover this time. I could feel it. This was a bad dream, for him as well as for me. One that would end as soon as we stepped away from Derek. But when? Was there still reason to stay? It could only get worse, not better. A man walked past me, picking at a plate of soggy chips. I felt nauseous. I had to act. Speak. But I couldn't move. And now Derek had returned with his beer. He cupped his glass in his hands, his eyes like misted windows. For a split second, he appeared lost, as if trying to find his bearings. Then his phone rang again, and this time he picked it up.

He spoke in such a low voice that it was hard to hear anything he was saying. He hung up and looked at us. "Trouble at the shop. Old bint wants an exchange. Says size 4 is too small."

Ben got up to get another drink. A song blared out over the sound system. The music jarred against my eardrums, and made me want to scream. Everything about the situation made me want to scream. This was not a man worthy of his mother. What would she have made of him? To think that until her last breath Flora had believed the Robert Schumann connection. That Robert had truly been an ancestor of the man now sitting in front of me. "These words are for him to know," Flora had written about her son. "How great and illustrious his pedigree is."

The encounter was beyond anything I could ever have imagined. Az's concerns had proved correct. But at least I had found him. That was the main thing. I had found Derek, and we could go home now. There was no reason to stay one minute longer. I was about to get up when he started speaking again. His face looked different. Harder. "So she was a Jew, was she?"

"Yes," I answered, as Ben returned and sat down again. "And she lost her family because of it."

Derek stared at us. "Don't you know?"

"Know what?" I asked.

"No one lost no one. The Holocaust never happened like they say it did. It's all a fucking Zionist plot. All of multiculturalism is a fucking Zionist and Islamic plot."

Ben stared back and said nothing. But I couldn't hold it in. "Where did you ever hear such a thing?"

Derek smirked. "Nick Griffin and the BNP is where. He's the only man who makes sense in this fucking nation. The only one who can see what this nation needs."

"What's that?" Ben asked. "A white nation for Britain?"

"Yeah!" He grinned and drank his beer quickly. His hand shook again. I wondered whether he was suffering from a neurological condition. And when I looked into his miscreant eyes

I detected vulnerability, a glint of fear I hadn't seen before. He was nervous. He was holding something back, I was sure of it.

"Well I think that Nick Griffin is a fucking animal," Ben was saying. "And so are you," he added in a lower voice.

Derek scowled. "What was that you said?"

Ben stared at him. "I hope you understand that by having a Jewish mother that makes you Jewish too. Do you understand that? You're Jewish, Derek."

Derek burst out laughing. Then he banged his fists loudly on the table. So loudly that for one split second the noise around us stopped.

"I never asked to meet you," he hissed. "I never asked to hear this shit. I don't like either of you. You come barging into my life. No one asked. Do you hear? How do I know you're not a bunch of fucking liars? Who says we're fucking related? Where are the documents? Fucking poncy London liars."

The barman stopped by the table. An apron was tied around his waist. "Everything all right?"

"Yeah," Derek sneered. "You should hear the shit I've just heard."

"What shit?"

Derek hesitated. "I'll tell you later."

I asked the barman for the bill. "Pay at the bar," he mumbled.

I got up and went to pay. Derek nursed his last beer while I pocketed the change. I motioned Ben to get up. "We're going now," I said to him.

"Not yet," said Derek. His voice was coarse, loud, slurred. "There's something about your face," he said, pointing a drunken finger towards Ben. "I've seen it before, and not on telly. I'm good with faces."

Ben shook his head. "I don't think so. You must be confusing me with someone else."

Derek leant towards him. "What did you say your name was?"

"Ben."

"Ben what?"

"Ben Karalis."

"Ben Karalis." Derek stepped back a little and took his cigarettes out of his shirt pocket. He lit one and looked at my brother. "I can't put my finger on it," he repeated, "but I've seen your fucking face before. Little nob of a fucking face."

Ben stood up. His face had turned a deep red. I knew that colour. I had seen it before, when he was a child, a shade short of crimson. This time, the alcohol had tinted it redder. "We've got to go, I'm afraid," I repeated.

"You're afraid?" Derek laughed an inebriated laugh, then took a deep drag of his cigarette. "Nah, I don't think you're afraid," he said, blowing the smoke straight at me. "I think you want to get the fuck away from me, right?"

"Yeah, that's about right," Ben said, his words sounding slurred. "I don't even understand why you fucking accepted to see us in the first place. Waste of everybody's time. So fuck you too. Can't say it was a pleasure," he added, walking towards me with some difficulty.

Derek bolted upright: "Hey! You come here, the two of you, and tell me this crap about a fucking Jew mother I never heard of before! You think I'm interested? You think I ever asked to know? Do you?"

"You didn't ask, but you agreed to it," I snapped. "We thought you were interested. It was obviously a terrible mistake. As my brother just said, it was a waste of everybody's time. Come on," I said, taking hold of Ben's arm. "We're going home."

"Listen," Derek said, in a more subdued tone. "You've come all the way from London to basically tell me that you knew my birth mother, yeah, and that I'm actually a fucking Jew. Then you tell me my own mother was a liar, yeah? That she was a liar, when we all know my Jew mother abandoned me. So how's that supposed to make me fucking feel, yeah?"

"Flora never abandoned you," I said, looking straight at him. "I told you what happened. She never abandoned you. She loved you. All of her life she loved you and waited for you to come looking for her. But you never came."

"She did not!" Derek shouted. "She never waited for me! Shut the fuck up!"

I looked at his face and saw it all then. His was a cry of despair, so deep he couldn't keep it in. It wasn't only she who had waited, but he too. He had waited for Flora all of his miserable life. He had dreamt of her and imagined her and probably spoken to her sometimes, in the dead of night.

But he never thought it would come this close.

He stopped and stared at us, still swaying. He looked so pale I thought he might faint. "What's going on?" Ben asked, barely standing on his feet.

"Everything," I whispered.

The expression in Derek's eyes was now one of a desperate man, whose history had finally caught up with him. A history of shame and shadows, but also of light.

He didn't know that light. The glimpse-of-beauty light. He had probably never seen it. I wished I could tell him, as he slowly turned away from us and staggered outside, where we followed him.

I wished I could tell him about the light. How it had filled his mother and probably filled him too.

He just didn't know it. That it was there, in his bloodstream, shining.

4

Harry rang to say that Derek wanted to see me. "He has some-thing important to say to you."

I hesitated; I was still coming to terms with the events of the previous day. I had felt so overwhelmed that I found it hard to put my feelings into words. When Az had asked about the encounter, all I could say was that Derek had taken it very badly.

"I'm not surprised," Az said. "I had a feeling."

"I know. I can usually trust my instincts, but this time I was wrong."

"I'm so sorry…"

"So am I."

He cooked the two of us dinner, but I couldn't really eat or speak. We sat in silence, as gypsy music strummed in the back-ground. I poured myself a glass of wine and drank it quickly. Az ate his food in a hurry. When he was done, he sat down beside me. "I should have been there with you today," he said, holding my hand. "It was a mistake."

I couldn't tell him the truth. That it was a blessing he had stayed away. That Derek was a racist and more. That had Az been there, the situation might have further deteriorated and involved racial taunts. That the mistake was mine: I should have listened to Az. I shouldn't have gone searching for answers, but followed the Arab proverb instead. I should have looked forward rather than back. Because back had made everything worse, including

Ben. As soon as we left Canterbury, he became violently sick and we had to stop the car several times for him to vomit on the side of the road. When we got home, he ran straight upstairs to his room and didn't appear again. Az enquired after him, and I blamed it on a stomach bug.

This morning Ben had rushed to an AA meeting before boarding his plane to Latvia. When I tried to discuss the matter with him, just before he drove off in a cab, he raised his hand to stop me. "Let's pretend this never happened," he said. "Let's pretend we never found him and this didn't happen."

But it had happened, and now Harry was telling me that Derek wanted to see me.

"You must accept," said Harry. "You'll understand why when you see him. He would like to explain himself."

This morning Derek walked through my front door with Harry.

As soon as I saw him I shuddered. The toxic words he had used rose again like fumes, and it was all I could do to maintain my composure. It was too soon, as I had told Harry. Even if Derek had seen the light, it was still too soon. He had spent his life using hatred as a repository for his pain – how could he possibly change overnight? Or perhaps this wasn't about change, but something more malevolent: was he here to claim the notebook? If that was the case, he was going to be disappointed. It was staying with me, in the third drawer of my desk, just as Flora had kept it. His mother's words belonged to Derek, but not her pages. That's the way I saw it. I needed to guard her truth. It was safe with me. She hadn't asked, but I knew that's what she would have wanted. We understood each other, Flora and I.

I hoped her son would understand too.

And here he was, standing in front of me, wearing jeans, a black shirt and looking very nervous. No matter the reason for his visit, I had to give him a chance. I had no choice. "Hello again, Derek," I said.

A packet of cigarettes was sticking out of his jacket. He kept his hands in his pockets as he began to apologize. He rarely came to London, he explained, but this was no ordinary situation. "I had to see you in person, yeah? I didn't mean all the things I said, back there in the pub. It was just the shock talking. Not me. It was somebody else. I hope you and your brother were not too upset," he added, sounding genuinely contrite.

His words took me aback. For the briefest of moments I wondered whether he was bluffing, but then seeing how agitated he was I quickly came to the conclusion that he wasn't. "It's fine," I answered carefully. I didn't want to appear too immediately forgiving, nor did I want to intimidate him. "Ben and I are both fine. And I appreciate you coming here," I added.

"I'm sorry, yeah?" Derek continued. "I don't know what came over me. I really don't. Like I said, I was shocked. So all that shit came out. I don't really mean those things I said about Jewish people. I don't know much about them. It was somebody else talking, not me," he repeated, in a hoarse voice. Derek had lived his whole life believing he had been abandoned. Now that belief had been shattered; he had been loved after all, and it was going to take some getting used to.

He followed me into the sitting room. He looked at the river, the room, the flecks of sun on my desk. "You have a nice house," he remarked.

"Thank you. Have a seat," I said, pointing towards the sofa. I offered him something to drink, but he declined. "Maybe later."

He sat upright on the edge of my sofa and cracked his knuckles. "There's something I'd like to ask you," he said.

"Yes? Please do."

He cleared his throat and motioned towards his cigarettes. "Before I ask, yeah – is it all right with you if I smoke?"

I looked at him, at the way his hand trembled as he replaced it on his knee. "That's fine," I said, even though I didn't usually let people smoke inside the house. But this was an exception. Everything about Derek was an exception.

Harry, who had been standing there the whole time, announced that he was leaving. "I'll speak to you later."

I waved at him. "Thank you, Harry. Derek, let me get you an ashtray."

I went into the kitchen, returned with a small bowl and placed it in front of him. "This should do," I said.

Derek removed a cigarette from his pack and lit it quickly. I went to sit opposite him and crossed my legs. I could see it again, the disquiet in his eyes. But yesterday's wrath had been replaced by something different. Something soft, like an expectant child.

"I would like to know about my mother," he said. "I'd like you to tell me everything about her, my mother."

He took a few quick puffs of his cigarette and blew the smoke towards the garden door.

I stood up and walked to my desk drawer, and then it hit me: he was about to find out that we were, in fact, not related at all. That his mother and I had met for no more than an hour. That until I read her memoir, I had known next to nothing about her. Nothing. I needed to come clean, just as he had. I didn't want to, but I had to risk it, no matter the consequences.

"Derek, you came all the way here to see me, so I think I need to be honest with you," I said, trying to keep my voice steady.

He looked at me, and the colour began to drain from his face. "What? What is it?"

I cleared my throat. "I met your mother twenty years back, and we got along very well. She was wonderful. But the truth is that we're not related. She dedicated the manuscript to me, as you will shortly see, and I felt that it was my mission to find you. But in order to do so, I had to pretend that we were distant cousins. It was the only way. Otherwise, I wouldn't legally have been allowed to track you down."

He continued to look at me, and was quiet as he took a long drag on his cigarette.

"So we're not related?"

"No. We're not."

"So you lied in order to find me, yeah?"

"Yes. I had to." He went quiet again, and I feared the worst. But then he smiled. "I like that."

"You do?"

He nodded. "Sort of thing I would have done."

I smiled back. "I'm relieved. Very."

He looked at me now with a different expression in his eyes. "So she still de... del... what was that word?"

"Dedicated."

"Yeah. That one. She still delicated her book to you? Even if she barely knew you, yeah?"

"Yes. It's not a book, but yes, she did."

"She must have liked you, my mother," he said, crushing his cigarette in the ashtray.

"It was mutual. We liked each other very much."

"Yeah, I can see that." He cracked his knuckles again. "Can you show it to me?"

"Yes of course."

I opened the desk drawer. "Here it is." I retrieved Flora's notebook and handed it to her son. "It's all in here. All you need to know about your mother is in here."

Derek held it gingerly, then placed his palm on the front cover. He raised his head and looked at me. "She wrote this? My mother wrote this?"

"Yes Derek, she did."

"Can I read it now?"

"Of course you can."

He opened the notebook and began to read.

The house was still. I was still. The river flowed silently. Silver shapes shimmered on its surface, dancing like fireflies.

Acknowledgements

I owe a huge debt of gratitude to the many who have helped bring this book to life. For their friendship, generosity and invaluable insight, Lisa Dwan, Rupert Thomson, David Sexton and Gael Camu. For her unstinting encouragement and support, my agent Caroline Michel, and the team at PFD. For making it happen, my editors Alessandro Gallenzi and Elisabetta Minervini at Alma Books. For those friends and acquaintances, old and new, who were there in spirit and more: Tim Miller, Cécile Laborde, Karine van den Abeele, Maggie Mills, my mother Anne Atik and my sister Noga Arikha. For inspiration, the Academy, the London Library and the British Library, and all the books which helped fill in the gaps – Janet Flanner's Paris journal in particular. For their professional advice and expertise: Major Kevin Pooley and the archive at the Salvation Army; Jean Misfield, from Adoption Services for Adults; François Jobard for his gastronomic tips.

For everything that matters: my husband Tom Smail, companion and editor *par excellence*; this book took shape with him. And finally, for my loving children, Ascanio and Arianna: it's been a privilege watching you grow up.